MOSH
IT UP

MOSH
IT UP

MINDELA RUBY

P
Pen-L Publishing
Fayetteville, AR
Pen-L.com

CONTENTS

Oakland Monitor

February 19, 2001 Edition

The Social Scene Page

PIEDMONT - Ms. Dickinson ("Boop") Park and Mr. Abel VanTurk were married in a civil ceremony at the Seaview Avenue home of Tom and Emily Latribo on the evening of February 14, 2001. The bride, 28, is a student completing the nursing program at Merritt College. The groom, 36, a Cal State University, Sacramento, and Western Medical College graduate, has been employed as an Alameda County Home Care Services nurse since 1994.

Following the nuptials, members of the wedding party, including former musicians in the local bands Up The Wazoo and Those Darn Accordians, provided entertainment and dance accompaniment for the other guests. A six-course vegetarian feast was prepared and served by Beautiful Cosmos Catering. The newlyweds have purchased a "fixer-upper" Craftsman-style bungalow in West Oakland.

Foolproof Antidote to Boredom

New Guy blows into my neighborhood drink-tank, his sights set on the beer taps. I'm sitting cross-legged on the floor of the bar, solo like him. He's clad in a high-gloss iridescent leather jacket. A big, dark bubble.

He's ready to freddy—I can tell by how he teases at the groin of his jeans and vets the chicks in the joint as he orders up. A couple of barely-drinking-age buffys exit the Ladies' and breeze to the bar. New Guy multitasks, mentally undressing the cuter buff while guzzling his just-served brew.

Not that his cad antics get me hot. Waiting to chat up my friend that works here is all I'm up to. Laying low, biding my time. The giggly career gals on the stools don't notice New Guy leering as they toast whatever the occasion is with mixed drinks. Near the front of the bar, a floozy with mud-color legs pouring out of her tight purple whoredrobe coolly dances her shoulders, which catches New Guy's attention.

All I catch is bartender Tiny's glower. More than once, he's tongue-lashed me for making myself a tripping hazard. Breathing room, I keep telling him—that's the reason the floor is my favorite seat.

Gita, my friend, the waitress, crouches to visit on-the-fly. "Tell me, oh wise one," she says. "Where can people get abortions?"

"You're preggers?"

She nods and pulls a stagy frown.

If I was in Gita's shoes, I could be all over raising my own little baby, though not the wrong way I got mothered. "Near the university on Durant? There's a clinic where I get free AIDS tests. Technically, since it's run by a church, it's anti-choice. What I hear, though, is some clients get referred for D&Cs. You positive that's how you wanna solve this?"

"Thanks, Poop," Gita jokes.

A female rock climber swaggers into the bar and says, "What's up?" to me in a husky voice. If I *was* licky-sticky lusty, the grail I'd crusade for, the person making me gotta, would be New Guy, not this butch girl in shorts. Her gal pal shows up a minute later to join her at a table. Gita hustles to take their order.

Jimmy the Gardener, the other regular in here, keeps his own tabs on the crowd. The working girl with Brandy Alexander foam clinging above her lip treats New Guy to a drunken smile. Jimmy sneers, resenting the male competition. New Guy slides his swill toward the Mai Tai of the buffy with the looks-like-natural-sun-streaked hair. Their cup lips nearly touching, his spit cooties could be transferring to her drink. She shoves her glass away and squinches her sorority buns to the far edge of her stool, next to her friend. New Guy leans toward the girls and runs his mouth about "custom sport truck . . . amateur boxer . . . live nearby?" Before he runs out of pick-up line buzz-kill, the co-eds zip their peach and sea-green hoodies and quit the premises in a pastel minute.

March chill steals into the place as the young-uns make their escape. Tiny blends Margarita slush that he tips into salted glasses—the suit crew's third round, if anyone's counting.

"Hey, Boop," Jimmy calls.

The few weeks I drummed in a band, my stage name was Boop. I still go by the single name. Like Flea. Beck. Bjork.

New Guy glances at Gita, whose dress fits like baby clothes on a bulldog. He gets back in the face of the well-dressed girl with green gills.

"I know from experience," I say to no one in particular, "Long Island tea, Brandy Alexanders, and Margaritas are a lethal mix."

Why be here, when lechers notice everyone but me? When Tiny plays gaggy disco like The Nitro Glitterings? Being home alone feels worse. That's why. And maybe getting crocked is the right idea. Nothing spins my spokes faster than agave tequila.

Gita's not used to me ordering a third drink. I can't really afford such vice. Plus the cops made it clear they'd rather not bust me and have to deal with my step-dad again. He was frothing at the mouth the time he posted my bail for public drunkenness.

But I'm more than one round away from passing out tonight. And a ruttish feeling's coming over me. The last swallow burns like rocket fuel. "Gita!" I gesture with my glass. "Hit me again!"

New Guy looks at me as if at furniture in the corner, his skull bobble-heading to the music. I'm about to tell him, "Quit that, bro," when, flouting the new law, he pulls his smokes from a shirt pocket. There's writing on his neon yellow lighter that I can't read from way down here. He drags deep off his cigarette, like it's freeing him from pain.

Gita exchanges a fresh glass for my smudged empty. The gold tequila is as still as mercury in mild weather. "Someone's gonna have a good time," she says.

"Surely you must mean me."

She tucks my money down her bodice and crouches. "My name's not Shirley."

I taste my six-buck ounce of drinky-poo and call, "Yo, Tiny! Did Gita get breast implants?" One of my dumb jokes.

Gita punches my shoulder, not playing along. "I'm knocked-up, remember?"

The mustache girl buries her head under her arms. New Guy stubs out his banned smoke and stares into space like he's chillin' or hangin' when I'm certain he wants to be scorin' not chillin'. Humpin', not hangin'. His beer is clamped to his paw like a neck to a choke chain. Poor boy's tense. He heard my comment about Gita's ta-tas. He scores a point for not staring at them.

"Tiny! Play Bad Religion or Rancid. Music with something to say."

Tiny is washing the blender. "Huh?"

I turn to Gita. "No one in here makes requests?"

"For cocktails."

The flesh donut around New Guy's middle overflows his jeans. Not that love handles offend me. "What do you think of that leather jacket guy?"

"Bad news," Gita says.

"Beer number three is clouding his vision. Or is it number four? Dude's got a remarkable bladder." I sip my poison. When I look up, Jimmy's laughing. He knows his rival, New Guy, is a joke. "I could use a good joke," I say. "World needs more plain old fun."

A newer guy appears at the door. He immediately hits on purple dress, voicing sweet nothings to her about "actuarial" and "Santa Clara." No one leaves. We keep imbibing, pretending we're not casing each other like houses to burglarize. Purple dress rolls her ass.

"Some babes know how to come off all that," I say to Gita. "Though who wears braces, unless she's eleven?"

I'm twenty-six, a hundred and fifty-three pounds of Single White Passion, with a heart-shaped face and fingers that bend inhumanly far backwards.

"I should stand up," I say. "Show off my goods."

"I don't advise it," Gita says.

The rock climbers pack it in after the one drink. Gita clears their table, her hips so square they could be graphed. New Guy stares at the bag of chalk dust hanging above one departing gay girl's caboose like extra genitals. New Guy has no shame, but the way my third dose of fire water's fixing me up, no shame seems a foolproof antidote to boredom.

A car alarm somewhere outside bleeps like a broken toy. Being ignored used to send me home from bars in tears. A lot of good that did. All New Guy needs to do is pull me to my feet. I could go to his place, do a two-step in the buff like I tried one time with my buddy, Spaceman Steve. Steve was too stoned on Quaaludes to appreciate the hoofing.

My tailbone hurts. New Guy's mug is almost empty. Why dawdle?

I check my fake leopard jacket pockets for smokes and come up empty. My thrift shop Swatch says 1:30, but that's New York time. The Eastern time zone's a dumb joke I have going with the drummer of Up the Wazoo, the girl band I manage that's on the brink of pop-punk stardom. We've been trying to book a gig in Brooklyn through someone I met from Yonkers. This band's gonna redeem all my little setbacks.

I jockey my knees under me and pray for enough strength to stand. When I'm up, New Guy eyeballs me. Took him long enough, but patience is one of my few virtues. I button my faux fur. Gita waves good-bye.

New Guy floats to me like a hot air bubble. "Leaving?" he says. "So soon?" He slides his box of Camels from his shirt pocket, opens and offers it.

Grateful, I take a cigarette. His beard, close up, gleams. He lights my smoke. The red print on the lighter says, "Vote For Me."

"You got my vote." I exhale a thin oblong of smoke.

He pockets the lighter. "Why do they call you Boop?"

"Bravo for paying attention."

I picture us having a laugh at my legal name before we make grunty music of our own. Maybe I'll play him my TSOL record. True Sounds Of Liberty. Their musical art is ten shades better than the electronica ticking like a bomb in here.

"Wanna go somewhere more secluded?" I say. Prowling wasn't my intent for stopping in, but with New Guy grooving on my chest puppies, lust calls the shots. "Go take a leak, and we're outta here."

In his truck, we make up for time lost in the bar. Our main order of business is lawlessness—reckless driving, a lewd act or two, open container. He says, "I'm Gordon," and floors the accelerator before the light turns green.

Feeling in my element, I sing Black Flag's "Gimmie, Gimmie, Gimmie" lyrics over the mariachi music spurting from the car radio.

"You're not a punker are you?" he asks.

"Don't you like punkers?"

"Hell, no."

"Me, neither!" I pat down my spiked, orange-tinted hair, turn up the radio's fiesta horns, and grin at the whole enchilada of New Guy. "Vayamos, Señor Gordo." For some screwball reason, I picture Hernando's Hideaway from *Pajama Game*, a movie me and Ma watched on TV when I was yea high.

"Gordon. Not Gordo. I'm no immigrant."

"Okay, Daddy-o."

"I'm not your Daddy, either."

We hang a left, my mind blanking on the thought of "Daddy." With good reason—my pa ran off when I was a tadpole.

Whatever's in this bottle that rolled out from under the seat converts tastebuds into scorching sparks. Car lights skitter like ray-guns across the intersection. Another look at Gordo, and that Mighty Dog yen for some playful shaboink blindsides me.

"Full steam ahead, Gordito," I whoop, bouncing on my seat. "It's show time."

Two a.m. California time. I crawl off the mattress he's asleep on. I rummage for my t-shirt among the dust bunnies on the floor. A sucked-dry Wild Turkey bottle lies on my velveteen skirt. Wherever my bra landed, Gordon can keep it.

My butt stings. I hadn't noticed his unclipped fingernails beforehand. Usually women claw men during nooky, not the other way around. I personally detest pussycat sex games.

Another memento of our spree is what might be a broken nose. The middle of my face throbs. I must have passed out on my stomach 'til he rolled me over and knuckled my nose as a prelude to the main event.

Funny how, for a minute there, getting hit made me feel alive—more than celibacy does, that's for sure. Even funnier is that at the bar, I felt sorry for that bruiser. Big mistake. I should feel sorry for myself, right? Except I don't wanna go there.

I locate my boots and jacket. Leaving my lost tights and bra, I close the door on the crude dumpling's snores and farts.

The street is deserted and cold. Dark bushes in front yards creak as if concealing trouble. Walking the graveyard shift spooks me. "Gimmie Gimmie Gimmie" runs through my head. I wish I could shut it off.

My real name—did I tell him? I'm hazy on the he-said-she-said stuff. Maybe he'll look me up. I'm listed. Not sure I want him to.

"One thing I do know," I say out loud. "Gordo's game."

Still, after this cruncher, I don't plan to hit my watering hole for at least the week it takes to heal.

Four more blocks to go 'til I'm home. The sky's unloading a steady, dirty drizzle. Wet electric wires snap above my head.

That swinish mutant knew how to burst a bubble, but we at least had a couple rowdy minutes before that. Life's gotta be more than waiting for glory with a struggling band. Don't eat animals, I often say. Fuck 'em. Another of my dumb jokes.

A Funhouse Face That Probably Isn't Any Fun

My neighbor's bawling pierces the dead of night, and I'm all, What's *her* problem? She's never made this kind of racket before. I try returning to dreamland, head buried under the couch bolster. No go.

When I get up to take a squirt, the cracked toilet seat bites my sore behind. Our building supe never fixes anything—*that's* worth crying about. I swat myself with tissue and flop back down on the sofa. The next-door pity party won't quit. It's frying my nerves.

"Shut your piehole—please!" I kick the hide-a-bed backrest and notice my boots are on. Swinging them to the floor, I go plug a Toxic Reasons cassette in the boom box to drown out that lady's whinnying sobs. What's she trying to do, get me started?

I stomp to Track One and think about how it's 1999, the end of a supposedly dynamite millennium, yet the world has devolved into a loserfied suckhole of road rage, air rage, work rage, school rage. Anyone with sense should cry about that. I dive over the armrest, sprawl on my belly, assess my own condition. On top of my battered nose, scratched butt, and wounded spirit, I'm starving. I roll to my feet again and raid the 'fridge.

A slimy godknowswhat in plastic wrap and some cream cheese dotted with mold are all I find.

There—a down-in-the-dumps groan between the songs "War Hero" and "Riot Squad." Poor lady.

Poor me, getting to hear and deal with that emotion. You'd think, with the walls soggy and thick after the century's rainiest winter, that noise wouldn't bleed from the next apartment.

Watching mildew collect along the baseboards is pretty much all I've accomplished in recent weeks while awaiting punk fame. I cram soiled socks and shirts into my laundry duffel. I should take out the trash, buy some food, at the very least get a lungful of fresh air. Not stick around here going loco.

With my shades on, it's dark-and-a-half outside. I pat the wallet in my pocket and set out for the supermarket, open 24/7.

Steering a cart through glowing aisles, I smell the tang of detergent and sourdough. The few other shoppers avoid me, put off by my black and blue nose and lax hygiene. I'm so hungry that groceries jump into my basket.

Waiting behind someone else's grub at the only open check-out, I laugh at the mondo amount of food we humans stuff our gills with. I lay my items on the conveyor belt—frozen fried chicken patties, aspirin, sherbet, Pepe Lopez tequila, and two garden fresh zucchinis as dildo stand-ins.

The Gumby-looking cash register clerk squeezes each purchase he scans. "Health food diet?" he says.

"Unhand my squashes, sir. And gimmie a pack of GPCs."

The total, minus food stamps, is $21.20. I swipe my credit card, holding my breath. When the transaction gets okayed, I exhale. Account's not closed. I'm not destitute yet.

On the trek home, my boots splash through a puddle. Treacherous unlit Oaktown streets.

As I juggle keys and the heavy bag outside my apartment door, a wail rips through the hall. Someone should call nine-one-one for that neighbor. I make my way inside, pull the Pepe Lopez from the sack, and bite off the cap seal. The first swallow sears my gut, then warmth hums through me. I pop chicken patties into the toaster-oven and down a palmful of aspirins.

The bathroom bulb burns out when I flip the switch. I flick water on my face and strip off my clothes. My gut hangs. In the dark, I look shockingly pale. My gel-drenched hair sticks to my neck. But I slap myself in the booty and say to the mirror, "You're alright, Boop." Some self-respect's left in this manhandled bod.

The heating chicken smells greasy and gamy, like Gordon at The Graduate a few days ago. Details of our drunken brush come back to me. How his tongue in my mouth made me feel gooey all over. How the whisky at his place smelled like the iron supplements you take for anemia. Loose as fishnet, I threw my punk-ass at him. The chump delivered what I wanted. And then some.

Shivering like tinsel as memories parade my brain, I grab a t-shirt from the towel rack and pull it on, a color-screened reggae rag my ma pressed on me the last time I visited her and her chicken-choker husband. It barely covers my promised land.

I slap music in the boom box and skip around 'til a screechier sound than PJ Harvey can produce halts my choreography. Could some emergency be brewing at the neighbor's? In my own hacienda, I can't sleep or kick up my heels.

With my semi-warm chicken dumped onto a plate, I track down some quarters and flee to the hall where I boot my duffel bag toward the basement laundry room. Plate in hand, I stop to listen at the crying woman's door.

Only silence inside there now. Is she about to croak while I keep a coin-op washer company? Someone ought to do something. Just my luck to be the one standing here.

My hurried knock goes unanswered. "Hello?" I call. A garbled sound reaches me. "Are you okay?" I turn the doorknob. Unwisely, her place is unlocked, inviting trouble. Abandoning my laundry, I venture in.

Nightlights fan weak yellow halos around her apartment. Arms low to keep my privates under wraps, I inventory the room. Motel-plain dresser. TV on a metal stand. My neighbor lies in bed, under a floor lamp. Five months have passed since I moved in and first got a glance at her. It's been downhill since for us both. I've gained weight and let myself go. Her Lizard Woman face droops like melted wax, the skin thick as a callous. It shines as if shellacked. A funhouse face that probably isn't any fun.

"I'm from next door," I say, torn between stepping closer and moving back, repelled. "Are you hungry?" I hold out the plate. The chicken's oily mist swirls through the Lysol-smelling apartment. I myself was famished 'til coming in here.

Her eyes, trapped under the mask of skin, wheel from the plate to me. "Hello, Dickinson," her weird voice crackles. It's like she's a radio broadcasting from almost beyond transmitter range. We've never introduced ourselves. She must have seen my name taped to the lobby mailbox.

"Hey, you," I say. Knobs of bone growths line her neck. The same crazy cactuses of bone wind around her wrists. I look away. Not a picture is tacked up anywhere in her apartment, as opposed to my walls plastered with band posters salvaged from music store trash bins. The shrub outside the window rises like a bear on its hind legs.

Turning back, I see the knuckles gripping her bed sheet are covered with raw sores. On the up-side, my neighbor's hair is copper-clean, her blouse ironed. She's better groomed than I've been in months. "Aren't you styling?" I say.

The pillow floofs as she lies back with a rictus smile. A squeaky laugh escapes her lips. Tré cool, that she thinks I'm funny.

"The county nurse came by yesterday and spruced me up," she says.

That voice—like she's trapped in a suitcase. She gazes at a cracked, brown ceiling that's just like mine.

"Have some fried chicken?"

"Can't swallow it." Her ulcerous fingers gesture at the meat on the plate then lift to her mouth in a mime of eating. "You go on."

"Maybe later." I'd actually like to chuck this battered carrion out the window. I scratch my matted hair. "What's wrong with your skin?"

"What do you mean?"

"Nothing. Sorry. My eyes are tired."

"Hush. I'm kidding. It's scleroderma. Reared up in the last fifteen months. Along with related abnormalities."

"Why?"

"Good question. They say I have Progressive Systemic Sclerosis, an autoimmune condition. The experts call this disorder PSS, sweetheart."

I've never heard of her disease, but no one's called me sweetheart for, gee . . . ever, and it makes me smile. Too bad she's got to see the shiner under my eye. "Is that why you were crying?" I say. "How painful is this?"

Her hazel eyes pierce me like pushpins. Shaking her head, she removes a Walkman headset I only now notice and says, "I was singing."

"It sounded . . . ." I don't press the issue. Her sobbing is her business.

She crosses her wrists over her sunken chest. What other growths and sores are hiding under her blouse? My spotless boobs lift half out of my t-shirt's stretched neckline with each breath I take.

"Were you singing?" she says, gnomish ears peeking out from her hair.

"That was a cassette. Hey—you want some aspirins? There's fresh ones in my apartment."

"No, thanks." Her elbow points at the partition. "My meds are all in there."

"Should I get them?" I park the chicken plate on the dressertop and enter the kitchenette, palms battening my shirt down over the junk in my trunk.

Our appliances are clones, except hers are scrubbed shiny. There's no boot dent in her 'fridge, and it's stocked with yogurt and juice. I swipe a bottle of apple cider but immediately reconsider and replace it unopened.

Amber and white containers prescribed to Sada Pollard sit on the Formica counter. I read a label as I stump back to her bed with seven drug vials corralled in my spread hands. "Would you like some Penicillamine, Ms. Pollard?"

Her fingertips brush her rawhide cheek. "It doesn't help."

"How about 'Cimetidine'?" I read the small print, "'300 milligrams daily for reflux esophagitis.' Procardia? Tetracycline? I've heard of this."

"Tetracycline. Sure."

I sink cross-legged to the floor and drop the stash into my lap except for one container that I shake a red capsule out of.

She leans to survey the cache of meds between my legs. "And one from the white bottle."

"Methrotrexate?"

"Please."

Piled at the bottom of the labeled container are two different makes of pills. "The white caplet or yellow cylinder?" I ask.

"I don't remember. They've gotten mixed up." She pulls her fingers toward her face and seems about to weep.

"No need to fret. Just take both, to be sure."

"You take one. I'll take the other."

Like that makes sense, but to appease her, I toss one of the yellows down my throat. Laughing, I extract a white caplet for her. "This way we prove which works better."

"Or kills quicker," she says.

I rock forward on my butt-cheeks and place the little bullet in her hand. "Want some water?"

"No." She painfully gums the medicine down. "I should be doing great in no time."

I heft myself to my feet and line the remedy containers along her headboard. "You like rainbow sherbet? There's some in my freezer." Before she replies, I scram to the hall and bang through my door.

I drop to my sofa, relieved to be out of there. Just because I shot my mouth about sherbet doesn't mean I'm on the hook to bring it. Nothing I do can undo that woman's plague. I militantly don't budge. I've got my own blues to sing. Hers are too intense for me.

Gotta be something around here to occupy myself with. I jump up. Mail's already picked through. On the top of the pile, the MasterCard envelope is stuffed with computer billing and surcharging. Next to the glassine address window, "FINAL NOTICE" is printed in red. Since getting fired from my bulk mail McJob, I've run out of dough. State assistance just covers the rent. Hooch, smokes, eats, and Trojans don't come cheap. Up The Wazoo, the band I manage, better start raking in commissions. My many hopes are pinned there.

Collecting dirty cups helps beautify the place. At the sink, I play air drums while waiting for warm water. *Plink-tadda-tadda-boom!* With the faucet clanking and water cascading, it's hard to tell whether or not I hear a howl next door.

I plug the drain. No one hears me advertising my plenty of reasons to gripe. All I want is to do a little dance and make a little love. Not take heat from meat-brains. I squirt Joy on the bobbing cups and think, *Why not make whoopee when I can?*

The hitch is, I barely get off anymore, no matter how much raunch gets factored in. And now I've crossed some line I shouldn't have with Gordo, that last dude.

Running a soapy cup under the water, I reminisce about my cute years, when getting it on felt like turning inside out in warm butterscotch.

These days plenty of slap-nuts still catch my eye. The wall I'm up against is them not digging this new overweight, frowzy me. So I've set my sights lower. Easy sell, in-out, bim-bam, no strings. Anyone's funner than doing myself with vegetables.

I dry my hands on my skirt and stop to listen for distress calls. Sada Pollard's luck is worse than mine. Would it put me out to go back and act nice? Common decency. A little company for us both. It's not like I'm busy.

I smear a layer of Erase over my black and blue facial blemish, then go rake the sherbet out of the freezer and peel back the lid. I plunge two fingers into the cold swirl of dessert and am about to lift out a snack-sized delectable gob for myself but decide against it. I smooth out the dints my fingers left, re-lid the tub, grab a spoon for Sada, and wrap myself in my phony leopard coat.

The laundry I left in the hall trips me. The cylinder of sherbet almost slips from my hands. Inside Sada's place, the smell of left-behind fried chicken greets my nostrils.

I approach the bed where my neighbor sits, hair scattered over her pillow like some deformity poster lady. "Sorry," I say.

"What for?"

"Leaving that stinky chicken."

"Have a seat." She pats the bed.

I hang back. "I'm not my cleanest."

"You should see yourself. The picture of vitality."

"Are you blind? Someone should put me out of my misery."

"Then we're in the same club. Sit." Her cupped hand extends toward me then nestles against her mid-section.

I perch on the edge of her mattress and notice dried food smudged on my coat sleeve. My wrist is pudgy. "I used to be loads prettier."

"It's going around." Her head sinks into the wadded pillow, but she turns twinkling eyes my way. "Tell me, have you got a boyfriend?"

Of all questions, when I'm sitting on a Gordon-shredded ass. "I've had a slew." I shuck off the sherbet lid and dip in the spoon. "Ready for some yum?" I turn the spoon to her lips and run orange sap over them. The sweet chill draws a cluck from her throat that could be interpreted as enjoyment. "You look awful nice," I say.

"The clothes look nice. The body looks awful."

As she swallows the next spoonful, I touch a bony knob halfway up her neck. "You've got a built-in necklace. My friend's boyfriend gave her a bracelet."

"Got a young man of your own?"

"Young man by the name of Stoney." I offer more sherbet.

She turns her head from the spoon. "What's he like?"

"He's a music honcho. Produces live shows. He's missing a few fingers from a motorcycle wipeout. No one's perfect, eh? He's darn close. Guy loves the hell out of me."

"Does he take you out?"

"All the time." Comments that started true have veered toward fantasy to please her. It's no skin off me to manufacture a rosy image. Saying little white exaggerlies out loud might make them more likely to come true. I lift the spoon. Sada lets a tiny sherbet pellet slide across her tongue. "Tasty, huh?" I say.

"The Methrotrexate's starting to work. You're a guardian angel."

No real food for days, and now being praised for inserting sherbet into this freakish stranger . . . . It leaves me feeling silly. "My pill made me better, too."

"Isn't that something." Her feet wiggle. Odds are more malformations lurk in those black socks.

I thumb a dab of green melt off Sada's chin. Not wanting to wipe the goop on her sheets or on my dress, I swipe it across my bare wrist. It flattens my little wrist hairs like glue. I tongue it away and taste sweet artificial lime and salty sweat.

"Aren't we something?" I don't know what I mean.

She lies back, old-eyed and slump-shouldered, her stamina for swallowing sherbet and Stoney Chavez kissy-spin fading fast. "Who cares what we are?" she murmurs.

The half-gallon tube of defrosting sherbet flexes in my hand. "I do."

"No."

I press a wet hand to her leathery, pocked cheek, as if branding my handprint onto her. "Yes."

Her fingers fumble at mine. "Me too, then, sweetheart."

Sweetheart, again. That slays me. "Excellent, Ms. Pollard." When I take my hand away, a magenta flush tassles up her face.

"Call me Sada," she says. Her gold eyes gleam. She looks like a wood icon catching fire.

Minoralities

"Best night of my life!" I crow in one of the wings as Tess, Bridgit, and Angie strum, drum, and sing on stage at The Frontline, a North-Of-The-Panhandle club. Rock impresario, Stoney, my old pal, had a band cancel on this gig, and he knows I manage a group, so Up The Wazoo got added last minute to the line-up. Is this real? You bet. Punks are roiling in the crammed mosh pit to our high-test songs—a dream come true I never want to wake up from.

"It's not like I veined the heroin," I tell Bridgit hours later.

She sits pouting at the kitchen table of this house we followed some slackers over to, after the club closed. The other partiers cleared out a while ago.

Bolted to the ceiling is a fire hydrant a cha-cha girl like me could kill herself running into. Not that I'm running anywhere. Stationed at the deep steel sink, I stare down at the barfed munchies I hoovered backstage and say, "Look what just smoking that scag made me bring back up."

"Why would I wanna see that?" Bridgit glances at the long, black window. "I wanna sleep."

"We'll split as soon as my stomach stops agitating like a toploader."

Bridgit's hands bongo the table. I try not to toss my refreshments a second time.

"Long night," she says.

"That's show biz." Our first taste of fame. So worth the effort it took to pull off. Like arriving early to unload gear with no help from the other bands. Then there was a sound check wiring glitch that almost didn't get resolved. "Once we're established, we'll hire roadies," I say.

"Amen to that. I saw you glad-handing people backstage."

"Networking, baby. Wait 'til we're the indie chart toppers with people falling all over themselves to meet us. I'm keeping a list of the ignoranuses that blow me off. When my chance comes, I'll deep-freeze *them*."

Bridgit fiddles with a matchbook. "Opening for Mr. T Experience *was* cool, Boopy-Dupe."

Life's good when she calls me that. Though sweat runs down my back and queasiness threatens, minoralities can't wreck our first opportunity tonight to gloat. "Sure was. Don't say I never did nothing for ya."

"Alright, okay, I won't." Bridgit slips her paycheck from her pocket and comically pets it.

"Most new bands play freebies for exposure," I say. "We're doing better."

"Thanks to brilliant management."

Gotta love the sound of that. "Lemmie wash out my mouth, and we'll leave." I turn the faucet handles. Nothing comes out, hot or cold. "No water. So much for Tess snurking upstairs to take a bath with that pretty boy she met."

"Roar?"

"That's his name? Or a comment?"

"He's Norwegian. Their band's recording a US EP called *Sales, Service, Parts*."

Everyone's boogying but us. Angie's in the living room with Stoney, last seen wearing a vest with no shirt, a look few hombres can pull off. I've had a thing for him ever since our Mass Communications class at community college. "Where'd the other dudes disappear to?" I ask.

Bridgit crinkles a scorched square of foil into a tiny ball. "Home. Where we should be."

"You'd think after this fab debut, that we'd find ourselves some love."

Bridgit bites her lip.

"You look slammin' in your boots," I say. "I can't feel anything below my knees." I reach down to poke the amoeba-shaped splat in the sink.

"Don't touch that," Bridgit says.

I wipe my finger on my dress. "Have you heard 'Drinking and Puking' by The Disappointments? Story of my life." I sniff my finger. "Though tonight I barely drank, and I ralphed anyhow. I know—it's the smack, stupid."

Bridgit flicks the foil bead away. It scuttles across the floor. "How's that song go?"

"Drinking and puking is all I ever do," I croon.

A short dude with muttonchop sideburns wanders into the kitchen, plastic bottle of gas additive in hand.

I sing the next line to him. *"And it's all because of you."*

"Nuh-uh." He sits and unscrews the bottle cap.

I duck under the hydrant and drop to the last chair. The shortie cups his fingers around the bottle rim to funnel a hit. Head yawing, he offers us his inhalant.

My reflex is to grab the bottle, boost my octane, like the label says the stuff is for. But Bridgit's head is waggling *no, no, no.* I sit on my hands and giggle at the "Ponderosa Ranch" belt circling this fellow's waist. Half of its multi-color beads are missing. He hunches for another snuffle of drug but clumsily knocks the uncapped container off the table. The liquid splashes over the floor.

Bridgit squeals and lifts her boots. My combat footwear stays put. The chemical vapor smells combustible. Good thing no one's smoking—or kapooey.

"Jesus, Boop," Bridgit says. "What happened? I didn't want to ask in front of the others, but your face looks . . . ."

"Spanked?" I've been wondering if she noticed my do-the-wild-thing trophies. "Worse."

"A sucker I picked up at The Graduate left some wear and tear I've had to hide with make-up and shades." I pat my nose. Thanks to the wonders of narcotics, it's now a desensitized blob.

"It's not well-hidden," she says. "What's this willingness to get roughed up about? You know that's not good, don't you?"

Our companion rescues his overturned bottle and huffs the remaining fumes. Clots of frothy spit ooze from the corners of his mouth. Bridgit's the pleasanter sight to focus on. "It was just this one time," I say.

"What about that hazardous episode last December?"

She sounds like the Environmental Protection Agency. "The what?" I pretend to ask.

I assumed she'd forgotten my pre-Christmas rout at a hyped San Jose rave. When we got there, the scene looked poky, and Bridgit wanted to leave. But after paying thirteen bucks, I said let's see if this party improvifies. The cavernous building was crawling with high school goths, jocks, ravers, heshers, and geeks. Either fake IDs were had by all, or beer was served to anyone with three dollars— flat lager people threw at each other as much as drank. A pockmarked foreigner grabbed Bridgit's breast. She smacked the degenerate's arm, so he turned to me, and I dry-humped him in the bathroom line.

During our turn inside the john, we banged against the sink and door. It didn't matter that we were in a condemned industrial warehouse or that me and this horny piston didn't know each other's names. All that counted was the ride. We were at Disney-fucking-land. Great-Fucking-America. Knott's Berry Fuck.

One steroidal lunge landed me under the sink as someone pounded the door to get in and use the facilities. My he-man zipped up his pants and fled, cursing in a language I couldn't identify. I crawled out from under the drain-pipe, feeling great except for the wrist I'd fallen on. The music and shouting sounded as if it came from under water as me and Bridgit waded to the exit.

Three days later, a cranky E.R. doc set my compound fracture. I never paid the hospital bill or explained to anyone how my bone broke, though the cast was a giveaway to Bridgit, who had witnessed that rave meanderthal I disappeared into the crap hole with.

Remembering, I rub my wrist.

"Admit that was hairy," Bridgit says.

A scraping sound above us could be a bed getting bucked about. My thumbnail dislodges a red fleck from the tabletop that I put on my tongue. Pizza sauce. "Maybe all I needed was a hit of wire to keep up with that toadmeat."

"You should have run the opposite direction."

"Yah, well, getting laid is mandatory for some of us. Don't sweat the collateral damage."

"Someone has to. You scare me."

I scare myself, but I don't admit it to Bridgit.

The wasted lamebrain at the table grabs my shoulder and stumbles to his feet. The spilled fuel additive is corroding the floor. With the heroin suddenly wearing off, my nose hurts. In this condition, I'm not grand slamming anyone.

"I'll be careful with strangers." I watch the drugged elf weave toward the door. "Okay?"

Bridgit squeezes my wrist, eliciting pain. The fracture might not be healed after all. "No one needs bad boys," she says.

The wimp trots back and brays, "I'm a gooood booooy."

I wonder how gooood.

"We love you," Bridgit says, ignoring him. "Me, Tess, everyone."

The huffer sinks to the floor, his pant knees soaking up the butane-smelling liquid. I stare at a bewitching fringe of gold hair along his earlobe. But Bridgit's vibe is warning me to take the safe side over the wild side—or be sorry.

Her boot slaps my leg. "Your cheek's puffy and nasty. Swear to me you won't let anyone hurt you again."

I'm about to swear. Then Angie loudly climaxes with Stoney, the mover and shaker I have a crush on. "These chemicals are dangerous," I say, nodding at the wimp on his knees like a freaking friar. I stick my nose in my elbow crook to block the fumes.

"And breaking your arm at a rave wasn't dangerous?"

"That was accidental," I say into my arm. "I slipped on the tea room floor."

In the living room, Stoney growls, "Mio Dios!"

I lift my nose off my skin. "Let's get out of here."

"Okay. Alright," Bridgit says. "Finally."

Outside, gray-brown marbled fog slops over lifeless houses. We ford the Mission District in the van. A yellow *Osvoldo's Liquor* sign makes me thirsty. The red *Cerrado* sign under it makes me morose.

Bridgit's jaw pops as she yawns. On the sidewalk, a man in a trench coat keys himself into the foyer of a structure with bay window overhangs. When the door shuts, lonesomeness sinks its grips into me.

Bridgit cranks her seatback forward and sits straighter. "This night's getting old."

"So are we."

A sign directs us to the Bay Bridge. From the skyway ramp, the bay comes into view, its surface shimmering. On the eastward underdeck, the cars drive in spaced formation, like arcade road racers. The van tires clack on the scored asphalt.

The morning's first light stabs through the gaps between the bridge panels. I shut my eyes and feel the van descend and arrive ashore. "If some horse-hung fan had been willing tonight," I murmur, "you honestly would have said no? You'd take a pass on the rewards of rock and roll success?"

Instead of Bridgit's predictable negative answer, I hear grinding steel. My eyes rip open. The van is strafing a car in the next lane.

Bridgit jolts awake. The car honks and evades us. Bridgit strangles the wheel to control our skid. The brakes oink like slaughterhouse pigs.

"Crimey!" I shriek.

The scraped car swings to the road shoulder. We pull in behind. Its trunk letters spell *Buick*.

"You're at fault," I say, "for being asleep at the wheel."

The Buick ejects two burly males in their 30s or 40s. Bridgit and I exchange wary glances and slide out of the van.

The driver frowns at his car's fresh dents and scrapes. He chops his fist at me. "What the hell kind of driving you call that?"

"I'm the passenger!" I holler.

The highway just off the bridge is so wide that a cyclone-fenced storage area fits between the east- and west-bound lanes. Roadwork apparatus sits parked in it. Bridgit extracts a card from her wallet. "Here's my insurance info."

"No red tape," says the driver.

"What?" Bridgit yells over the loud traffic canting off the bridge.

"I don't do claim agents and estimates," the driver yells. "Probably cost a thousand bucks to fix that side panel alone."

"Fifteen hundred," his rider says. Fangy teeth poke from his greenish whiskers.

"What are you," I say, "a mechanic?"

"I don't have that much money," Bridgit says.

We have paychecks from Stoney, but no way am I letting grifters pillage Up The Wazoo's first earnings. "That's what insurance is for," I say.

"I'll follow you to an ATM," the driver says. The fists in his pockets bulge like grenades.

"The limit on withdrawing is two hundred," Bridgit says. "We'd better call the police."

Wind flurries carve whitecaps in the San Francisco Bay. For some reason, the smack of these guys' nylon jackets against their backs makes me wanna scrag at least one of them. "Let's bring these guys into the van," I say to my friend. "We can blast 'Hot Wire Your Heart' on the cassette player and have a laugh." I guffaw and shake my hair, as if demonstrating. "Maybe settle our fender bender with some rumpy pumpy?"

"That sounds stupid, Boop, and you know it." She shuts her wallet, unaware that our crashmates are fixated on her chest in that vintage Avengers t-shirt. She walks away.

"What about the damage?" the driver says.

"Bridgit! Come back before some Caltrans paratrooper chases us out of here," I yell.

Bridgit reaches the van. "You're insane, you know that?"

The Buick brothers look on, speechless. A truck rumbles by and sprays grit in our faces. I spit it off my lips. Temporary insanity is hardly the end of the world.

Bridgit opens the driver's door. She wants no part of this? Fine. The dudes can make a me sandwich. My rocks need getting off, and here's a chance.

The rider bolts to the van and jumps on Bridgit's back, his body stuck to hers like a wet slug. She tries to shake him off. I expect drive-by busybodies to stop and inspectigate this human rodeo, but no motorists even slow down.

"Get her wallet," the driver calls. His tongue flicks over his bottom teeth.

I grab his sleeve. When he turns, I joke and grab my crotch.

Bridgit's squawks ruin the mood. Her ramrod has her in a wrestling lock. Tears cling to her temple, and her silver nose-ring slings up as if it's about to rupture her septum's cartilage.

"You're hurting her," I scream, running to them, prepared to fight. "Get the hell off her!"

Miraculously, the ape obeys.

I hand Bridgit's insurance card to the driver. If he wants his car fixed, he'll have to play the claims game.

Bridgit bellies up to her van's passenger door, which makes me designated driver. I get in and punch the lock down. The Buick drives off, springs cheeping like canaries. Bridgit sniffs and sighs, hamming up her snit fit.

"We're out of here," I say, "with our virtue intact. Happy?"

She doesn't answer. But things need saying before we leave, about priorities and values, like that. "So sometimes I'm a slave to my clit." I start the engine. "Like the 'Buzzcocks' 'Orgasm Addict.' What's so bad about a healthy sex drive?"

"Just drive."

This's my first time operating a motor vehicle since my car got impounded. "Driving your heap is like trying to steer a buffalo."

Nonversation from my friend. Less sleep-deprived, she might have been more willing to talk or laugh at our inner idiots.

"I only meant spending five minutes with those dickwads," I say.

"They were disgusting."

"They'd do, in a pinch. What's the harm?"

At the interchange, I take the cloverleaf—not going any particular place, just driving in a big circle. We sail across the rebarred overpass.

"They wanted money, not company," Bridgit says.

"They might have settled." My nose smarts. The gears strop each time I shift. "Unlike you, I don't have a wooing Ashland school boy to satisfy my needs."

If this van was mine, I'd make it a shaggin' wagon. With the band gear cleared out, there'd be space for a mattress.

"Unlike you, I'm no hooch," Bridgit says as if mind-reading.

Overhead signs name streets I've heard of. "On the bright side, we're not lost," I say.

"If I was you? I'd take a long, hard look at myself. You're out of control. Look what you tried to drag me into. I could've been raped."

"You know I'd never let that happen!"

"Slow down. You're speeding."

"You're mad about the crash." I pick up speed. "And unleashing the dark side on me after I arranged the band's first legit job! What kind of gratitude is that?" I slide my hands to the top of the wheel. "Your driving almost killed me."

"Don't worry, I won't drive you anywhere else. Don't call me if you're gonna be in denial and screw up your life."

"Don't hold your breath about me calling. And don't insult me with psychobabble."

I take the 52nd Street exit. Don't this, don't that. Bridgit said she loved me, back at that house. Is everything conditional?

I brake hard two blocks from my building. "Then I guess our relationship's just band business from now on." I unhook my seatbelt, wracking my brain for a way back to one hour ago. If we were still friends, I'd untangle the locket chain raveled in Bridgit's hair. All these years we've been each other's bestest buds . . . . And there's upcoming music success to share. Ending like this is tragic.

"This isn't your house," she says.

"I moved," I lie.

"Good for you." She unfastens her belt. "Goodbye."

"Some friend." I open the door. "Throw me over, just like that."

"This is your own doing."

I get out and slam the door, knowing she's right.

Bridgit scrambles into the driver's seat. The parking brake detaches with a clunk. The van takes off, leaving me crashing off heroin two blocks from my building and a million miles from my one true friend.

I march on, thinking up tardy replies—Have a heart. Come back. All a dumb mistake.

"You win, Weenie!" I yell. Bridgit's too far away to hear.

I kick a retaining wall in front of a duplex and just about break multiple bones in my foot. I yowl and don't care who I wake up. Tonight's glorious escapade turned into a fiasco. My toenail's gonna turn black and rot off. Putting weight on it makes me swoon.

"I lose," I say and limp home.

.

In The Mythic Land of Boop

All women are created equal, but I get first dibs on dudes.

Money grows on trees. And bushes.

Candy is a nutritional supplement.

Good hair days—365.

USA adopts punk rock national anthem.

Friends last forever.

The Swell Foop

I stumble to the can at a nebulous pre-morning hour. Under sixty fresh watts of a light bulb bummed off my neighbor, a cockroach hunkers in the sink. "Vamoose!" I tell it and sit to do my business.

Instead of pushing the toilet handle when I finish, I mind Ma's water conservation byword—*Flush down the brown/Let the yellow mellow.* The reassurance of sour urine—that's the extent of my family legacy. I pull up my shot-elastic briefs.

The stink that irked me as a pre-teen was the loose wino turd in Ma's undies. Hippie Bob, her precious husband, never changed her Fruit of the Looms or helped lift her off the floor. He would step over her prostrated body and say he was the only one in the family with any self-respect. According to him, we were trashy losers who ought to kiss his ass.

Kick his ass is what we should have done. I flush and glance at the sink. The cockroach hasn't moved and doesn't skedaddle when I tap its shell. Aren't these pesks supposed to be indestructible? This one's a limp-antenna goner. I flip his pellet body over, and, not on purpose, it lands in some basin muck. Stuck in mire—sounds like a familiar state of affairs. A proper burial is the least I can do for my little apartment cohabitant.

Alley cats screech a fucky-fighty duet outside as I kneel in the plant bed near the lobby door under a purpling sky. Waterlogged and missing a leg, the dead roach waits on a square of toilet paper on the sidewalk. I start digging a grave with a teaspoon. Goosebumps smear down my bare legs as I sing a song by The Damned—

"*No living thing has lasted here, yet we shall both survive . . . .*"

One of us already hasn't survived, I think, as a car slants out of the dark and pulls alongside the curb. Oakland Police—what a knack they have for showing up unwanted.

Daryl Prettyman, a night patrolman who booked me on a drunk and disorderly charge last year, opens his window. "Everything alright, Ma'am?" his drab voice says over the dogged thrum of his motor. This chauvinist let the lunkhead I was carousing with that night off the hook and arrested just me. His ears ride so low, they're on his neck, not his head. "What are you up to?"

I scratch my behind. "Burying a dead pet."

"As this hour?" he asks, as if the sanctioned pet burial portion of night has passed. He glances around for a beloved feline or gerbil and doesn't notice the deceased critter waiting on the sidewalk to take its dirtnap. "You have permission to place remains in this yard?"

"Yes, sir," I lie, spading a wayward blackberry vine with the spoon.

Prettyman's arm drapes down the cruiser door. "How 'bout you stop that?"

"Who's it bothering?" I keep digging. A berry thorn pricks my wrist and draws blood. "Fucking shit!"

The car door opens and out steps "Oakland's finest" in full regalia. As if my current fate isn't demoralizing enough, this cop fingers his puppety ear, casts his jurisdictional gaze on me, and says, "It bothers *me* when a citizen disses the police force."

"Sorry." I wriggle into a squat, ligaments burning.

Pretty Badge peers around for incriminating evidence to bust me for. "It's my job to keep my beat safe."

"Why's everyone so absorbed with safety?" I mutter. Safety advocate Bridgit called out on my recent sexcapades. She thinks I'm endangering myself, and I can't say she's wrong. I sure do miss her company.

"You'd better go indoors. You're not dressed."

Above the East Bay hills, the first of dawn gleams, the color of just-forged steel, as if this new day might hammer itself out less tarnished than previous ones.

As I stab a chokehold of dandelion weed, the spoon handle buckles into candy cane shape. "Hey," I say, "you ever see that TV magician who bent spoons with the power of his mind?"

"I don't think I have."

"My step-dad, the expert spirit-crusher, claimed it was a trick."

Pretty's face is frozen in its official blank expression.

"No magic here." I fling the spoon away. It gyres through the air, strikes the car fender, and plonks to the asphalt.

"Step forward, Ma'am," the officer says.

I know from experience that stern-voiced cops expect to be obeyed. But no giddy-up's in me. My knees are stiff as padlocks. I can't straighten my legs. "That was accidental," I say.

His hand twitches near his gun belt. "You've been instructed to stand."

Though Daryl probably won't shoot, he might be gunning to put hurt on me, and I don't want any. I limp out of the flower bed, my arms POW high. The surrender pose is actually exciting. But my right foot is pins and needles, frozen like a clubfoot. I stomp down repeatedly until feeling comes back to it.

"Miss?" Pretty says.

Wagging my boot in victory, I detect a paper scrap wedged in its cleats. "My bug!" I pluck out the shred and turn it over in my hands. Search and rescue's hopeless. The cucaracha is a smear at best. Woe-Is-Mea-Culpa. I, too, feel crushed. The small things in life are what break us.

My arms start flailing like let-loose water hoses. Prettyman vises me in a body lock. I hang half-naked in his police custody arms, cursing under my breath. His service revolver is holstered inches from my face.

I've never touched a real-life pistol. The second I do, my cop tackles me to the pavement. He locks my wrists into metal cuffs, frisks me from the waist up, and, before any mild thrill of that wears off, hoists me by the sweater with excessive force into the backseat of the police car.

I rub my snotty palms on the plastic bench seat cover. Thick wire mesh separates the front and back areas of the car. He dispatches a radio report that I decipher only "10-50" out of. I look out the window and wonder if Sada's watching me get in trouble. I hope she's asleep, dreaming, missing the drama. "Five-O," I say. "Why are you persecuting me?"

He re-clips the mike to its mount and twists around. "What's your beef?"

"You wrecked my attempt at a good deed!"

"Oh? What's your name?"

"Park."

"Park what?"

"Born Under a Dark Star Park."

He turns and starts the car.

Eventually, I'll have to tell him my full name, Dickinson Park. "Did someone from my building call the cops? Or was you showing up my crummy luck? I wasn't trying anything funny with your weapon."

The cop turns again with a searching glance I feel required to explain away.

"It's just that my whole groove's gone bust in one swell foop."

"Fell swoop?"

"Not even that fast. My life's been going downhill for months. There's no stopping it."

"It can happen to the best of us, Ma'am."

There's this about cops—you can bare your heart, and they'll hear you out and protect and serve. With my undies clumped in my butt crack, the plastic seat's perforations are scratching my exposed glutes. "Getting busted doesn't help, you know."

The police radio fuzzes and fizzles. "Try to simmer down," he says.

The sash of sunrise widens. I sigh. "I have a right to know what you're charging me with."

"314 probably."

"What-what-four?"

"Misdemeanor lewd exposure."

I rub my knees together. He thinks this is lewd?

"Maybe 374. Animal carcass violation."

I bat tears off my cheek. Another line from "Wait For the Blackout" runs through my mind—*The darkness holds a power that you won't find in the day.*

"Probably transfer you from the stationhouse to the psych facility in San Leandro," the cop says.

"John George? Please, don't. I'd rather cool my heels in the slammer than go to the heebie-jeebie bin again."

"A clinician should evaluate you. You could be a danger to yourself."

Not this old story again. "I'm no psycho! Swear on my mother's grave."

He nods, not knowing that Ma's alive and kicking. "Alright, then."

I smile. There might be a way out of getting arrested. "You know how cops put the moves on girls sometimes?"

"No."

"Sure, you do. It's common knowledge copsicles use the badge and their vested authority to get girls to do them." I lean on the screen and blow on Pretty's neck. Slutty talk pours out of me like unstoppered syrup. "Some girls are up for a little copophilia if it keeps 'em out of trouble."

"I quit listening five minutes ago," he says, shoving his gearshifter. My building drops from sight.

"Rear entrance, recreational spanky-spank. You can get it here, Daryl baby."

He brakes so hard my forehead bonks the screen. "Keep it zipped," he says.

I slide back on the seat as we pass the boarded-shut corner grocery I used to buy Doritos and cigarettes at before Mom and Pop got deported. "You're on duty. I get it. Rules and regs, respecting my rights. I was just foolin' with ya. Making conversation to pass the time. Onward to the clink."

My cuffed hands pull my sweater over my thighs. "Can I get a blanket at the station? And this time, can you not call my parents? Don't want my ma paying bail or my step-dad blow-harding advice. I'd rather languish at Boy George than take more wrong-rub from him."

We pass renovated buildings a century old, filled with nice, clean men. "If you change your mind, though, pull over here." I point to a massive gray stucco house with white shutters, circa 1930. "'Cause you're the man. And I'm just a half-naked skank with bound hands and a juicy—"

"Shut that filthy mouth!" He stops the car, throws off his seatbelt, throws his door open, throws my door open, and throws me to the curb. He unlocks my nippers and throws them down near me.

"I thought you were carting me to the loony farm?" I say.

"I don't want to deal with you."

I rub my wrists. "What if I wanna deal with you?"

He slams my door shut. "Go home."

I crawl to his shoes. "Abandon me blocks from home? Police brutality!" I grab his legs to pull myself up, one hand accidentally slithering over his wiener.

He pulls his gun. This time I'm not so sure he won't shoot.

"Easy," I say, backing away. It's one thing to playact smuttiness, another to get capped for it. I flap my arms like a moth. "See? I'm flying home, like you said."

He gets in his car and is off to harass other small fry in the 'hood, leaving me across the street from the wall I smashed my toe on three weeks ago when my ex-friend Bridgit dumped me off with no more than a toodle-oo. A garbage truck comes clanging down the block.

A strip of grass on this side of the street is springy green from the recent rains. I lie down and let dew penetrate my sweater. At the sidewalk's edge, my fingers hook onto something hard and cold that I pull toward my face.

Handcuffs. The discombobulated po-po forgot he'd thrown them down. I flip to my stomach and inhale the brawny sweetness of the ground through the unlatched loop of one handcuff ring. "Too bright out here," I say through the bracelet, thinking of the "Blackout" song. I hum a few notes and lay my head down. Under this grass live relatives of my cockroach—worms, earwigs, millipedes.

"Can't get myself arrested," I tell them conspiratorially. But there's no indication they hear.

The Onslaught of a Tailspin

Headline from My Daily News—BOOP HITS PAY DIRT.

Someone left a five-foot tall novelty wood fork on the sidewalk for the reclamation truck, and I scavenged it. The burly curio bounces in my arms all the way home.

My boots mash pink blossoms dropped from ornamental plum trees. They release a jasminey perfume underfoot. The rain has stopped. Morning sun plays peek-a-boo above the dark branches. I'm Green-Giant jolly, heading up Webster Avenue with my colossal trinket.

When my arms tire, I drag the fork up my walkway and through the unlocked lobby. The butt end scuffs, but minor damage can be lived with. I've had practice.

I waltz my find into the apartment. Work of art that it is, the decorative flatware should be hung on the wall to spruce up the joint, but I don't know how to mount something so goliath.

I sit down on it to rest and gaze out my open door. What do you know? Either I'm hallucinating, or my most recent Graduate bar conquest is here, muttering hello.

I gamily take stock of him—two hundred pounds, age thirty or thereabouts, holding a long paper bag. "Gimmie a hand," I say.

Gordo grasps my previously broken forearm. Upsy-daisy I go.

"Easy on the wrist." I pull away.

"Remember me?" His thumb jerks towards his groin, like that's the feature to remember him by.

The contusions he caused faded only a day or two ago. I slap dust off my skirt. "I'm not sure."

He whisks a bottle of Juarez out of his bag. Nifty, seeing as how tequila's my refreshment of choice. Though he hasn't brought a premium brand, it's the thought that counts. I'm not above indulging in cheap moonshine. It cures what ails you the same as big bucks hooch. "Wasn't I unconscious some of that night we met?" I say.

"I didn't mind."

"I did." I spot more dust on my skirt but leave it. "Can I get a taste of what you brought?"

He hands the tequila over. While I slurp, his eyes drift to my relic lying under the window like fresh timber, and he says, "What's that?"

"I got forked." Was Gordo lurking outside, watching me lug it in? "Sixties' bric-a-brac, pop art, pseudo-Tiki, collectible kitsch—whatever you wanna call it. Wish I had the matching spoon."

"Want your door shut?"

I hug the bottle. "Sure, Gordo."

"Gordon. With an N." The slammed door booms like a distant avalanche.

I point the bottle nose at the fork. "Can you believe someone threw such a treasure out?"

"Yah." His eyes comb my room. Looking for more heirloom folk art? Bird-dogging for a bed's more likely.

The sleeper sofa mattress is stashed under the cushions. Maybe we can unstash it. Though, looking over his same hard knuckles, maybe I shouldn't rush out the innersprings.

He sits on the couch. Amazing, this prick showing up with tequila in hand. The sofa casings groan as he sinks back.

I sip more Juarez. Sheesh, it burns. "How'd you find me?"

"Bartender."

He went back to The Graduate and made inquiries! "That's right. Tiny carted me home once at closing time."

"Pass me a drink."

I have a seat—not too close—and hand him the bottle. Pipes in the wall gurgle. Sada must be up and about. A good ounce of liquid disappears into the pink slit in Gordo's beard before he politely gives the bottle back.

I wipe the rim on my sleeve. "Mud in your eye."

"Glad to see me?"

"What's it been? Three weeks?" I take another chug and feel the Juarez's heat. "I don't miss anyone that fast."

That's a lie. I miss Bridgit in less time.

He slides closer to me. "Happier now?"

"Sure," I say, unsure if the opposite is true. This tequila's grubbin.'"

"Drink up, pretty."

In small measures, his booze isn't savage. And this guy called *me* pretty? Gotta enjoy that.

His fingernails tickle my calf through my skirt. "Been thinking about you."

"Yah?"

"Your soft skin. How free you are with your body." A grope along my leg. "Let me treat you special."

A cold shiver arrows up my spine, mostly dread, but mixed with a smidge of excitement. "I'm not used to special treatment."

"A sweet thing like you? Why not?"

"Ha! You're sure different from last time."

His fingers crawl under my skirt. "Forget last time."

Being in the moment always used to work wonders for feeling less alone. My thighs part under pressure from his hand. His other hand tips up the bottle in my grip and doles a long swig into my mouth. Tequila dribbles down my neck.

"You were smashed last time." I deposit the bottle on the floor. "And ornery."

He leans over and licks tequila off my wattles. His tongue's roughness makes me giggle. I'm about to suggest unfolding the hide-a-bed when he says, "You left underwear at my house."

"Tights. I'd like those back."

"I'm keeping them. To remember you by."

"They cost ten bucks. If they've become your kinky fetish, Gordo, you should pay me a user fee."

"I told you. There's an N on my name." His fingers clamp some flab at my waist. "Why don't you stop insulting me and act happy I tracked you down?"

"I am."

"Then take your dress off." He pinches my flesh hard. I'm about to push off his hurting hand when he lets go so I can do his bidding.

The one day chudda comes to my door, I should jump and strip on command. Of all the times to feel bashful. There's a clamminess, like my apartment's slipped down a well, that's making me not want to shuck off the last defense of clothes. The spot Gordon pinched feels sensitive as surgery.

"Should we order a pizza?" I ask. "Put on some music?"

He pats the cigarettes in his pocket but doesn't take them out. "Later."

"Yah, right."

"You want me to float your boat? Be good. I'll stay all night if you're good."

A game plan percolates in my head. Four Cheese Pizza, the Juarez, morning coffee, erotic interludes. "I'm good."

In a heartbeat, he's a hunka burning love pinning me down on the couch. The last time anyone macked on me like this was eons ago. My tongue eels around his gums. His beard bristles sproing up my nostrils and almost make me sneeze.

He extracts a hand from our suctioned-tight bodies and cops a feel of breast through my dress, like a sixth grader. This is not my usual three-minute screw. Old-fashioned necking's more like it. I feel so cornbelt wanted. Soon we'll be watching *The Matrix* at the Jack London multiplex, heavy petting in the back row. Unless I need to quarterback a band to a gig, in which case my new boyfriend can be my *plus one* on the guest list.

He plants hickies on my neck. I try to pick my favorite romantic song. Bridgit got a bangle bracelet from her boyfriend. Maybe Gordon will gift me. A jar of body glitter or some new tights. Once Up The Wazoo earns me some moolah, I'll reciprocate with something nice for him.

"Help with my top." My arms lift. My belly sucks in tight. My legs flop wide apart. Strip me, my motions say. Take me. I shut my eyes and await a move that doesn't come. "You with me, Gordo?"

His knee piledrives between my legs. The pain makes my pelvis seize. My sight blanks to white then blinds to black. My throat knots. I breathe in and out 'til the sick goes down, and I can blurrily see. He looks pleased with himself. Dumb me, dropping my guard. Or did I ask for a wallop?

Either way, I hunch over, fresh out of lust. I'd make myself scarce if this rough stuff wasn't happening in my apartment.

Bulldozing me off the couch is Gordon's next trick. He slithers onto my balled-up body. "You like this," he wheezes.

"Not anymore." Like a pill bug, I resist being pried open. His face swings close to mine. I spit at him.

No surprise he grabs one of my chi-chis and squeezes hard as payback. Rather than wait for this scum to finish whatever he's going to do, I ram my elbow into his chest to show him I'm no masochist. Big joke, the stab hurts me more than him. I don't wanna cry, so I mew some forced laughs.

He lets my breast go and rubs his sternum where I landed my attack. "Who says you get to be so moody?" he says with what might be a trace of humor.

But I don't trust the sharky emptiness in his eyes. "Who says *you* do?"

His thighs straddle my ribs. "Feisty cunt."

My stretched fingers contact the shaft of the wooden fork. If the knick-knack wasn't so outsized, I'd lift it up and bludgeon him to smithereens. That's how feisty I am.

He looks terrified, as if privy to my warpathing thoughts. But pinned down like this, what kind of threat am I? He's not even looking at me. He's staring past me.

"You must be Stoney," Sada's Tin Man voice says. It's anyone's guess when she barged in and how much of our love fest she witnessed.

"W-what?" Gordon seems stupidfied by her leper face as he lurches to his feet. I flip over and see Sada's eyes drinking in the scene.

"This's him alright," I say. Sada thinks he's my beloved Stoney. No use backtracking with facts at this juncture, so I say, "Stoney's a goofy nickname I call him behind his back."

Sada's pants droop on her hips. Gordon can't take his eyes off her petrified flesh. I'm all but forgotten.

"These were in the door." She drops my keys on the shelf. "Pardon the interruption."

"No problem," I sigh.

All bets are off on whether she remembers the detail about Stoney missing half a hand. Gordon has two whole dukes to show for himself.

Sada watches me sit up. I'm glad there's no new black eyes or gashes on me, just the lingering pain of a kneecap smashing my crotch. "Nice fork," she says.

Though *I'm* fed up with this scum's shenanigans, Sada sees what she wants to see—Boop and her fella making merry. For a second, I see us as she does and wonder . . . if she went away, could he and I go back to smooching on the couch, sweet as pound cake, seeing where young love takes us? He called me a feisty cunt as if that's something he likes. He came to see me again, didn't he? Talking about my soft skin . . . .

Except Gordon's stuttering to Sada, "I-I've got to go."

She hobbles after him. "Hang on a second, Stoney. I've heard so much about you."

"You have?" The look on his face is aghastment. I'm sure he's thinking, whatever the hell I want to call him—Stoney, Gordo, Daddy—just don't let this stiff-face gargoyle near him!

"Boop loves you to death," the gargoyle says.

His arm shields his chest, making me feel fended off. He must be thinking, *What kind of whangdoodle, haunted-house friends does this crazy chick have?*

"Jesus, Sada." I nervously reach my hand to fret the abraded base of the fork. "Don't publicize a girl's secrets."

"Sorry, sweetheart."

A splinter bores into my finger.

"She's fine," Gordon stage-whispers to Sada as if some homage to me must be paid as he keels toward the door.

Like I'm supposed to believe he thinks I'm fine when he knees me and deserts? He doesn't even look at me in parting, just Sada. She believes he's the dreamboat music promoter man I've pitched her on. He's good for that fantasy, at least.

"I scared your boyfriend away," she says.

He opens the door. "I'll come back another time."

I feel the onslaught of a tailspin. "You will?"

But he's gone, Sada grinning after him like a freakazoid.

I suck the splinter in my finger pad. Was not doing Gordon when I had the chance a dose of dumb? Or a stroke of smarts?

<u>Cable movie of My Life</u>

Act 2, Scene 1000

EXT. RAMSHACKLE HOUSING TRACT – DAY – 1985

BOOP, a scrawny pre-teen, runs wild in the streets, looking for trouble.

Not finding any, she wanders home.

INT. BOOP'S FAMILY HOUSE

Boop enters through the kitchen door, sees MA and EVIL STEPFATHER going at it on the sham-brick linoleum floor. Ma's Indian print dress is shoved up to her waist. The pants of Evil Stepfather Bob's armed guard uniform are pulled down to his knees, exposing his white rear-end.

                    EVIL STEPFATHER BOB
          You next, Kid?

                         MA
          (covering her breasts in fake modesty)
          Leave her be.

                    EVIL STEPFATHER BOB
          Don't lecture me, bitch.

                        BOOP
          Don't call her bitch, you fuck.

                    EVIL STEPFATHER BOB
          Shut the hell up, you little tramp.

                         MA
                      (to me)
          Get lost, Kiddo. Go back out and play.

Riding The Disorient Express

Spread-eagle on the couch at night after that lummox Gordo's pop visit, I try to predict whether he'll come back for more, and if I should move out to avoid him.

In my sick puppy moments, his devilment is exactamundo what I want—or what I believe I deserve. Gotta put junk thoughts like that behind me.

My brain's riding the Disorient Express. I wedge my hand between my thighs and try concentrating on band business. With the momentum we built at the Mister T show, a headlining gig or second-bill is Up the Wazoo's logical next step to success. There's nothing I want more than for this band to fulfill its destiny.

Possible west-coast venues where we could play pop to mind, starting up north. Velvet Elvis, Tractor Tavern, RKCNDY, Crocodile Club, OK Hotel, Sit 'N' Spin.

Clubs down the coast—Koo's, The Casbah, The Barn, Soma, Gabah, Bar Deluxe.

Schedule us now, I'll tell these places' booking managers, *'cause in no time we'll be the next big thing touring stadiums.* The sooner the big time hits, the better. 'Til then, I'm barely hanging on.

Once I line up the next gig for the band, Bridgit is sure to return to being my bestest bud. I'll earn 10% on the draw, dineros I desperately need. Another night in the spotlight might attract the side benefit of boy groupies. My hand slides under the elastic of my panty. I could get off on the thought of negotiating a booking.

Or—I get off the couch, find the phone, and turn thoughts and daydreams into reality.

The Slim's Nightclub number from directory assistance connects to a recorded run-down of upcoming shows—not useful for my purposes. I need direct access to producers and promoters. Like Stoney. Come to think of it, he once wrote his number on a napkin for me. I search my clutter. Pizza boxes, caseless cassettes, cassetteless cases, 'zines stolen from the mail bin, outgrown slacks, and shriveled zucchinis cover the floor and shelves. No napkin, but my Operation Ivy cassette turns up. I put it in the boombox, press *Play,* and attack the closet's hodgepodge of unmated earrings, dirty towels, bus transfers, political fliers, overdue library books, and a half-eaten maple bar with a brown worm plowing the dough. I find a pair of swirly orange-and-green toy eyeballs from one Halloween when me and Bridgit trick-or-treated with the neighborhood tots.

A song featuring full-throat harmonies between Tim and Jesse comes on— ideal example of how great music lives forever. Up The Wazoo can be immortal, too. Making that happen is my reason for being. I drop the toy eyeballs, run to the bathroom, and lean over the vanity. My orange hair is half grown out. "Mirror, mirror on the wall," I say, "where did Stoney's napkin fall?"

Reflected in the glass as if by a magic spell is a black sweatshirt wadded behind the toilet. The napkin's tucked into one of its pockets, stained with ketchup, but with Stoney's number still legible. Pressing the numbers on the phone buttons, I whisper, "Pick up."

He answers on the eighth ring with a breathy, "Yah?"

"Amigo. It's Boop."

"What's wrong?"

I solder my ear to the handpiece, eavesdropping for a rustle of clothes or a bedmate's whisper. "Nothing. Are you alone?"

"What can I do you for?"

Anything, I think. "More bookings, for a start," I say. "Since you love Up The Wazoo."

Seconds of silence. I decide that fake Stoney—the serial dimwad Gordon—is friendlier than real Stoney sometimes.

"Dígame," I egg him on in Spanish. "It's a going-somewhere band, don't you think? What's next?"

He yawns. "Record a demo?"

"10-4. I already reserved a studio in West Oakland," I lie, lie, lie with my pants on fire. "And the East Bay Express is *this* close to running a feature story on us."

"Good. Build a press kit. Upload mp3s to the band's website. You know all this."

Tess must own a computer. I sure as hell am on the wrong side of the digital divide. "Got it covered, Catdude."

With a grumplestiltskin laugh, he says, "Can I get back to sleep now?"

"You'll think of us for the next show you produce?"

"Si. Noches, Boopito." He clicks off.

What a smooth operator, jazzing me up about Wazoo promotion. Ought to call him back and ask for a ride to Wednesday's band practice.

Instead, I push my one pre-coded phone button to let Bridgit know how hard I'm working to make her a standout indy rock star. Soon neither of us will need low-wage jobs.

On the twenty-third ring, she answers. "Boop, are you out of your mind calling this late?"

I drop the phone in a blaze of shame, disconnecting the call. It's safe to assume Bridgit's more pissed now than before. I run to the closet like a kid hiding from a parent. The maple bar still lies on the floor. I pluck the worm out—afterall, I'm vegetarian—and wolf the stale cake down without a chew.

PRINCE OF WALES

"You haven't been home in a year," Ma slurs through the phone. "Bob doesn't yell like he used to. Let bygones be."

It's a Fuji-color afternoon. My window's open. I was enjoying the simple fact of being alive 'til hearing Bob's name. He's not my father or guardian or ally. "Whatever," I say.

Ma coughs out a husky laugh. "Come for dinner Sunday. I'll fix rice and beans like the old days."

"What old days?"

"Bring a banana cream pie."

"I can't get free pie anymore."

"We'll open a bottle or two and read Rimbaud . . . ."

Her Marlboro and chianti voice fades away before she finishes whatever she's blabbing about Rambo.

"Stop upsetting your ma!" Bob's raging voice. "Don't call here."

"She called *me*. Get off the line, Bob, or I'll come over there and dismember you."

"Ass-monkey whore. You think we want gutter trash in this house?"

"What are you, the Prince of Wales? Put Ma back on, Fancy Pants."

He hangs up. Is Ma ever wrong on the subject of his self-improvement.

I star-69 Ma. A busy signal goes *raw-raw-raw-raw-raw*—

I bang the earpiece down and hurl the whole phone at the window. The too-short cord extends full length, snaps, buckles, and spills the phone to the floor with a razor-sharp ding. The cord curls like a rattail behind it. "Stupid shits!" I howl.

Top Ten Reasons To Hate Ma

1. Child neglect

2. Hippie Bob.

3. Wino diarrhea.

4. Worthless blather.

5. Letting my real Pa hightail out of my life.

6.

7.

8.

9.

10.

Ix-nay on the Urch-chay

Our TV options suck—golf, carpentry, bowling, animals. If only Sada had cable, like my ex-friend Bridgit.

I tune to a bird show and settle on the floor to watch. A parrot with its feet clamped around a dowel speaks in a Cockney accent. "You're a naughty, naughty bird."

"Boop?"

I don't immediately realize it's Sada, not the bird, saying my name. Taking a break from bed, she sits in the only chair.

"What?"

"Do you drive?"

The parrot bows like a little man tributing a queen. "Why?" I say.

"Curious." Sada rests her fists on her knees.

I turn from her cankered sclerotic knuckles. My only eyesore near as horrible is a red keloid in my armpit. "Not much anymore. Last year I got caught driving without a license, and they impounded my car. Couldn't afford the tow and storage charge, so my ride got forfeited to a dismantler. Now I'm stuck sitting around, mostly."

"And going out with Stoney."

She hasn't figured out the me and Stoney thing's a sham. I bite my cheek. "Sure. He's been calling me 'Boopito' lately—little sugar name between us. Last night, he took me to this cushty party . . . ." He *has* called me Boopito once or twice, but beyond that, I'm garnishing my facts to cheer us both up. "All these local musicians were kickin' it there. Davey Havok. Jello Biafra. East Bay Ray."

Sada's index finger circles in front of her mouth. "Who?"

Jello and Ray walked by me at a Dead Kennedys show when I was twelve, but I never partied with them. They're not even a band anymore, or on speaking terms. I add more daydream partygoers. "Ian McKaye was there. Mia Zapata."

"Have all the fun you can, sweetheart. It doesn't last forever."

"Damn true." I think about Mia getting kevorked by a brazen murderer.

As for fun, everyone but me is having it. Bridgit and her fawning college boyfriend when he comes down from Oregon. Stoney and Angie. Tess and whoever she lays eyes on. Even Sada, getting off on my bogus love stories.

I flop onto her bed and claw into my lap the blanket that smells like a just-washed dog. On TV, a flock of gray birds flies into a car through a half-open window. They peck the driver's seat 'til the vinyl peels off. Their beaks shred the cushion batting into a blizzard.

"Must not be Volkswagen fans," I say.

"Birds breathe in and out at the same time."

I try breathing in and out together. Impossible. The birds vacate the car through the same window.

Sada mimes putting food in her mouth. "Time for a snack?"

I jump off the bed and peek inside her 'fridge. Scummy eats like applesauce are all that's ever here, regularly replenished by the county health department. I grab two yogurts.

When I get back, a different TV show's on. Sada has hobbled over and changed the channel. Her remote control went missing years ago.

"Golf fan?" I deliver her yogurt and spoon.

"I used to play." She works off her container's plastic lid. "Back when I had joint mobility."

PSS can cause musculoskeletal decay, she has told me. I sit on the bed and dig into my yogurt, picturing Sada with a bag of clubs on the golf course of life.

"Another birdie." She points her spoon at Tiger Woods punching the sky.

Four swallows make shortgevity of my yogurt. "You haven't touched your lunch."

She gets a lick down her gullet. "How do you get around? Bus?"

"You going someplace?"

"Nowhere important."

"Get your grub on, and I'll take you."

"You will?"

"If you finish that yogurt."

"Thank you, sweetheart. I'll pay for your time." She lifts a gelatinous spoonful to her face.

Sweetheart again. What a kiss-up. "We're friends. You don't gotta pay me."

A toss-and-turn night, and come morning I grab my sweatshirt and the eyeball goggles and tap on Sada's door, ill-prepared for invalid-chaperoning. Keen to attend some "workshop," Sada booms out to the hall in a too-big, unzipped frock.

As she limps to the bus stop, I catch the zipper tab and pull it up so the dress doesn't fall off her frail frame. The bus arrives as we do, brown exhaust whorling from its tailpipe. The door folds open, and Sada reaches out for the aid-and-abet that I'm tasked to supply.

My arms wrap her ribs and awkwardly lift. We climb the stepwell like tandem gymnasts. The driver stares as Sada pays both our fares. I'm wearing the clothes I slept in, feeling conspicuous. Everyone on the bus gawks at Sada's face. We sit side by side, and I sling the toy goggles over my eyes. Contentedly sightless, I say, "Truth time, neighbor—you're a missionary, right?" I try to conjure St. Henry's, our destination, but can't form a picture. "Do you earn salvation points for bringing Miss Sin to church?"

Her throat chirs like cricket wings. "Our grief workshop is led by a therapist, not a minister."

"Your *what*?"

"Bereavement management for the terminally ill. We call it having a good BM."

"Please tell me you're joking."

She pats my knee. "It's only once a month. After missing the last two workshops because of this and that, I'm constipated."

I laugh, though dragging herself out at ungodly o'clock to be exploited by a snake-oil shrink is not high on my list of things Sada—or anyone—should ever do. Especially anyone with so much "this and that" to cope with. But Sada's workshop might be like band practice for me—survival. "It's good we're going," I say.

"Why are you wearing those goggles?"

"To hide my bloodshot eyes." The bus door hisses open at the next stop. There's a shebang of footsteps, coin-jangling and voices, as if a mob is boarding. I pat Sada's leg.

"Take them off. People are looking."

"That's *why* I'm wearing them. To block out rudemankind. We almost there?"

"Soon."

"You want to take a turn wearing them?"

"No."

After further discussion last night, we decided she could compensate me after all. As her symptoms worsen, she'll need help, and for some bizarre reason, she wants it from me. Her offer of twelve dead prezzes per hour felt over-generous.

I agreed to a pay rate of seven and a half buckeroos but warned that my future availability could be limited once my band tours.

Sada sways in sync with me as the bus gains speed. "Arctic terns fly around the earth two times every year," she says.

"What for?"

"Here's our stop. Get up."

I stand, still hiding in the goggles, and grope toward the back of the bus. My elbow bumps someone.

"Watch it, girl," the person says.

Sada fumbles for my arm and leads me along. Some dorkus mutters commentary about freaks holding everyone up, but we're too busy de-busing without killing ourselves to care. The second we touch ground, the bus screams away. I pull the goggles off my face and cringe in the sunlight. "Howdy do?"

Sada grunts and trudges on.

"Or howdy don't," I say, trailing after her.

St. Henry of Uppsala is a gravel-rimmed wood church with a dingy, blistered whitewash exterior.

"Room One," Sada says, limping to a side entrance. "It lasts an hour."

I paw open the door for her.

She steps through the opening and turns. "In?" she says.

"Ixnay on the urch-chay for me. I'll wait out here."

Maybe it's the way I was raised, Ma being atheist and existentialist and a general scapegrace—I don't cotton to churches. People begin to arrive, not dressed for services, presumably terminal grief candidates. I bum cigarettes off two of them.

The six-sided window facing me is gunmetal grey. Do people in there take turns showing off diseased bods? I don't need to see that. I enter the building only to take a bio-break, hurrying past Bible display cases and racks of brochures. Two old ladies have a card table set up where the hall L's. Arrayed on the table are a bowl of sugar cubes, a shake-spout coffee creamer, a footed aluminum urn, and stacks of Styrofoam cups, all set on lacy doilies. "Where's the john?" I ask the gal wearing a hat.

I hope Sada saw this headwear, decorated with plastic salamis in red-brown shades of meat. The old crone ought to sell deli sandwiches, too. The other gizzard's pink hair net covers dainty gray curls. "The Ladies'?" Miss Hair Net says.

"Duh." I threaten to lift my black skirt, under which I'm going commando. "Want to confirm?"

She shakes her head and points a gloved finger to the left.

Locked in a toilet stall, I sing "Bodies," a Sex Pistols song about a talking abortion. Clicking footfalls interrupt my concert. I sit stock-still on my porcelain throne and hear the lock slide on the adjacent door. Elastic snaps. The Invader pees, exits her stall, runs water at the sink, and doesn't turn it off. I wink through the door crack to see what's taking so long. A redhead in a green pleated skirt peers at the mirror and makes "tut" sounds. If she heard me singing, she might be waiting to scold me. I tilt away from my stall door.

Sada's probably wondering what hole I fell in. The redhead fusses with her face as soft footsteps carry someone else into the next-door crapper. Under the divider, tiny beige shoes with cutesie laces are visible. A high-pitched squeak starts up in there and quickly hurts my brain.

I squeeze out a final burning drop of piss, unlatch my door, and slink behind the redhead.

She says, "Are you from SNL?" She holds a tube of something in one hand and a row of false teeth in the other.

I shake my head. Saturday Night Live—at this funky place of worship?

She says, "Are you grief or mad?" As if my feelings are her business. Goddam church. Goddam grief.

The grating *yeekity-yeek* in the other stall continues.

"Mad." I watch dentures get inserted into the redhead's lipsticked mouth.

"Me, too," she gums. "I'll be back once I get my dental plate to quit driving me plunkett."

"The TV show's not really here, is it?"

"How's that?"

I shrug. "SNL?"

"The 12 Step?"

The shoelace woman bangs what must be her head against her metal door. Me and the pissed-off redhead jump. "Someone else appears to be mad," I say.

The redhead presses her molars. The other wombat bangs her head again. I bound out the maniac door to go find Sada.

Retracing our way to the bus stop, I offer Sada my arm. "Hardly worth fifteen bucks, am I?"

"Why not?"

"Wearing goggles on the bus, holing up in the bathroom . . . I'm discounting you down to ten bucks for all the inconvenience."

"Can I see those goggles?"

I pull them from my pocket. Sada positions the toy eyeballs onto her head, the strap twisted behind one ear. The effect is macabre.

"Now you fit in with the people wearing salamis on their heads," I say, "and strangling rubber duckies."

"What?!"

"People at that church. A toothless chick in the bathroom admitted she's ticked-off."

"About what?"

"How do I know? She said she's mad."

"You mean Mothers Against Drunk Driving."

"I do?"

"M-A-D-D," Sada says. "They meet in Room Two."

"She asked about S-N-L. What's that, mothers against comedy?"

"Sex Addicts Anonymous."

"Sex addicts at church? Yah, right. Yuk yuk."

"They're Room Three. It's an AA chapter."

"The Alcoholics thing?"

"For sex addicts. Sex AND love addicts anonymous. S and L."

I scratch the keloid in my armpit. "Those people were love junkies?"

Sada laughs. "Some of them."

"Strange. Interesting. I've actually had this thought that I . . . ." I stop myself. Why divulge worst habits when it's smarter for Sada's caretaker to come off as Little Miss Responsibility?

"You what?"

"I hear the bus." A diesel engine rumbles not far off.

When it stops, I guide the goggled Sada up the steps and onto a seat. I'm sweating like left-out cheese.

Lost in her dress, oblivious to our new set of staring bus riders, fulfilled by her grief group, Sada smiles all the way home.

Too bad I don't believe in heaven. This gimp drill could have been my ace in the hole.

TV Shows I Miss Getting to Watch

X-Files

Real World

South Park

Jerry Springer

Highlander

Mad TV

The Simpsons

PHANTOM MAN

Not again—same strange man shows up in a dream. There's no knowing how old this man is or anything else about him. His yap stays zipped. He's a phantom mute.

I struggle to wake up but can't.

Is the man some panty raid muscle brain who I got suckered into thinking was hot once upon a time but now just wanna sucker punch? I'd rather be tranced out on hooch or pills than clenching my teeth in a nightmare featuring rough trade like him.

I roll over and dream-a-ling on. The man keeps dim watch over me. He ought to say something. Like he's sorry for hurting me. Or would I like to fuck? That's usually the ticket in.

Say he's Gordon. He's gonna treat me special. I'd better get ready.

Hoo boy, I'm tense as a high-e guitar string. I'm flopping back to front on my sofabed, completely in the dark about whatever trip this figment man is taking me on.

Daily Duties at Sada's

Insert food & meds according to instructions sent by her doc.

Chitchat about everything and nothing.

Fill time with TV.

Lead excursions to the john.

Act nice—find it surprisingly easy.

Dress her in glad rags from the closet.

Don't screw up these needed wages.

PUNKSPLOITATION

There's plenty of chow in my 'fridge, but I'm lolling on the couch in the doldrums with no appetite. Those dirty dogs Bridgit, Tess, and Angie don't return calls, leaving me unsure if I'm still in the band's loop or not. Joy Division's "She's Lost Control" plays on the boombox. It could be my theme song.

Side A of the album ends, and instead of getting up to flip the cassette, I stay reclined and belt out a verse of what'll probably be Up The Wazoo's first gravycool hit—

What did the world teach the girl to do?
To shove it up her morass!
What did she say to her fascist boss?
To shove it up his morass!
You, too, twerk—Shove it up your morass!

It was me who wrote the song's catchy-as-herpes chorus, though I'm not officially "in" the group. If my childhood had been less dementoid, maybe I'd have gotten whatever leg up it takes to play in a rock band, like Tess and Angie with their years of music lessons and parental encouragement. I was lucky to eat regular and stay under my step-dad's radar. My only lessons were hard knocks.

Band neglect is a bolt of fuck-you to the heart, I can't lie. Before long, though, Up The Waz is sure to be the alternative flavor of the month, so, aloof or not, I'm keeping my girl lollipops as clients.

Not showing up at tomorrow's band practice will look like I don't give a hoot—when the opposite is true. My stumbling block is transportation. Bridgit used to pick me up. Taxis cost big bucks. Busing takes three complicated transfers. I have to use the old bean to hatch a scheme to get to practice.

Nightlights streak across Sada's apartment at 3 a.m. Technically this isn't a break-in since the door's unlocked. I keep telling her that's dangerous. No one listens to me. But I listen. Yesterday Sada mumbled something about a "car out back."

I tiptoe to the bed. "Sada?" I whisper. She sleeps flat as a cadaver. In the carport this afternoon, I located a cobwebby Nissan that hasn't moved in months. Presuming it still runs, all I need are keys to drive myself to Tess's house.

There's a flashlight in the first kitchen drawer I search. Its beam scampers across soup, spices, oatmeal, sugar, expired prescriptions, a crock pot, and placemats in the cabinets. I transfer a dirty plate from the microwave turntable to the sink.

In the main room, I place Sada's slippers next to the bed for when she gets up. In her closet, a Tilden Pro Shop tote bag hangs on a hook, two plastic-headed Nissan-stamped keys lying at the bottom. Ready or not, Wazoos, here I come! I return the flashlight to the drawer, secrete the keys in my pocket, pull the cover over Sada. "Goodnight, sweetheart."

"Drink your broth," I tell her later while working for my daily clams. I keep mum about the pre-dawn prowl for keys. No use asking to borrow the car outright—she knows I don't have a current driver's license.

Sada eyes the steaming bowl I've brought her. "Yeck."

"Don't pan what you haven't tried. This broth's been enhanced with onion powder, marjoram, and nutmeg."

"Fine, I'll have some, since you fancy yourself a chef."

After lunch, I brush her hair while we watch a TV judge. The plaintiff in the case accuses her ex of dognapping the schnauzer. A neighbor testifies that the dog tunneled under the fence and ran off.

"I believe the neighbor," Sada says.

She's got no clue *her* neighbor is a carjacker-in-waiting. But my plot has rationale. A useful piece of machinery shouldn't deteriorate unused. There's a rock band to pilot to Easy Street, and Sada's Nissan will take me on the voyage's first leg. The keys and car will be returned right after practice.

I sneak to the ricemobile before eight. The car battery not being dead seems like a cosmic nod to my gambit. First stop—Whitehorse Liquors to get Juarez, what's-his-name's pet tequila.

The Whitehorse cashier wears a Davy Crockett coonskin hat and sings the Macarena song as he bags my bottle. I dance the moves, not recalling ever consciously learning the routine. The King of the Wild Frontier is oblivious. I exit with my purchase.

Stars freckle the sky's broad face. I cruise up Telegraph Avenue, leaving the tequila bagged so I don't get stopped for impaired driving in a stolen car. With my priors and the new criminal code, the cops could pitch my sorry ass into jail, Strike 1 being my Drunk & Disorderly, Strike 2, the D.W.L. that cost me my vehicle, and 3, for which I'd be "out," Grand Theft Auto.

Not that Sada's a blame-gamer who'd slap a felony charge on me.

I hang lefts and rights, thirsty with anticipation. One quench from the swaddled bottle won't be a sin on San Pablo Avenue, where half the hoi polloi have been unwinding in corner bars since the close of the work day. I bust the paper seal off the cap and duck down for a discreet swallow. At the corner of Washington Street, I brake smoothly without drawing attention to the sedan or the 93% full bottle between my legs.

A no-wave number playing on the radio makes me want to call in a request for Up The Wazoo. What a coup, to appear at practice with us playing on the FM dial! But there's no car phone. And we haven't recorded our demo. A second swallow of hooch has me yodeling "Shove It Up Your Morass" and turning at the Blockbuster corner, like Bridgit always does.

———

They are practicing "Heart Slayer" while I wait on the porch. The song's too metal, too country, too Seventies. Good thing management has arrived to prevent more lapses in judgment.

Tess opens the door, glammed out in a beaded sweater. "Get in here, Booper Scooper," she laughs.

Only Bridgit looks up when I dash into the living room practice space.

"I got some wheels." I swag my faux fur jacket over Angie's amp and flick off the tequila cap.

Tess gets back from bolting the door, takes the Juarez from me, and downs a slug, which I shouldn't allow 'cause of her diabetes, but who put me on rotgut patrol?

"Anyone else care for a drink?" I fill my mouth. Down the hatch the hot swirl goes. "Rock out, girls!" I bray.

Angie pushes her Stratocaster to her back and digs under her t-shirt to tighten her bra straps. The undergarment doesn't exist that could make my chest that pointy.

"Play one of your oldies," I say.

Tess supplies the tra-la-la base line of "Insulin Shock" and Bridgit adds snare. Angie rips a few power chords then stops to tuck her shirt in.

I click my tongue. "That was just getting good. Press on, mates. We need to produce a demo. No more lackluster practicing."

A toilet flushes. Stoney emerges from the WC, a big smile on his Mayan-looking face. "Boopito! Hola."

I shake his kinkalicious amputee stumps and say, "Here to see Angie?"

"To see all four of you."

Gotta love him counting me in the group. "You and me should discuss these scrubs getting more shows," I say.

"Let's get through the Mariner gig first."

"Your Mariner show? We're playing there?"

"No one told you?"

Bridgit whaps her drumsticks and looks guilty. I'm ecstatic about the booking, even if no one had the decency to inform me. "Don't think you're stiffing me out of my cut," I tell Angie.

"Play Boop the new song," Stoney says.

The three perform a ditty obviously composed behind my back, with Tess of all people warbling the lead. *"Do you ever stop to think about the ripples on the water?"* she sings.

"What's our pay for this gig?" I ask Stoney.

He keeps his eyes on Angie. "Couple hundred, split among you."

"Punksploitation!"

"Hot song," he says to the others.

He must be thinking with his dick. Angie's guitar lead is so ten years ago. Tess has a reedy voice at best, and the goofball lyrics leave a bitter taste I literally spit out on the floor.

"Boop!" Tess bellows into her mike. "This is my house, not a grubby club."

I glance at the globule of spit near my boots. "It'll evaporate."

"Wipe it up." Tess's mike feeds back, "up-pup-pup."

I ignore her miffy tone and say to Bridgit, "How's your boyfriend?"

"Wipe up the spit," she says.

They all must wanna see me on hands and knees.

"Beeee gooooood Booooop," Angie sings into her mike.

"Muchachas," Stoney says. "La paz, por favor. Peace."

He's right. I use my boot sole to smear out the spittle, but the thready yolk of mucous won't dry fast. "Gone," I say, wanting all of our attention turned back to music.

"No, it's not," Tess says.

"Spit. Not snot." I smile. "Let's quit wasting time and strategize our break-through."

Tess thumps her bass down hard, like she's Pete Icon Townshend with spare Rickenbackers to smash.

"Boop, your contract for the show is in my car," says Stoney. "Come outside and put your X on it for me?"

"Sure, okay," I say. "Let tempers settle."

"And stay out," Tess says.

Stoney's ride is parked close to my car. As he reaches into his truck cab for the paperwork, the seat of his pants looks like mother-of-pearl. If he didn't dig Angie, I'd drop my professional posture and make him feel the love.

He hands me a contract clipped to a folder with a ballpoint pen. "Autograph the bottom line, superstar."

I deposit the Juarez bottle at my feet and write my name.

He inspects the signature in the urban sprawl dark, perplexity twisting his face.

"It's my real name," I say. "DBA—doing business as—Boop."

"Bueno."

"Is Stoney *your* real name?"

"Anthony. Named after an uncle the Viet Cong decapitated. In sixth grade, my homies started calling me Stoney, and it stuck."

"My homies called me Dick Park, as in where to park their—"

"I get the joke."

"It's my *legal* name, swear to God! Dick is short for Dickinson." I point to the contract. "See?" I pass him the bottle. When he swallows, his Adam's apple glides like a mechanized pump. "Wanna take a ride in my wheels?" I picture us parking on a view bluff and cozying up in the back seat.

"I've got business to take care of tonight."

"Giving Angie the business?"

"None of *your* business." He hands back the bottle and pats my head like I'm in first grade.

So he's not what Sada thinks—near and dear. At least he's straight with me. More than Traitor Bridgit, Queen Bee Angie, and Ticked-Off Tess are.

"Angie's using you," I say. "That's her M.O. She used me to get ahead. I wrote half the songs and brought you in, and now she wants to jettison me." I offer the tequila again. With more liquor in him, maybe Stoney will see I'm the one.

He plants the bottle on the hood of the truck. "Angie deserves more credit."

"All three of them gimmie a royal pain, if you wanna know the truth. Their new songs are as soul-stirring as canned peas. If they tried, this band could push deep, like The Contractions or The Breeders!"

He crosses his arms. "Ah, Boopito. You have a true artistic ethic."

"That means so much, coming from you."

"But a band has to appeal to the public."

"The public's smart, Stoney. *We're* the public." I bump his hip with mine. "Let's sit in your truck."

"Can't."

"They're looking for excuses to 86 me, aren't they? The one person who wants them to be real with the music! Isn't that why they threw me out?"

"Tess is mad because you spit."

Stoney's eyelashes are dark and thick. We're bathed in the same blue moonlight.

"I'm pissed, too," I say. "I'm the glue holding the band together. Doesn't Bridgit realize?"

"Ask her, not me. Maybe you have a persecution complex."

"Ha ha." I lay a hand on his thigh. After a few seconds, he steps back and makes my hand slide off.

I lean across the hood to grab the tequila, but my aim miscalculates, and the bottle tumbles to the ground. On impact, Juarez and glass confetti detonate across the asphalt.

"Bummage," I say. "There's a paper sack in my car. I'll get it to put the glass in."

On my way to the Nissan, I pat my pockets, remember a ticklish detail, and circle back. Stoney's heading inside.

"Car's locked," I call, hearing my voice tremble. "My jacket's in the house."

He turns. "With your keys?"

"Dumb, huh?"

"Wait here."

I bolt up the step. "I'll come with. Maybe me and them can make up?"

Stoney shakes his head. "You should come back tomorrow when every-one's calmer."

"I can't borrow the car that long."

"Then wait while I ask Tess if it's okay to let you in."

"Hurry. It's getting cold." I lean against his truck and blow on my hands, hoping I haven't betrayed Sada's trust for naught. Sideshow street racers burn rubber in the distance. Sirens wail. A bug or bat flaps near my head. "Am I supposed to squat here all night?" I ask out loud.

Those curlicues are probably telling Stoney what a hoochie loser I am, how I'll only hold them back from the mainstream success they so richly deserve, how I get pissed to the gills every chance I get, and he should be their manager from now on.

Tess's door opens, and Stoney appears, holding my coat, a broom, and a section of newspaper.

"What's the verdict?" I say.

He hands me my coat. "Vete home. They're tired."

"Damn."

"You four need to work as a team."

"I'm trying!" I reach for the broom, but Stoney plays keep-away. "Lemmie do it."

He glances up the block. "You good to drive?"

"Will you stay with me a bit?"

"I can't. You're okay, though, right?"

Like a yes or no answer's gonna solve this. I'm too upset about screwing this up to have a discussion. Stoney's eyes make one thing clear—he's not about to jilt Angie for me.

I dig Sada's car keys from my coat pocket. The one answer I have—bailing.

Infractions Galore

Stoney is a drug I want to U-turn back to, but that's not among my options. I keep driving away from Tess's, obeying every stop sign, traffic light, and speed limit along the way. The DMV should unsuspend my license, given this behind-the-wheel expertude. I park near the door of The Graduate. Trick that funk with the band. Nothing else to do about them tonight.

In the nearly empty bar, Tiny, Master of Mixology, is at the ready, rows of flasks sparkling behind him.

I elbow up to the bar. "Hit me with the good stuff."

He nimbly grabs the blue label bottle. Faded script across the back of Tiny's t-shirt reads *Mountain Water*.

I decorate the bartop with my upper body like I'm a raffle prize someone can win. "Make it a double."

Tiny sets down a coaster, the tumbler. With any luck he'll charge me for a single, as he sometimes has. "Fourteen bucks," he says. Double it is.

I slap down a twenty. "Keep the change, ya filthy animal."

He commandeers my greenback, and what's this? Cracks a smile? Maybe I'm not a loser after all. Instead of heading to my usual post on the floor, I loiter at the bar with my amber agave.

A second slurp sends a primeval pulse down my spine. I lean forward, wound tight as a cuckoo clock, itching for a ruckus. "You ever see that guy I left with last time?"

Tiny glances away to gauge his other customers' needs.

My haunches press down onto the stool Gordo's smucky rear was all over when I first saw him. My boots hook under the rungs. "Nevermind." I salute Tiny with my drink. The tilted liquor bulges at the rim but doesn't spill. "To you," I say. The honked-down ration stings my tonsils.

"What are we celebrating?"

"Nothing yet."

He opens the cash register and counts raggedy dollars.

"I oughta flog you for giving my address to that vandal," I say.

"Thought I was doing you a favor." He returns the heaped bills and shuts the drawer, the coins going *chink-chink* in their little pools.

"You abetted a thug and encouraged battery. Infractions galore, Cupid."

Tiny passes through the bar drawbridge and moseys toward the tables. A nondescript couple sipping house red waves him away. The other table's beer-drinking bowlers also reject his services.

Tiny returns and gives my empty drink the evil eye. "That guy was a horse's turd," I say, pressing the glass to my chest. Giving it up will mean I have to clear out, making this night a pathetic waste of a borrowed car. "Where's Gita?" I mumble, wondering about her pregnancy.

Tiny opens the 'fridge under the bar. He can't throw a customer out because he's sick of her face, like Tess did, but he can throw him*self* into arranging juice cans.

"You know The Mats' song 'Customer'?" I say. "Oughta play *that* in here."

The thought of Paul Westerberg's heartsick voice filling this dive warms the old cockles. But Tiny's too busy fresh-test sniffing Bloody Mary mix to entertain my jukebox plea.

What a muscle bear Tiny is. He could squeeze every idle worry out of me.

"Are you deaf?" I say.

"What?"

"Bingo."

He slaps his paws on the bar. "Did you want something?"

Staring at his hands, I try to decide what I want. Shoulder to cry on? Consolation sex? Being left alone? I adjust my underwear out of my butt crack, mentally weigh whether more booze will improve my chances at (a), (b), or (c), and glance at the door as it opens.

In blows a flavor I've never seen here, wearing a three-piece suit and hatchet-job hairdo. He goes for the middle stool and plops his briefcase onto the empty seat. Forty, graying hair, and having a lousy day, his balled fists and knotted neck seem to indicate. Should this unobjectionable Man X be horny, help might be near at hand.

"Coke," the stranger tells Tiny.

"How's it hanging?" I say.

Tiny shoots the soda gun at a glass—*Phisst!*—and delivers the soft drink. "Two bucks."

I wave my arm. "Put it on my tab."

"I'll cover this round," Man X says. "What's your pleasure, young lady?"

"You know my pleasure," I tell Tiny with a wink. "Double the trouble."

A new coaster and fresh pour appear. I yield the empty glass.

Man X slides a gold card toward Tiny. "Thanks, Captain," I say. He scrawls on the charge slip and mimes a salute to the eyebrow.

I smooth my orange hair behind my ears. "At ease, soldier. What's your name?"

"Randolph."

"Boop." I salute from my chest. Maybe the gesture is too Heil Hitler, but my new buddy's replacing his billfold in his pocket and doesn't notice. One big hit of the new drink trips my flip wire. I blow a kiss and say, "I'm a band manager. What's your trade?"

"Pet product sales."

"Leashes?"

He twirls the red straw in his bubbling Coke.

I slide over one stool. He grabs his briefcase before my flesh descends on it. Heat seeps from his suit, plus a ranchy smell of wool.

"I always wanted a dog," I say. "Best I got was a hamster."

"A hamster's nice."

I laugh as if he's said something staggeringly witty and collapse against him as if I'm inebriatedly freaky. He shrugs to urge me off, but I stay put. "I'm a band manager," I repeat, praying it's not a lie.

Tiny stalks toward us, the bar towel whaling around in his hand—his intimidating demonstration. He scoops more pretzels into the fake wood bowl on the bar.

I look in the mirror and see a filthy cool hellcat in fake animal print, drooped on a de-wormer specialist in a near-empty tavern. Maybe this can go somewhere. "You need a shot of rum in that Coke," I tell Randolph.

"I don't feel like it."

"Why not?"

Tiny says, "Quit leaning on the man."

Or I'm outta here, the tone implies. I straighten back up.

Randy smoothes his coat and aims at Tiny a pop-eyed look that says, *Phew!*

"I'm minding my own private Idaho," I say. "Be a sport, Tiny."

"I always am."

"You always run interference on me." In the mirror, I see Randolph slide off his stool. He jams out the door.

"At least I scored a double off him," I say, nose poked into the brothy vapor in my glass. The remains of tequila that I hork down cause a muzziness in my head that reminds me why the floor's a better seat than a high stool. I'm almost to the pain-free point, though. "One more double," I say, grabbing the wood bar that's flocked with burns and grimy nicks left by years of drunks.

"Fourteen bucks."

I empty my pockets and count what money I have left. "How 'bout I take back the tip I gave you to make up the difference?"

Tiny looks at my funds. "You'd still be short a buck."

"Then gimmie a single." I suck on a pretzel while he allots tequila to under the blue line on the shot glass.

One gulp's what I make of his sheisty shot. It hits its mark, though. The mirror behind the bar wavers like Death Valley sun rays. The neon beer signs in the window pinwheel. I grab what turns out to be the snack bowl instead of anything stable. My stool clonks to the floor, and I crash-land, pretzels scattering around me like weevils.

"You conscious?" a voice says.

I suppose I am. Unconscious people don't feel like puking. A cowboy boot prongs my hip. "Tiny," I say. "I'm sad."

He forklifts his arm under my ribs and raises me to my feet.

Slumped against him, I hear his heart beating along with the first melody I've recognized since arriving. *"Da da da da,"* I sing, pecking my chin like a disco pigeon. *"Duh funk funk brouhah."* The zipper on his fly rasps against my stomach. *"Duh duh duh duh!"* I sing.

He leads me to the exit, his hand shepherded under my ass. Some men go wild over my ass. The table people watch us. I wave. No one waves back. I drag my feet, not wanting to be put out like someone's unlovable dog.

"Would you cooperate?" Tiny shoves our tangled legs apart.

The two bowlers with bronzed cheeks and lilac lips stare. I lick Tiny's ear. "Let's give 'em a floor show they'll tell their grandkids about."

He swings his face away from my slobber.

"Wanna tell you something on the down low," I say.

"Tell me over here."

I hold my head up like I'm this aces deb getting escorted to her coming out. He props the hydraulic door with his knee.

"Let's duck into the archway, and I'll do you," I say. It's me pulling, him resisting, now.

"I can't leave the bar."

"Wanna know the secret?"

"No." He holds me like a slop bucket he doesn't want to drop and have to clean up.

"I don't have secrets. That's my deep secret."

He drags me over the threshold and lets go.

I melt to the sidewalk like Dairy Queen on Labor Day and grab his boot. "What happened to men wanting a sure thing?" I say.

The boot snaps away, the welt scraping my chin as it goes. Steps fade back into the bar, leaving the world's feeblest sex addict and least appreciated band manager down and out on College at Claremont, staring at the spangling stars I—six, eight, nine, ten—count.

<u>Cable Movie of My Life</u>

Act 3, Scene 1

INT. GARAGE — NIGHT – 1987

DICKINSON PARK, a rangy 14-year-old, pogo dances at Janna Potzi's unchaperoned party. The family car is out for the night. Billy Idol BLARES from a portable cassette player.

Bad weed and worse liquor make the rounds. A dozen TEENS mosh on the cement floor, knocking into brooms, rakes, stepladders. The garage door lifts partway, and three OLDER MALE TEENS duck under.

HALF-HOUR LATER — CORNER OF GARAGE BEHIND SHELVING

One of the older males, a greasy, skinny, multiply-pierced 18-year-old, gives virginal "Dick" a crash course in hang-on-for-your-life, stand-up intercourse. All year, this neighborhood sultan of screw has caught our heroine's eye—DEREK FRICK, cherry-popper of Dick Park's dreams.

                    BOOP/DICK
          Can't believe how long I held out for this.

                    DEREK
          What were you waiting for?

                    BOOP/DICK
     You, Daddy.

MIRACLE PARK JOB

Opening my eyes to get my bearings = dumb move. The light sears my corneas. Away flies my memorydream of Dicktastic Derek, my first hot-daddy loverboy.

"Get up," says Sada.

I'm down on some floorboards like a bushel bag of flour. My peepers clamp shut again. Whatever smells sulphuric, I wish it would stop.

"It's not okay to lie there," says Sada.

Must be her floor I'm on. Though the smell is different from her apartment's eau-de-disinfectant. "Cut the lights first," I say.

"I can't. They're the hall lights."

Punching the floor = another bootsy move. Now my hand hurts. "If I'm bothering you so much, leave me be."

Was it last night I basked in the moonlight with Stoney? And danced the funk with Tiny? When did I pass out in front of Sada's door? Think.

I recall crawling to her car in the wee hours. And plainly, I almost made it home-free. A few gaps in memory.

"Whose keys are those?" Sada says.

I squint at the ring of keys looped around a puffy finger. Familiar keys (hers) on a familiar finger (mine).

"They're yours." My head flops back to the floor. I could tell a lie, but I've been making crap up since meeting Sada. The band's thinking of firing me—that's no fucking lie—and it's partly my fault for drinking, spitting, and criticizing.

Sada creaks closer in her slippers. The keys fidget in my fingers. I wish she'd take them and let me suffer alone, every vein cringing.

"You're shaking," she says. "What's happened?"

"I hate questions. I love the floor. Gonna marry the floor."

She claws the keys out of my hand and glonkity-glomps down the uncarpeted hallway on her spastic ankles.

"Wait," I call.

She gimps past Apartments E and D. I lay my cheek down, slice-of-bread flat.

How long I've slept—unverifiable. But I know the hickory spiciness I smell in the hall. The fetching scent of bacon. All I've consumed lately is yogurt and applesauce.

I stand, fix my dress, and knock on Sada's door. This one time it's locked. "Olly, olly, oxen-free!" I call. No response.

I need aspirins. First, though, I should make sure her car is where I think I left it.

My memory's not solid on how this achievement occurred, but the Nissan is backed into the carport. No harm, no foul.

I lay a neighborly slap on the car's hood. Glancing through the windshield, I see Sada sitting in the driver's seat, nearly lost in the glassy glare, puckered behind the wheel like last month's apple. Shocked by the sight, I step onto the bumper to peer at her zombified face. "Hello?" I say.

Her nonelectric window lowers. She's wearing a white turtleneck. "Come down before you get hurt."

I step down, open the back door, slide in behind her. "Gentlemen, start your engines!" I quip.

"You thought I wouldn't notice you'd taken the car out?"

Exactly what I thought. My head feels like a pot of burnt lentil stew, like Ma used to make. Hot and mushy. "I didn't plan on passing out with the incriminating keys in my hand," I say. "At least give me points for honesty."

Sada clicks the turn signal on and off. "I never back in like this."

"A miracle park job, you gotta admit."

She opens the glove box. "I suppose I was an easy target for a hot-shot."

"Me, a hot-shot? No way."

She slams the glove box shut. "I can't have you working for me. Turn in your uniform."

"Ha, ha. What uniform? Wait—you're actually firing me? But I love hanging out with you!"

"I don't have faith in you."

"You should! I swear!"

She peers over her shoulder like a dubious owl. "Oh, Boop. Remember the workshop you took me to?"

The grief thing. "What about it?"

"That day, I decided to give you this car."

All's not lost. "Sweet," I say. "Why didn't you tell me?"

"I was waiting until your license was reinstated."

"I'll go to DMV today."

"Too late. I changed my mind."

"Don't say that."

"You can't run riot without repercussions."

Pissed at myself, I slap my palm against the seat in front of me. The whole modular chair unit jolts, and Sada, who's not belted in, catapults forward like a crash test dummy. Her chin caroms against the steering wheel.

I jump to my feet. "Are you alright? What a frickin' jerk I am!" I settle her back then genuflect myself through the gap between the seats to search her face. "So sorry. Truly."

She toils to breathe like a goldfish that's leapt from its tank. There's no blood, no cut on her face. Just a pink mark on her chin.

"Don't make yourself sick over this old car nothing happened to," I murmur.

She clears her throat several times. "Nothing ha-happened?" she stutters. "Why's it ba-backed in? To hide w-what you did! Don't deny it."

"What'd I do?"

"Get out and look at the da-damage!"

I get out. The vehicle's back end is parked almost on the carport wall. A taillight is cracked. The trunk is dented, the bumper stripping scraped. Evidence, altogether, of a Mysterious Drinking Accident that replays in my head.

Last night coming home from The Graduate, I turned onto a one-way street, got honked at, and had to back off. Too fitshaced to hug the corner in reverse, I cut it too tight. The car rolled up on the curb and clipped a tree. I cursed, I stopped, I got out, and observing the back end damage, I sank to a heap on the sidewalk. Drunk driving despair. What's more, I felt completely unwanted—Up the Wazoo, Stoney, Randolph, Tiny had pushed me away in succession. Even night crawler Gordon never returned like he said he would. Estrus = torture, I thought. When I finally got back in the car, the tree was visible in the rear-view mirror, lit by the rising sun, purple-red, like a kid had crayoned it all one color. By that point, hitting it had somehow slipped my mind.

'Til now. Stinging with shame, I shuffle to Sada's open window. "Cross my heart, I will never, ever take anything of yours without permission again."

"It's you I'm w-worried about, not the car. Were you out drinking last night?"

"I went to band practice. I did get some grog to, you know, lubricate the creative process, but it's not like I'm some problem drinker!"

Here's where Sada should accuse me—and who'd blame her?—of being in denial, like Bridgit did. "But," she says, "my car . . . ."

"I'm getting to that. Stoney was at band practice, acting all gaga over our singer, and everyone was secretive about band business, and Tess made me leave, so I stopped by a bar to cheer myself up, not that anything came of that. On my way home, a tree crossed my path. End of story."

"You go to a b-bar, hit a tree, and tell m-me drinking's not a problem?"

"Not as big a problem as sex," I say, surprising myself.

"What?"

I slide into the backseat again, my mind connecting dots. "That sex addict thing at your church? It got me thinking I have the same problem."

"Where'd this silly idea come f-from?"

"From my life!" I press my temples. "Please listen. Orgasms have messed me up ever since I was teenaged."

Sada's palm does a paddling gesture near her heart. "No, sweetheart. Enjoy sex w-while you can."

"I don't seem able to." Gordon's kneecap comes to mind. I go dizzy with relived pain. "I've never said this to anyone, Sada, but I'm freaking myself out lately."

"Oh?"

"Rowdy sex sent me to the hospital last year. It's like, even though I'll be sorry afterward, I let the prick I'm with do anything for a thrill."

She glances back. "That needs to change."

"I know! But then the next time I smell a chance of someone getting me off, the same fucknut desperation strikes."

"Oh, dear."

"Sorry about the language. I'm trying to explain. And yeah, sure, I might have a drink or two, to loosen up, but tequila's not the bitch of it, Sada, believe me."

My punk goddess fantasy, the carrying-on, the drinking—I see now I've been chasing a glory fuck that's always just out of reach.

"Wanna know what's out of control with me?" I say. "Look between my legs."

Sada leans on the car horn—*Blaaaaap*! So loud I almost crap my pants.

"My hand slipped, s-sorry," she says. "Go to SLAA. You need the help."

HOPELESS IN ST. HENRY OF UPPSALA

At chicken o'clock, I set off on foot. All last night, to avoid oversleeping and missing the meeting's start time, I slammed down Jolt and stayed awake. People who write me off as a hopeless organ-grinding tramp should see me now, arriving early at St. Henry of Uppsala for sex addict 12 Step. Like I told Sada I would.

Not at my peppiest or sure how to blend in, I stage my entrance into Community Room 3 with eyes cast low. The chair I pick is near the window. As others take their seats, I feel their attention bushwhack me. *Who's the new girl? The overweight punk in the thrift store houndstooth skirt—what's her frailty?*

Displaying a chink in the armor's not my thing, but having to wait for the program to begin intensifies the lub-dub contractions of my heart. Remember why you're here, I remind myself—Sada, my employer (and well-wisher) didn't fire me, even after "stealing" her car. In fact, she says if I get in the 12 Step pink, her old Nissan will be mine.

Gain back Sada's trust and snag her ride? Blowing this sweet a deal would be a stupiculous move.

Besides, my sex life's hit rock bottom. All I'm good at lately, other than getting rejected by heartless douches, is going cruising for a bruising. Not a maneuver I recommend.

Will 12 Step help? No guarantees. What *is* a safe bet is that these folks expect me to talk about myself. Blather is what self-help's all about, as evidenced by Sada's workshop at this same church. From what I heard, they unload sorrows about being sick and then cheer each other on. I lift my chin and suck hard at air, trying not to turn blue with fright. What was I thinking, coming here?

Eight others are present so far. Wearing jackets in the unheated room, we look like a pack of embarrassed bears. I'm shivering and sweating.

To distract myself, I think of my music kingpin pal (and secret object of desire). When I called Stoney yesterday for a show prep update, he said our bass player's dad fell sick. Tess left town to visit her parents, this flounderous fish tale goes, and since no one knows when she's due back, Up the Wazoo's not rehearsing. Or so Stoney and the girls in the band would have me think—if I'm gonna get paranoid about them, and maybe I'd better. Johnny Rotten once said it best: "Ever get the feeling you've been cheated?" But this band's my baby, my chief hope. I won't be pushed out when we're booked at a fab gig! If necessary, I'll fill in for Tess. Barely playing the bass didn't stop Sid Vicious, so why should it stop me?

On a cue I've managed to miss, a lisping male voice across the room gets the proceedings underway with a divine appeal—*"God give uth grayth to akthept with therenity the thingz that can't be changed."*

One chair over from me sits the runt who squeezed a rubber squeak-toy in the toilet stall when I accompanied Sada to this church. Wearing the same size-four shoes with matching laces that I saw in the bathroom, she isn't acting like a hyped toddler now. She's quietly pursing her lips as the prayer ends—*"And withdom to dith-tinguith one from the other."*

Confident "Amen"s chorus around me, though, if you wanna know the truth, this room's a far cry from inspiring. The floor is worn to ribbons. The paneling droops. The chairs have seen better days. The one grace note of this excursion struck on my way in, when the refreshment table biddies offered me free coffee. While I tanked a couple of cups, the ladies explained that they're a Black ministry of Evangelical Lutherans, and St. Henry of Uppsala was a canonized bishop in Finland.

I'm Too Far Uppsala on caffeine when "Introductions" begin. My glands perspire in hyperdrive as participants state their names and the gist of why they're here—Tarik, Fred, Roxanne . . . internet sex, anger against women, romantic escapism. Details fly faster than bullets in a shoot-out.

"I'm Dales," the guy in front of me says, "a sex addict who can't get through a day without ten or twelve ejaculations."

I digest his sentiment with a grin. A hush descends like a thought of death. Everyone stares at me. My turn? Already? I've got zip! No handle that neatly justifies my presence. The blood in my lower extremities defies gravity and whooshes to my face. It's all I can do to sputter "Pass" to divert attention from me.

Someone laughs. I can't see who. My engorged head hangs between my legs. Introductions end. The topic "internet addiction" generates cross talk, but I hear only smatterings and my own heartbeats that insist, *Get out, get out, get out.* When I rise and follow these dictates to the exit, no one laughs or speaks or tries to stop me. Even the coffee peddlers in the hall ignore me shambling past. I'm hopeless. Everyone at St. Henry's knows it.

Oh yah? Anyone who thinks I'm too hopeless to stick out a meeting should see me now—combed, washed, wearing a new bra. Back in the hot seat after last week's false start in this community room. I'm determined to return home and look Sada in the eye without pretending to have endured the hoopla. I owe her this much.

A volunteer rises to deliver what I expect will be a reassuring screed about Sex and Love Addicts Anonymous. "Yesterday," he says, "I drove to some soccer fields to look at girl athletes and M."

Masturbate, he means. The same abbreviation got mentioned last week. Like wanking isn't wanking. Who do they think they're fooling in this semicircle?

According to the speaker, a soccer mom walking by his car saw him massaging sunscreen on his willie. The mom screamed, so the weenie-wagger sped to a 7-11 to buy a 'young stuff' pussy-pie stroke mag. Back in his car, he gaped at the photo spreads and got turned on.

Ha! I know what this choob's saying, about the gimungous jones that prompts misbehaving. Someone gimmie a medal for being so in step with 12 Step.

"Soon after that," says the volunteer, "I was on Grand Avenue, window-shopping streetwalkers."

He's bawdy alright, this slime-brain spellbinder. Last time his introduction went—"I'm Dales, and I'm into sex and porno." Like there's two of him, Dale sub sex and Dale sub porn. His twine belt hangs below his knock-knees. His eyes are afire with excitement.

"This smokin' 16-year old came back to my apartment . . . ." He trails off. Purple details and lewd blow-by-blow are prohibited. They "trigger" other addicts.

A flurry of rustling among people near the door is set off by a latecomer's entrance. My eyes stay fixed on Dales, who tugs his belt like he's raring to yank down his pants and demonstrate the slammer pud he brags about. Wrong or right, I find him mildly stimulating. Whoever just arrived is just in time for this stooge's striptease.

"One hour later," Dales says with a smirk, "the trick is gone, and I'm surfing the net for explicit dot com action." His pants stay put. "It's been a backslide week."

Thus concludes the uplifting message. You can tell Dales loves spouting his testimonial about acting out. What a scam. The whole underage hooker thing—who's to say it ever happened? He could be making this crud up and juicing everyone, especially himself, with lies. Last week he claimed to need to whip the dripper ten or twelve times per day to stave off a nervous breakdown. Come on!

A wankathon of emissions like that has gotta be impossible to maintain on any ongoing basis.

One would think they'd peddle stick-to-the-ribs, take-it-to-the-bank sobriety at these "Working The Steps" meetings, but so far these folks aren't wearing goody-good badges. Cure for addicts, my ass. I should walk out. This meeting is witless and too early in the morning. Worse, it makes me think about sex more, not less.

"Something grabs my crotch," Dales adds. "I can't always grab it back."

His face reminds me of a crotch—pubic-y whiskers, receding chin. Bowing his head, he could kiss his own neck. He *should*. Someone here said we need to be gentle with ourselves.

Dales returns to his spot next to a lanky jamoke in a faded postal uniform. "Forgot to mention," Dales says as he seats himself, "I'm back to Step One, admitting I'm powerless."

The mailman character turns a big 'Abstinence rocks!' smile on Dales. Like anyone's buying that shaky -ism.

Jonathan, the meeting leader, says, "Thank you, Dales," not very sincerely. "Let's turn to the Introductions."

The dreaded Introductions. My chance to slip out under the radar gone, I squeeze my fists and stay strong, even when Dales and others turn and stare. This time, thankfully, they're not looking at me. The person who came in late is in their crosshairs. Jonathan's body points that same direction like a foxhound. I rubberneck to see who's so interesting by the door.

A cover girl has joined our ranks! With pantabulous hair and a whoa mammy outfit. What a candy piece of heinie. I can't wait to hear *her* Introduction.

"I'm Jonathan, acting secretary, recovering sex addict." Jonathan nods at Dales.

"Dales. Sex and internet addict." He tips his head at Post Office Man, who waves hello to New Girl like this is a shindig.

"Hi, I'm Felipe. A bi- thex addict."

I twirl a lock of my hair so aggro that strands rip from my scalp. I can't mumble "Pass" and duck out again this time. Not if I plan to ever come back. I have to play the game as if I'm in it to win.

"I'm Fred," the big guy says. "A once-in-a-while abuser." Hairy toes stick out of the cross straps of his gladiator sandals. "If no one minds, I'll explain."

I wish he wouldn't, but Fred only notices pretty Miss America, who doesn't realize he's about to explain something abominable to her. "Minor aggravations constantly tick me off," Fred says. "Orders from my supervisor, traffic tie-ups ...." He flexes his pecs through his sweat-colored T-shirt. "They make me want to hit something. Some *one*."

Our new member jiggles her high heel shoe all jittery, as well she should with Furious Fred spilling mean beans in her direction. I know from experience—punches hurt.

"Good to hear you articulating, Fred," Jonathan says. "Volunteer sometime soon to probe this further, okay? Let's keep the Introductions rolling."

"I'm Tarik, porn addict."

New girl's turn. She blinks at porny Tarik and says, "I'm Emmie, and I'm, or I might be, a sex addict."

At last, someone gives this addiction a luster.

"I'm Samuela," the next-in-line says. "Recovering sex and love addict."

"I'm Roxanne," the bathroom rubber ducky squeezer says. "A romance addict."

"Boop here," I blurt. "Love junkie." I wipe my brow, wondering if New Girl is looking at me.

"Musef," the guy who's even wormier than Dales says. He sniffs one of his palms. "Sex and drug addict."

"Welcome everyone," Jonathan says. Even a procedure-wonk like him is having difficulty keeping his peepers off Emmie. I'd kill to be a pin-up stunner like her, with everyone salivating over how I "might be" a sex addict.

A room-rental collections basket gets passed around. When it reaches me with three bucks in it, I hand it on, too bankrupt to contribute.

Jonathan reads aloud from a clipboard—"You're all invited to an alcohol-free, drug-free, tobacco-free, caffeine-free, MSG-free, sexism-free SLAA potluck at St. Henry of Uppsala Social Hall at 6 p.m. May 30th. Lemonade, utensils, and paper goods provided." He looks up and adds, "RSVP by May 26."

"Make that Boop-free," I mutter.

Musef points scornful black dot eyes at me. I crane my neck and notice Emmie fattening the basket with a ten spot. So she's generous besides being sex on a stick.

"Do we have a second volunteer speaker?" Jonathan says.

Last week, everyone eyeballed me. Today, I'm history—Sex Bomb Emmie's the mystery. The guys watch her and pray she'll let something risqué about herself slip.

"Anyone?" Jonathan says. "Don't be shy."

"A new person?" Dales suggests, completely out of line.

Emmie wrings her tan, manicured hands. "I could say something, if no one else . . . ?"

No one moves. With a swish of his hand, Jonathan encourages Aphrodite to rise and be worshipped.

She catwalks to the front of the group in cream-colored wool slacks and a fever-red sweater. "I'm not sure how this should go," she says. "This is my first meeting."

As if we don't realize.

"Normally we 'work' one of the steps," Jonathan says. "In other words, discuss which we're focused on. But it's okay if you're not familiar with the codex. Talk about what brought you here, maybe?"

Codex! Someone's trying to impress.

Emmie nods. "What brought me here . . . . Okay. I started seeing a therapist because of thoughts that I might be, um, a man collector. Or sex addict, I guess is the terminology. Except, what's come out during the sessions is not so much that I'm addicted to sex itself . . . ."

A stifled male groan escapes from someone.

". . . it's more the power sex gives me."

This time the groan emits from me. Why wasn't I born her? Walking a mile in her high-heels, I wouldn't have a care in the world.

"I moved here from Honolulu to live with my fiancé," Miss Sexy Pants says. She tosses her luxe hair over her shoulder. "Our wedding date is set. He's a businessman I met at the hotel where I used to work." She looks surprised at how mesmerized her comments have us. "But the prospect of marriage . . . ." Her eyes ricochet from one to another of us. "It makes me think . . . ." She looks helplessly at Jonathan.

He nods.

"The day I left the islands, something happened." Emmie takes a deep breath. "I had an inappropriate encounter with another hotel employee. It was meaningless, but it forced me to wonder—should I get married? Do I deserve a husband's trust? I'm here for answers. My therapist suggested it." She smiles at the floor and sashays back to her chair.

"Thank you for sharing," Jonathan says.

"That was touching," Dales blurts, though I'm pretty sure another unspoken rule is that we shut our traps during and after presentations and keep judgments to ourselves. "I mean it," Dales slobbers, making a full-fledged quimby of himself. "Amazing stuff, Emmie. It's soooo great to have you participate in our group. Welcome in."

And people consider *me* hopeless?

With Dales setting the bar low, I should have no trouble being in like Flynn at meetings.

A Fantasy Where I'm the Foxy Chick

Hi, my name is Emmie. I'm a red hot mama fixing to move in with my sugar daddy.

I work in bling-bling Waikiki at a hotel activities desk. That's how I met my moneybags boyfriend. He asked me to make golf greens reservations. Later, I made him.

My flight out of Honolulu departs in two hours. All packed, I take a last look around my room. Hotel employees don't usually live in the resort, but a property manager who was sweet on me pulled strings. The queen bed's yellow sheets and blankets lie clumped like scrambled eggs. Every stem in my Bon Voyage bouquet is a hothouse show-piece. The fake bamboo trash can overflows with old make-up, runned stockings, discarded love letters. The ceiling fan rotates lazily, marking island time.

As I step to the lanai, my eyes go to the spot in the ocean where surfers congregate. A longboarder sits past the sluggish reef swells, waiting to catch a ride. A bellhop will be up any second. No time for a last jog on the beach. I light a cigarette and rub one bare foot against the other. My spiked-heel sandals wait at the door with my suitcases. The tropical breeze musses my hair.

The rap on the door comes. "Bellman."

It's the new guy—Stoney. No, let's give New Guy his own name. Lance. I hold the door wide for Lance's luggage truck. "Welina. Hi."

"Mind if I bum one of those?" he says to my cigarette.

"Come outside."

He leaves the luggage truck and follows me through the sliding door. I wave at the pack and lighter on the deck chair. The tradewinds swirl his fresh smoke over the lanai wall. Laid-back Lance lingers next to me. "Some view. How long have you lived in Wonderland?"

"Several years." I watch Lance being seduced by the ocean blue.

"Where do I sign up for a room like this?"

"Don't count on that happening."

Lance clears a strand of my hair away from my eye. Audacious, but charming. He has dimples in both cheeks.

"Eight days ago I was in college in Wisconsin," he says. "And not real into it." He scrapes the embery edge of his cigarette with his pinky nail. "I caught a red-eye, bought a used surfboard, found this job. My folks are pissed 'cause their tuition money's down the tubes, but no regrets for me. It's awesome here."

The wind bumps whipped-cream clouds across the horizon.

"Can't believe I'm leaving," I say.

Our arms touch—mine bare, his in a starched white hotel blazer. There's a small Band-Aid on his neck. His hair is long and dirty, already sun-bleached. "Where you moving to?" he says.

"Mainland. I'm engaged." I show him the rock my squeeze laid on me.

He barely glances at the diamond. "Too bad. We could've hung out."

"You and me? And do what?"

"The hula."

LANCE JOHNSON says the tag pinned to his blazer. "I've seen you at the beach," I say, tapping his badge. "Baggage supervisor."

"Wish I'd seen you in a bikini."

I haven't banged a drone like Lance in ages. The hotel conference center keeps me busy with blue-chip men, like my intended. Surfer boys and bellhops need not apply. I stub out my cigarette on the wall and drop the butt for the maid to sweep. Lance does the same and follows me into the room.

I take my lipstick out of my purse. The bellhop watches me color my lips coral, then he reluctantly hefts my gathered bags onto the cart. The orchids in the vase give off a rotten papaya smell.

I step into my strappy shoes. My dress is clingy raw silk. Lance loads my flight bag onto the cart.

"That's everything," I say.

"You sure?" He jumps to the dresser and jerks out a couple of drawers. The first is empty, but nestled in the second one he pulls out is a pile of underpants like a litter of baby animals. It's as if Lance intuited I'd forgotten them.

"You can have them," I say.

Lance's face flushes. College boy.

"Give them to a sweetheart. With those dimples, you must get girls easy."

He shrugs.

I grab a palmful of the underwear and stuff them down the front of his regulation flowered shirt. "I'll smile about this on the plane," I say.

He licks his chapped lips. "Put 'em down my pants, and we'll both have something to smile about."

I return to the drawer for the few delicates left there. "Unzip."

He opens his fly. I push my undies into his tighty whities, feeling his pump handle swell at the graze of my fingers.

Lance grabs my ass. Bristling, I wriggle away from his clutches. "I'm spoken for, remember?" I clutch my purse and march to the door. He pulls himself together and yanks the baggage cart into the hall.

The bamboo-veneer elevator doors close. The gears launch us down the shaft, the drop causing a bends-like sensation in my head. The air conditioning sends shivers across my shoulders. The elevator car smells of coconut oil. My genitals feel inflamed. I unsnap my purse and remove my hotel keys, inserting the special small one into a lock in the station panel to bring the elevator car to a stop between floors three and two. Looking into Lance's blue eyes, I say, "How about one last dose of Aloha Spirit?"

Mr. Bellhop knows exactly how aloha to go, thrusting his tongue toward my throat, unzipping his pants, spilling my orphaned undergarments to the elevator floor, ripping off his Band-Aid and pressing it over the security-lens aperture at the back of the elevator car under the hung ceiling. He reaches up my dress and tears off my stretch-lace thong.

We bang the stolen way of strangers, watching each other in the mirrors, grunting like tennis champs. No time to waste and nothing to lose. So bad, it's good. So in the present, time stops.

The $1,000 Question

Why can't I get off anymore?

The $1,001 Question

Why are aspirin bottles so hard to open?

SPLIT THE CHEDDAR

Cement apartment bunker, natural gas leak, dumpster out front—I've tracked down my last romeo's habitat. His hood looks worse by day than night. Everywhere I turn, it's spray-painted wall tags, junked cars, spewiferous piles of dog crap.

It used to be wham-bam, on to the next man, but lately I'm the Queen of Cling, mosying out here before my morning coffee, and for what? Not to solicit more *Pow!* or *Zam!* foreplay. This mission is for 12 Step, for facing my mistakes, putting rough love behind me. That folly has turned gnarly too often.

What's scary, as I sit my ass on the curb across the street from Gordon's building, is the 'now what?' If my tournament of daredevil lust is kaput, are memories *it* from now on? Like staggering all hotted up from Gordon's truck in this very spot that night we met. Like our soused free-for-all behind closed door. The rusty smell of blood in my nose when he coldcocked me. That dude's brand of affection has crossbones on the label. When he showed up at my place, he hit me again. Who knows what would have happened if Sada hadn't burst in on the scene.

A BMX bike in the street skids to a stop in front of me, its pedaler a young gun with pimples and unlaced Adidas. "Yo. You live near here?"

I shrug.

"I do," he says. "Half time."

Gordon's truck is nowhere in sight. Even if he's home, I'd be better off leaving. Mission accomplished, mission aborted, whatever. To have bothered to come here at all seems fuckwitted now.

"Lookin' for johns?" the spug says, watching me.

"You think I'm a ho? Working this dead area?"

He swings off his bike, parks his duff beside mine. "I could set you up. Forty bucks a go." His head dribbles like a basketball. "Me and you could split the cheddar, fifty-fifty."

"Who would cough up this forty-buck flash?"

"People from my school."

"How old are your 'people'?"

"Old enough." He scratches his biggest pimple, a yellow lozenge on his chin. "These kids aren't real demanding, and they'll pay us gar-un-teed cash money." He points to a gloomy 1960s three-story. "We'd use my dad's place. He's never home."

"Get lost, Squirt. I'm busy."

Like I look busy. Dumb joke.

"Do the math," he says. "Line up four or five of these choir boys—Bam! Best dough you ever made in twenty minutes. You're a firecracker, I can tell."

My juvie buddy's got salesmanship. I'll give him that.

He spirals a shoelace around his finger. "How about Monday after school? You'd make those horny pussies' day."

"What am I, a public servant? Got a cigarette?"

He stands, like he's gonna produce a smoke from his pocket. Instead he grabs the bicycle's handlebar. As his fanny hugs the seat, he leans down. "You're the mangiest hooker I've actually ever seen."

"Liar!" I spring to my feet and arch my neck like a cocked pistol. "Then why'd you suggest the trick?"

"Forget it." He pushes off from the curb and centers his fat-tongued shoes on the pedals.

When bike and rider vanish up the block, I sigh. Gonna kick myself later, at home with my zucchini, thinking about trembling underage pud and getting paid for it. Forget it, he says? Regret it's more likely.

Or will I? I tuck in my bra straps and imagine facing Emmie and Jonathan at the next meeting, knowing I'd serviced a fresh squad of nerdling cock for cash. That'd be a whole new low. Hooking's never been my thing. I've got real jobs, plenty else going on.

"I'm still bugger-able," I say out loud as I cross the street, "if a BMXer wanted to pimp me." A white airplane etches the sky, dragging its jet roar after it. "And you," I say to Gordon's building, "are a bluffer that says you're coming back to see me, then never does."

Bewitched by my own outrage, I follow the fractured concrete walkway past doors 1 through 5 to Gordon's abode in back with its metal "6" coming unglued. The digit clings beneath a duplicate "6" blanched in the wood where the number originally was attached.

I press my cheek to the warped door veneer and feel vibrations. The gas stench wafts up like evil fairy mist. My knees buckle. My sweater snags on the unsanded wood. My posture's grotesquely humpbacked when the door flies open. To keep from falling in on Gordon, I grab the jamb and hold tight.

Bed-haired, wearing gym shorts that expose his chunky-monkey knees, he squints at me, incredulous.

"I came for those tights I left here." I slide my right boot into the doorway. "Those ones you told me you kept to sniff?"

"I don't have nothing of yours." He swings his door to lock me out, but it rebounds off my boot.

"Last time you were all bout it bout it for me," I say, shocking myself with weak moral resolve, "'til my neighbor butted in. Remember *her*?"

"Why the goddam hell are you bothering me?"

I sniff at him. "Do you practice being a mork-suck? Just give me back what's mine, and I won't bother you anymore." Harp on those tights—I can't come up with a better riposte.

The doorway widens. "Find whatever it is, then leave," he says, retreating into the black hole of the apartment.

He's left me a painless exit strategy. Even a fool would know to walk away. "Just get the tights," I mutter, stepping in. "I have this under control."

In the living room, Gordon makes a show of rummaging for my lost garb, flinging TV Guides, chair cushions, t-shirts, and the like to one side or the other. When everything that can be flung has been, I tail him into his bedroom. He kicks the covers off the bed, as if my tights could be wadded under his daggy paisley quilt after so many lapsed days.

"Maybe you threw them out." I stare at the bare sheet.

"Ya think? If you're satisfied, get the hell out."

I'm not satisfied. I gaze at the plastic lamp, the hairy neck I've licked. "I was friendly to you at my house. Why can't you be nice?"

He chucks a pillow onto the bed. "Why does every bimbo want me to be their tame pigeon? My ex-wife. The freak I met at McNally's. Now you."

I smile, charmed to be included on a list. "Au contraire, Brutus. Be as wild as you want."

He tramples over the mattress, looking like he wants to throttle his former wife or whoever's conveniently available. I go cross-eyed as his finger lands on my chin like a laser bead.

"Tagged, I'm it." I wish I'd washed my face.

"You smell." His finger slides off me. "You said you'd split."

"What if I don't go?"

His eyes have the same black, blind, hunger-steered, swimming shark look I've seen in my mirror. There's always been a kinship between us. I picture the beaver cleaver in his shorts.

"Get out of my place, you thick-head bitch," he says, hands hanging at his sides, hard and stiff as meathooks. "You ever come back, I'll kill you." He punches the wall. The plaster cracks in three directions. That wall could be my face.

Outside in the cold light of day, I understand—Memories really *are* it for me.

What a relief. I retrace my steps, marveling at making my escape without more personal injuries. I wipe my nose on my sleeve. Being told I stink by Gordon is rich. That tossbag stinks. And the sump-pit he lives in.

I pause in front of #2 and sniff under my arm. My B.O. smells like chili powder mixed with sour milk. When did I stop using deodorant? When was my last shower? I inhale the air. The swamp gas smell is gone.

Maybe Gordon killed me without me realizing. I've reincarnated to some unpolluted place, like New Zealand. Or a galaxy far away. I hurry to the street, have a look around.

Still the same seedy block of 60th. All Gordon killed was my desire for goons like him. A seismic shift.

I'm no thick-head bitch anymore. That girl's back at Gordon's apartment, ghostly as his duplicate 6.

BODY RIPPER

From Gordon's lair, I sally forth to Sada's apartment and find her crumpled on the floor by her bed, a cloth puppet with no supporting hand inside.

I rush to free her from the twisted blanket. Where the legs of her fleece pants fork, there's a wet stain. "What happened?" I whisper, hangdog guilty for clocking in late.

"Collapsed getting out of bed. Legs don't seem to work."

When she tried to fire me after the carjack kerfuffle, I swore dependability up and down. Today she needs me, and I welsh on my pledge, disappearing on the pretext of taking a step toward redemption when I was really chasing down the phantom of a sick thrill.

I have to do better.

As a start, I husk off her uriney pants and underwear. Her exposed raw loins remind me of a half-skinned possum. I lift her off the floor—first time carrying a person in my arms. Her hands bounce on her stiff chest like rabbits' feet on ball-chains. I lower her to the chair and collect dry clothes, a diaper. She grabs the washcloth from me to mop herself clean.

I turn away to give her privacy. The umpteen times I swabbed my ma when she blacked out and soiled herself rise, uninvited, from memory. Whereas Ma brought indignity on herself, Sada got dealt a bad hand that took away her dignity. I part the curtains, considering my own lot in life. I lost out by virtue of birth but brought indignity on myself all the same.

I gaze out the window, randomly singing Elvis the Pelvis's "Viva, Las Vegas!" that I learned from Jello Biafra's version. Across the street, a satellite dish on a roof shines like lithium. Sada grunts her way into the track pants I set beside her.

I strip the bedding off the mattress, singing the delirious three-word mantra, "Viva, Las Vegas!" over and over with a desperate vehemence.

"When you're done, put the TV on," Sada says. "That's what I was getting out of bed to do."

I gather the bedding and the soaked pants into a dank cloth bulb. "Should I call Dr. Cho?"

"No reason to. He said to expect pain."

I detest how Sada so easily converts her fatalistic doctor's prognosis to self-fulfilling prophecy. Doctors should harness the power of positive thinking. "Pain can be fleeting, you know," I say. "Did that quack say it was gonna be permanent?"

"I don't recall."

I drop the laundry and use my pinky to tap the TV switch. Up blooms a flashy, toned female model demonstrating a workout gadget. Disease-wracked house-bound wretches like us have no business watching a "Body Ripper" being endorsed by a heavily made-up, Lycra-clad blonde demonstrator. The spot jump-cuts to a spray-tanned chiseled male in nylon shorts having the time of his life with the same handgrip-stretchband contraption.

"Hasta la pasta, go-bots." I tune off his exertion-is-morphine smile, replacing it with the next channel's scene of bleachers filled with Coors-sotted, God-blessed American NASCAR fans. The lead race car screams past a Penzoil sign, spins out in the turn, and crunches into a padded wall.

Sada doesn't need new visions of car crashes, either. I press the channelsurf arrow again, landing on a Chinews program with a photo of America's Wild Bill Clinton in a magenta backlit box. Our commando in chief has gotten caught in mischief, which I can relate to. Just this morning, some part of me still clung to the belief that life's purpose was hunting down the ultimate orgasm, no matter the consequences.

It's afternoon now, that myth withered away, Sada's care my main concern. I glance around her apartment and think of those boobytrapped rooms in adventure movies where the sides compact. In horror, the locked-in characters notice the walls closing in on them. If they're good guys, a trap door gets discovered in the nick of time. Organ-squishing death is the bad guys' outcome.

This apartment seems to have shrunk in minutes. Will Sada and I escape alive? I'm betting on it.

"Change the channel," she says. "That's no Ronald Reagan."

On PBS, a snake swallows a rat, head first. A voice-over says that a python can go two weeks between feedings.

I ask Sada if she's hungry. She asks did I go out with Stoney last night?

"That guy you met? Little misunderstanding. He's not Stoney."

"Who is he?"

"A dinghead I'm through with." I find the bristle-hair brush and run it through her locks 'til they're soft as smoke. The motion soothes us both. "I need to go more than two weeks between rats," I say.

"You know best, sweetheart."

If she knew Gordon threatened to kill me, she wouldn't give me so much credit. "I'm going to 12 Step tomorrow. How 'bout I carry you to the bus stop for your meeting?"

She whaps one forefinger against her other hand. "Too far to walk."

"Nuh-uh." I flex my arms. "Me strong like bull."

"Bull shit."

I laugh but feel tears escape down my cheeks. I bury my face in my sleeve.

"W-what's wrong?" she says. "Are you crying over me?"

"No!" My voice is muffled in my sleeve. "I have my own self to cry about, thank you very much."

"But why?"

My morning's expedition exposed how far from any real relationship I am. "Why can't I be somebody's baby for a change?" I say. *Instead of someone's punching bag,* I think. I lift my face and through my tears see a man in plastic green pants on TV. He transfers a wriggly shell from a bucket to a boiling kettle. "What's that?" I snivel.

"Crawdad."

"Let's eat, okay? Low blood sugar makes me emotional."

Sada's fingers snap against her thumb. I hope that means she'll take some food. "I'll make soup," I say.

At the back of the kitchen cupboard sits a lone Campbell's soup can that I pray is Chicken 'n' Stars.

"I'm like a baby," Sada says in the other room.

Grabbing the can, I lean through the doorway. "What do you mean?"

"W-weak, dependent. You don't want to be a baby."

What's wrong with being cared about? With being taken care of? My eyes drop to the label on the can. Cream of Broccoli.

"Here's one thing I'm sure I don't want." I show her the can. "Green soup."

Precious Moments

Samuela, the volunteer speaker, is a beady-eyed brunette with a morbid aura hanging over her like polder fog. She explains being stuck on Step Three, and "turning my will to God's care?" A neon white purse hangs from her shoulder, a ponderous brass cross from her neck. "Can I use a catechism to explain why I'm working the same step as last time?" she says. "Shouldn't we put ourselves in His keeping everlastingly?"

No one but you, God, has the answer to her questions. The rest of us listen with zipped lips because SLAA etiquette requires us to act impartial and not raise objections, no matter what anyone claims, denies, or asks.

"Is it wrong to keep His mercy foremost in my thoughts? To lean on Him through my vicissitudes?"

She must be wearing a wig since—Lord, have mercy—the pelt jolts like a hank of fake fur each time she scratches her eyebrow. She questions the travesty of her sister being awarded custodial care of her child—how can a devout Christian be deemed unfit as a parent?

The poor girl's sweating prayer beads, trusting you'll hear her pleas—Higher Power, Allah, Jehovah, Big Kahuna, Jesus, whoever's up there. Obviously, she thinks about you all the time, the way love junkies obsess about stankie. She's awaiting your coming.

She's not your only fan in the house. The bywords, hosannas, and testimonials at meetings refer to you ad nauseum. Addicts have big voids that you help fill. Our warped families turn us out, hooked on sex, thrills, anger, drugs, and whatnot to forget our pain. 12 Step offers divine assistance. Samuela's sold on you. Even I'm on psychic bended knee. Not on my own behalf. I always get by. But Sammy—she needs succor.

And Sada, who's resting at home, missing her workshop . . . . If I was you, healing *her* would be at the top of my miracle list. Then take care of the other hoodooed folks at this confab.

Emmie, in tight striped pants, is our one exception—a goddess unto herself, who got all the help she'll ever need by being born beautiful. Lovely doesn't go wanting and hurting the way plain or ugly does.

Did you will it for us to show up at the church entrance simultaneously? Emmie treated me to a coffee. I recommended donating her change to the Lutherans.

"God bless," the Salami Hat lady said as she dropped the loot into a foil-covered box. She smiled and pointedly told me, "I pray for you every Sunday."

Lit up like birthday cakes with candles, me and the goddess strolled to our meeting room and sat together.

"What good," Samuela says, "is a day not dedicated to extolling the Almighty?"

Maybe she's had chemotherapy and lost her real hair. Maybe she's a man in drag. Or a hairless space alien impersonating a human.

"God understands my love—why doesn't anyone else?" Her forehead bulges like a frog's. "Isn't it wicked for Human Resources to have branded me 'obsessed' with my boss and terminated my employment? Isn't my Tender Tails figurine collection evidence I have other interests? Really, my rare Precious Moments pieces, like the fish-in-a-Bible, should prove, wouldn't you think, that I'm not 'fixated' on some standoffish supervisor?"

She pauses and fingers the cross hanging between her breasts. Her face reminds me of a coconut I saw on display at the grocery store, hacked apart and set on ice, white flesh contrasting with dark hull. "Every night," Samuela says to Jonathan, our closest thing to a confessor, "I pray my new manager at Tran's Plumbing won't take out a restraining order, like my other boss, and since I still have my job, doesn't that prove the Lord is protecting me?"

I look up at the acoustic tile ceiling. Help needed down here before this nut cracks!

Her Ode to You finished, Samuela slinks to her shabby banquet room chair, her cheeks flush with a peachier hue than before.

The collections basket goes around, as do the Introductions. Each person states name and rank. I picture Stoney in his vest. "Boop," I say, at my turn, imagining Stoney's abs exposed, like Jesus on the cross. "International sex addict."

Twitchy Roxanne volunteers to speak second, her eyeballs sidewinding like a rodent. "I'm Roxanne, and I've been coming to meetings for a year."

"Hi, Roxanne," the rest of us offer in unison.

"I haven't volunteered 'til now because, in all honesty, I've never taken the steps seriously."

Dales snickers. I feel grudging admiration for Roxanne's 12 Step sacrilege.

"I've been celibate for years." Her eyes slide right to left. "When Ronn walked out on our marriage, I gave up sex cold turkey. No slippery-slope backslides. No dating."

The postal worker shakes his amazed head.

"I could probably deny my sexuality the rest of my life. Of course, repression isn't the healthiest solution to addiction, but it's been the easiest for me. My mother nags me to get over my guilt, find a new husband. She doesn't know my infidelity wasn't one isolated case—that I'm some kind of nymphomaniac."

Nymphomaniac! Gotta love it.

"I don't intend to relapse into carnal indiscretion," Roxanne explains, "but I have to say, the chaste life feels more like a dead end than a refuge. That's why I put off sharing my story for so long. I knew it would be disheartening for the group to hear that recovery, for me at least, turns out to be overrated. Then again, we're supposed be honest, right? With ourselves. And each other."

The room is still.

"Sorry I haven't focused on a particular step. Maybe SLAA isn't the place for an atheist like me." Roxanne looks up at Samuela, then Dales. "Maybe someone who's been clean and sober a long time doesn't fit here?" She looks at Emmie. "Even after a marriage, a string of romances, and lots of cooling-off time, I don't know how to do healthy sex. I'm still seeking my path."

"We're out of time," Jonathan cuts in. "That'll have to be it. But you'll find your way, I know it."

Roxanne returns to her chair to get her purse. Her gray shoes have cutesy laces just like the beige ones that pissed me off in the bathroom stall.

"Whoever has the basket," Jonathan says, "bring it forward as we close. See you next Sunday."

I pad out behind Emmie, smelling her perfume and leather coat. Dales presses toward her. I glance at the transom above the door. A water stain on the wall looks like a shrink's inkblot test. "Hey Emmie," I say, "could I get a ride home?" Tarik eavesdrops on us, as does Fred. "It's not far."

"Okay."

I look again at the water stain we're walking under. A monkey with its tail up—the shape of the blot.

On the church pathway, I button my coat. Roxanne passes us, purse strap across her flat chest.

"That was brave, your talk," Emmie tells her. "So great."

"Especially the part about being a nymphomaniac," I say.

Roxanne stops and says to Emmie, "Thanks."

"An eye-opening view of where recovery leads," Emmie says.

Roxanne cracks a miserly smile. "For whatever realism is worth."

"A lot," Emmie says. "We have to know the stumbling blocks ahead."

"But if you're so bummed after licking your addiction," I say, "what's the use?"

"That's exactly my question." Roxanne walks on.

We watch her shoes trot-trot-trot away. They stop about thirty feet beyond us.

"Excuse me?" she says, turning. "Would you like to get some breakfast?"

"Sure," Emmie says.

"Is there somewhere near here?" Roxanne says, not once looking at me.

"Boop?" Emmie says. "Interested?"

"The Hollyhock's close," I say.

Roxanne drives separately to the restaurant. Emmie and I hustle down a side street off Alcatraz. "I was in St. Henry's bathroom a few weeks ago," I pant, "and she was in a stall squeezing a squeaky toy like a lunatic. Maybe she's not as together as you think."

"Compared to some of the others, she sounds stable."

"True," I say, wondering if I'm included in the sub-class of unstable *others*. "Like Dales? Or restraining-order Samuela?"

"At least they come to meetings," Emmie says.

"Sometimes I sit there and imagine God smiting us with a bolt of the by-Jove for being immoral seedbags."

Emmie laughs and opens her purse. "I've been worrying about being smitten, too. Not by God, though."

I'm about to ask, "Smitten by who?" when she pulls out the keys to a champagne-yellow, hit-song perfect sports car. We climb into contoured leather seats the color of fresh semen. The dashboard looks like a jet cockpit panel filled with gauges.

"Your beau lay this junker on you?"

"Engagement present," Emmie laughs and clicks her seatbelt.

"You love this poobah?"

"Most of the time." She starts the engagement present. It purrs like a just-fed panther and runs steady as a conveyor belt.

"The dude you met in Hawaii?"

"Uh-huh. Wow, you really listen, don't you?"

"Turn right at the corner." The leather emollients and fluffy pile rug give off new-car euphoria spoors. "This, my friend, is no car. It's a pleasuredrome."

Emmie laughs again and consults her side mirror. "After a few weeks, it's just a car."

"Some old Nissan's just a car." My knees spread apart in the plentiful leg room. Everything we pass on the street seems to sit up at attention. "When's the wedding?"

"June 2."

"This June?"

"Four weeks from yesterday."

"Have you heard the expression 'enjoy yourself, it's later than you think'? A reminder to get your drink of water before the well goes dry. Before getting hitched."

Emmie doesn't reply. I fumble with the radio tuner and find the modern rock station. All my life, I've badmouthed fat-cat wealth, but with my velvet-leather seat reclined and Radiohead cooing "Karma Police" from distortion-free speakers, my resistance to the good things in life ebbs.

"*This is what you get when you mess with us*," Thom Yorke sings.

"I'm having religious experience in your sports car," I say. "I see God!"

Emmie glances out the windshield to the great blue yonder of the South Bay. "Where?"

"In here!"

You're not just *in* this car but *of* the car, Heavenly Father. You're the wheels beneath my tush. You're the mother of all drivetrains.

"Peek-a-boo, God, I see you!" I say. "You're Emmie's motherfucking Mercedes!"

Emmie laughs again, blushing, and says, "It's a BMW."

Breakfast Orders

Me

Buttermilk waffle
Brownie
Coffee

Emmie

Cheese omelet
Cranberry muffin
Cappuccino

Roxanne

Rye toast
Mint tea

DEMON IMP

None of us has a dong for a nose or scissors for hands—nothing outlandish a breakfast hour observer might pinpoint. Yet, as our food orders go in, I can't shake my nature-out-of-whack feeling. What have I gotten myself into, who are these women, where the hell am I?

"Where" is simple enough, I guess—the Elmwood-Rockridge neighborhood at the Oakland-Berkeley border. A bakery café with three small dining rooms and antique decor.

The mid-May morning glows on the storefront windows like spray-gunned gold dust. It's 1999—end of one epoch, beginning of a next.

Fried onion and seared coffee smells hang in the air. Forks clink on earthenware plates. Red-aproned waitresses bustle back and forth on crepe-soled shoes, delivering downhome cooking.

At a three-sided table in the restaurant's middle room sit the "who"—a curly-haired tinkerbell, a rangy vamp, and me, their dag nasty sidekick.

If I was a stranger noticing our junta, I'd wonder about this covey of mismatched maidens. This beanery's granny pantry atmosphere is more about eat-and-mind-your-business than see-and-be-seen. I, however, am people-watching.

One table over, a huge-headed baby ejects every spoonful of mash his parents insert in his mouth. Behind the tired family, a pair of laborers wash down a platter of homefries with fragrant hot chocolate. No one knows that at this table, three card-carrying sex addicts are waiting to slake their hunger.

To "break the ice," Roxanne suggests exchanging some basic stats. City of residence: El Cerrito; Piedmont; North Oakland. Age: 35; 27; 26. Job: school teacher; ex-hotel concierge; band manager. Number of times we've been to The Hollyhock: 3; never; 30 or more.

The waitress distributes sloshy cups of water. I notice the pleated copper Jello-mold forms propped on a wicker shelf above us. In the event of seismic activity, they'd fall onto Roxanne's head.

She flattens her hand to her chest as if about to pledge allegiance to her water. "I hope you don't think I'm weird for inviting you to breakfast," she says to Emmie. "I never talk to SLAA people outside of meetings."

"Aren't *we* people?" I say.

"What made you want to this time?" Emmie rewords my question.

"She just admitted having a hole in her life," I say. "So she reached out to the new girls because, compared to Samuela, we're as normal as"—I pick up the salt shaker—"as this." I put down the salt and blow my nose in my napkin.

"That's partially true," Roxanne says.

I smile and don't mention the obvious reason she invited Emmie to breakfast—the pretty thing. Everyone likes to keep company with picture-perfect folk. I got dragged along 'cause I was in the right place at the right time, and Samuela didn't 'cause she wasn't.

Roxanne pulls a pillbox from her purse. "After that meeting, I need my Vi—"

"—codin?" I finish.

"Vitamin B." She puts a spansule on her tongue and swallows. "And moral reinforcement, like you said."

"I need a brain purge," I say.

"The meeting wasn't so bad," Emmie says.

"Are you kidding?" I say. "Samuela is grade A psychotic."

Roxanne narrows her eyes. "When we talk about the group, let's not use loaded terms."

"I agree. Who are we to judge?" says Emmie.

She and Roxanne unfold their napkins onto their laps. My ex-napkin sits on the table, morphed into a snotty ball.

"It's just us here," I say. "We can be real. You wouldn't call Samuela cured, would you? The dottiest banana of the bunch?"

"If 12 Step's teaching me anything," Emmie says, "it's to have an open mind."

"Meetings make for interesting company," Roxanne says.

The smile that passes between them, the us-against-her (them-against-me) vibe I'm picking up on . . . it's plain I'm not one of the girls. I'm worse than Samuela. She's just a holy roller. I'm a holy terror. I don't know where to put my hands. Plop them on the table like cloddish intruders, hold them in my lap as if hiding something disgusting, or let them hang like pig's knuckles? Any minute, I could scream a curse word like a Tourette's sufferer to release my nervousness. "Talk about interesting company," I manage to say, to stay in the mix. "Dales is comical."

Roxanne frowns. "What do you mean?"

The waitress serves the hot drinks. I empty three sugar packs into my cup. "I mean, he needs to get that romancing-the-bone habit beaten out of him. Maybe with those?" I point up at the copper Jello molds and laugh.

Roxanne just stares. The answer to *What's Wrong With This Picture* comes to me. The problem is the gremlin parasite in my head, the subversive voice I always hear. A demon imp prods me to say and do regrettable things.

It hasn't been easy, lately, for my gremlin. I quit the anything-goes sex (for now and maybe forever). This morning I even got weepy over God, arch-enemy of demons. My imp's looking for new ways to make me bad. It's open season on my soul.

But I'm brunching with the ladies and not going down easy! If it's just for one day, one meal, I'm keeping the satanic clutches out of me. "Don't get me wrong. I feel sorry for Dales," I say to my 12 Step friends. "He's like a dog that chases his own tail all day long."

"I feel sorry for him, too," Emmie says. "There but for the grace of God . . . ."

"Go I," I say.

She lavishes me with one of her cream custard, us-against-the-world smiles.

Our waitress directs a couple standing at the *Wait To Be Seated* sign to the far room. They pass our table, a tall man in aviator specs and his Earth goddess consort, garlanded with strands of beads on a braless chest.

"I've been out of control like Dales," Roxanne says, picking up a rye toast triangle. "Most of the time I was married. I was on a tear and acting out."

Roxanne on a tear? Hard to picture. "Like doing what?" I say.

"The usual infidelity. Men on the sly." She nibbles a toast corner.

"How many men? Do tell."

"Boop," Emmie says. "Maybe she'd rather not delve into private details."

"She can, if she wants to. We're not restricted like at meetings."

"It's alright," Roxanne says. She drops the toast and counts on the fingers of one hand. "Simon, Eli, Mike, Gabe. And can't forget Mohammed. Five lovers besides my husband. For me, that's compulsive."

"Mohammed? Like the prophet?"

"He worked at my school. P.E. teacher."

"I thought you were swooning over a savior, like Samuela."

"No. He's a Syrian lacrosse coach."

"Your husband found out you were cheating?" Emmie asks, her voice guarded and low.

Roxanne nods. "I was so busy fanning each little flame, I wasn't thinking straight or being careful."

"You fucked all these guys?" I say.

"Boop!" Emmie peers over her shoulder, concerned about the racy tattle being overheard.

Roxanne's pledge of allegiance hand clamps over her heart again. "Yes, intimacy was involved."

"Involved?" I repeat. "Wasn't it the headline act? You're a *sex* addict, aren't you?"

"Sex was part of the intrigue," Roxanne says. "Those relationships were mini-vacations from being married and responsible. Meeting someone new, feeling that flustered titillation, the secrets and the danger . . . . It was a package deal."

"Hot times in the old town," I say.

Roxanne sighs. "However long it lasted—at most a couple months—the intoxication was offset by anxiety and regret about sneaking to trysts. Then the break-up, or fade-out, always with the same guilt."

"I could get that all done in ten minutes," I say, "and skip the guilt."

"To answer your question," Roxanne tells Emmie, "it doesn't matter how, but yes, my husband found out. And filed for divorce."

"That's what I'm scared will happen to me," Emmie says, "if I get married."

"Don't let it happen," Roxanne says.

"Don't get married," I say.

The cooked food arrives. I almost weep at the nectary smell of waffles and syrup.

"I bared my secrets," Roxanne says. "Your turn, Boop."

My first steaming bite hangs on the fork prongs, and Roxanne wants me to open my veins for her amusement? I sink my teeth into the dripping lump of waffle and pretend I haven't heard.

Roxanne refolds her napkin into quarters. "I'm curious what brought you to SLAA."

Picking up my mug, I think of the lads she said she boffed—Simon, Mohammed . . . . My tally would include hella more, even just the ones whose names I knew. Like the country songs go, I've looked for love in all the wrong places. "I don't kiss and tell," I say and polish off my coffee.

"You don't have to," Emmie, bless her, says.

Is java burning my gut or shame for my debauchery? "Trust me, you don't wanna hear about my past, especially while eating."

The waitress sandwiches a saucer holding my brownie between the other plates. She's gone before I can request a coffee refill.

"This isn't a meeting. You can say anything," Roxanne says, echoing my earlier comment with a stink-bomb smirk.

The tall galoot who came in with the Earth mother appears at our table, alone, and locks eyes on Emmie. "Excuse me, don't I know you from the potter's guild?"

"Potter's guild?" we all three echo.

"On Jones and Second?"

"No," says Emmie.

"Do you swim at the City Club?"

"I'm new to the Bay Area. I don't know those places."

"I'm Bruce." He reaches to shake her hand. A silver band with inset red stones bracelets his wrist. Emmie doesn't take the offered hand. We all stare at it until he pulls it back and stuffs it in his pocket. "I wish I could place you," he says.

"Maybe she doesn't wanna get placed," I say. "We're in a meeting, if you don't mind."

He lingers, unable to tear himself away. He wants a private meeting that includes caveman sex with Emmie.

"Bruce," I say. "Our secret society, Nymphomaniacs Anonymous, does not include you."

"Sorry," he says. He pads back to the bead freak lady waiting like a fox at her hole in the other dining area. Our table's quiet, watching his retreat.

"Lame pick-up attempts happen to you a lot?" I say.

"Nymphomaniacs Anonymous?" Emmie says.

I pull my ear. "Cute, huh?"

"It's not funny," Roxanne says. "That's an invasion of our privacy."

"That's why I told him to clear out while you just sat there!"

"You don't have the right to divulge information about SLAA to strangers," Roxanne says.

"He has no idea what Nymphomaniacs Anonymous means."

"You don't know that," Roxanne says.

My face burns. My sister nymphos are in a pet. I drop my fork and croak in self-defense, "It didn't mean anything."

"I resent it." Roxanne turns to Emmie. "What about you?"

Emmie flashes me the briefest disappointed look and says to Roxanne, "A bit."

I pick up the brownie and, in a fit of gremlin-driven lunacy, toss it into Roxanne's lap. "Resent that," I say. She stares at the brown slab resting on her thigh like a turd.

"Oh, Boop," Emmie says.

Roxanne folds the brownie into her napkin. To impress Emmie with her politeness, she says, "I'll take it to my mother."

Our waitress skids to the table. Sucking the inside of one liquid-foundationed cheek, she slaps our bill on the table and a suspicious look on me. Emmie hands her a credit card and announces that breakfast is on her.

"Thanks," Roxanne says. She opens her purse, puts the brownie in, and removes her school district business card.

While Emmie signs the charge slip, I dip a finger into the syrup on my plate and flick a teardrop of it at Roxanne. She doesn't notice it land on her sleeve as she pens a home phone number on her card and slides it to Emmie. *Next time let's not invite Boop* is what I'm sure they're both thinking.

"I want the brownie back," I say, jumping out of my chair.

Emmie stands and slings her arm over my shoulders, murmuring my name like I'm a fitful horse in need of whispering.

Roxanne thrusts the purse at me. "Take it."

Ignoring her keys, tampons, pillbox, wallet, and what looks like a spray vial of Mace, I remove the brownie and hand the purse back.

Emmie picks up the card Roxanne left for her. "Say goodbye, Boop."

"Goodbye, Boop," I say.

"Call me," Roxanne says to Emmie.

"Will do," Emmie says, waving the card.

I'm led away like a mule. I've mucked up their nice girl brunch and need to be locked in the barn with no hay. At the *Wait To Be Seated* sign, Emmie glances back at Roxanne.

"Roxanne," I call, tearing the napkin off the brownie, "you can have it." I lob the lump of cake back at her. It rips past our table and strikes and upends a water glass on the family's table.

My svengali imp must be happy now. The glass doesn't break, but the water spills. The mother pulls napkins from the dispenser to mop it. The dad whirls around to glare at me. Their little darling gurgles happily at the commotion.

"Cute kid," I call.

Emmie's digital clock lights up money-green at the turn of the car key. "Yipes," I say. "I gotta get to work."

"On Sunday? Is the band playing a wedding?"

"We're not a reception band." A truck rumbles by with a green and white side panel that says, 'Make 7. Up yours.' "My other job is helping a sick lady next door."

"Sounds noble."

"That's me, noble. Except when squabbling over baked goods."

Emmie glances at me as she drives. "Know what I think?"

I don't answer.

She turns on College Avenue. "Roxanne's questions made 12 Step a little scarier for you." She buttons the air conditioner fan on.

I stare at the pizzeria being constructed on the avenue and, apropos to nothing, say, "I saw this bumper sticker the other day. It said, 'If you're not outraged, you're not paying attention.'" Cool air zephyrs from the vent. "Did I tell you I'm getting a car? Not in time for my band's big gig, though. I'll have to take BART."

"If you ever do feel like telling someone why you've been going to SLAA," Emmie says, "I'm a good listener."

"Not *this* again."

"It's what we have in common."

"There's no complicated reason I go. It's just to prove I'm not a fuck-up."

"To who?"

"To everyone that thinks I'm a fuck-up."

"How will you change if you don't undertake the process in good faith?"

"I've changed plenty already, don't worry. I just haven't told those homies at the church about it."

"Good." Emmie throws her hair over her shoulder. "I just have to worry about me, then."

"What've you got to worry about?"

"Keeping my marriage vows."

"I thought you're marrying Prince Charming?"

"Duke Charming, maybe." She opens the glovebox. "Picture of him in here somewhere."

I find a framed photo of a tall, dark gent. Spiffy haircut. Broad shoulders. "Hello, handsome," I say to the picture. "I wouldn't mind being balled and chained by you."

"You're hopeless."

"Not really. Don't think that." I put the photo back and shut the glovebox. "The turn's just ahead."

"The marriage fairytale didn't stop Roxanne from cheating," Emmie says, taking the left I point out.

"Roxanne's no Cinderella," I say.

"I don't have a fairy godmother, either."

"Me, neither. Or a father." I gesture to keep driving up the street. "Got a devil in me is what I've got. Who's not happy unless I'm acting berserk or getting on every man I meet."

"A version of that devil haunts me, too."

"The yellow building's mine."

Emmie parks across the street and turns the ignition off. "Nice to have a friend to confide in. Someone to trust."

Confide and trust. Out of her mouth, it sounds so easy. "The lady I work for? I said I'd go to 12 Step so she wouldn't worry about me as much."

Emmie gazes at my 1930s two-story building that lost its charm around the time Truman nuked Hiroshima.

I open the door but don't get out. "Can I ask you something?"

"What?"

"Are you cheating on Tommy Boy?"

"No."

"Your face is red! Omigod, I'm right?"

Emmie sighs. "It's the pool man, but nothing's happened. He's just . . . eye candy."

"You have a pool?"

"Our neighbor does. We see it through the fence. But I'm just looking. I've never even talked to the guy." Emmie sighs. "Please don't repeat this to Roxanne."

I picture Johnny Depp in red trunks, zinc oxide on his nose, leaf-trapper in hand, on deck for pool service. "My lips are sealed."

Emmie laughs. "When's that band thing?"

"Tomorrow."

"Why don't I give you a ride?"

After embarrassing her at the Hollyhock, this offer's not deserved, but it's too good to refuse. "Sure. Will the hubby come along?"

"He's away on business. And he's just my fiancé so far. Remember?"

"Right."

"This'll be fun. I don't know anyone else in town." She restarts the car. "And if I see that devil on your shoulder . . . ."

"Swat him off!"

"Will do," my nympho comrade promises.

I get out and shut the door. She roars back to Camelot.

"You heard her, Demon," I say out loud. "We gonna git you!"

Shopping List

Deodorant — me

Depends — Sada

Cigarettes — me

Protein powder — Sada

Sneakers — me

Wheelchair — Sada

Sparkles. Chameleons. Transparents.

I've passed this retail outlet in cars and buses a hundred times, never predicting I'd set foot inside. Chances are the same storm cloud would mushroom above the shopkeeper's head if *any* skuzzy punker opened West Coast Wheelchair's tempered glass door. Yet it's me the salesman hustles around the counter to intercept. In his diagnosis, I'm a germ; this store's a cut; he's Bactine to the rescue.

Boo-ya! I could half-nelson this puce-haired clerk to the floor with the greatest of ease.

"Can I help you?" Despite the friendly teddy bear-shaped name tag on his pocket, Stan's face is contorted with doubt. I look like trouble. By Stan's calculation, if I have money, it's worth less than other people's.

He's mistaken on that count. Walking the three miles down here, I brainstormed several practical ways to save funds for a wheelchair purchase. Cut down on bus fares. Cut back on smokes. Cut out tequila. Cut the crap and work more.

"Just browsing," I say to Stan, buying only time so far.

The store's floor space is limited, the selection skimpy. Bright advertisements hang on the walls—fanfare for Sovereign, Invacare, Quickie, brands I've never heard of. Stan would be equally clueless about the Jawbreaker and NoFX posters tacked on *my* walls at home.

I spot a no-frills wheelchair wedged, unshowcased, between piled crates at the back of the store, a chair straight out of a '50s movie featuring a cripple. It looks so right.

Stan positions his body to block access to this old-fangled hack. He flings a short-sleeved arm at the two examples of state-of-the-art handicap transit under the lights up front. In case I'm both a valid shopper *and* unwashed slut, he wants my eyes feasting on his high-end stock.

Questions get asked—who the disabled is ("my neighbor, Sada Pollard"), where the chair will be used ("where*ever*"), and if I want Sada Pollard to have the most comfort and mobility available in a power chair today.

I point to my choice. "I want her to have *that* fine old chair."

Stan honks a loud Ha-choo! As if just the thought of the cut-rate ride is sickening to a quota-hitting professional. When he lifts his glasses to dab at his sneezed-wet eyes, I skip past him.

Lobotomized Randle McMurphy got parked in a contraption much like this—I found *One Flew Over The Cuckoo's Nest* in Ma's garage when I was in high school and savored its denouncement of cruel authority. As I drop onto the wide black seat of what I'm already naming Sada's Freedom Roller, Stan hurries to intervene. "Home users," he says, pressing in on me, "favor power chairs four-to-one over the self-propelled."

I sprawl back and imagine propelling my housebound neighbor through Oakland sunshine, red robins and bluejays tweeting overhead.

"That particular vehicle does have a chrome-plated carbon steel frame." Smelling a transaction, and seeing as how my booty's all over it, Stan is pitching me on this product after all. "Flame-retardant, mildew-resistant upholstery," he recites, "gusseted braces and axles—all standard. Chest strap and amputee attachment optional."

"Too much information, man," I say to halt his amputation talk. Sada's the one person who's believed I could be something other than a fuckup. I refuse to believe she'll require hinky attachments or straps. "Let's not bring up worst cases when I feel so good about this."

"That makes one of us," Stan says.

I read the price tag hanging on my backrest—$169.00, nineteen bucks of which I've salted away—a start, though hardly. "Why do these wheels splay?" I ask, suspicious of a defect.

"A feature called camber, for stability. Perhaps you'd better get up."

I give the wheels a whirl and roll to his oxfords' toes. He grabs for the chair, but I swiftly bowl myself up the aisle. "Medication time, Nurse Rat Shit!" I work up a respectable drool.

Stan vaults after me and seizes both handles. "Stop this thoughtless clowning!"

I leap to my feet and frown at the chair like it's to blame, though I know better. I just have to *do* better. High anxiety's no excuse for rambunctious behavior. I'm here for Sada.

"You're insulting our customers," Stan says, "and wasting my time."

"I am in the market for a wheelchair." I lift sad cow eyes to Stan.

He looks dubious. "For whom, did you say?"

"A lady with advanced sclerosis. Excess collagen's attacking her lungs and joints. She's immobile and desperate to escape the prison of her apartment. Can I take that chair on installment?"

"We don't arrange financing."

My mission is failing. I jab my chin in the direction of Stan's super-duper merchandise. "What's so great about *those*?"

He grins. I'm finally where he wants me, inquiring about the prized line. "Their main advantage to the mobility-impaired is independence," he says.

The Declaration of Independence jumps to mind—life, liberty, pursuit of happiness. Learned all that in eighth grade. I examine the mechanized wheelchairs for guaranties of inalienable rights.

"The left unit travels up to seven point two miles per hour. The right model, five. Both chairs are vibration-free with dynamic anti-tippers, shock-absorbing forks, semi-pneumatic casters, and anodized finishes—sparkles, chameleons, or transparents."

Sparkles. Chameleons. Transparents. How poetic wheelchairs can sound.

I step to the high seat-back version, turn over its laminated price tag, and feel my heart pinch. Dynamic anti-tippers set a pilgrim back a whopping thirty-eight hundred bucks. "These buggys are complicated," I say—code for costly.

"Better living through technology," says Stan.

"Just swinging your basic 'companion model' will be tricky on my chapter 11 income." I shrug and find myself practically crying, "I'm not expecting a miracle. Just hoping to dial back the misery meter."

Stan's eyebrows go up. "It's your mother you say needs the chair?"

"A neighbor. She's like a mother. Only person on earth who loves me. And no one but me watches over her."

"I see."

How could he see what it's like for her, being devoured by disease, or for me, watching helplessly? I'm on the verge of telling him to cram his on-board battery chairs up his unhelpful Stan-the-West-Coast-Wheelchair-Man ass when he says, "Most insurance plans cover wheelchair rental with a small deductible. Hundred dollars typically."

"I might save that in another week or so."

Stan reaches out, squeezes my arm. I've been found worthy of trust and help, the squeeze says—shocking to a fringy sex junkie, who any other day might be trying to engineer my way into Stan's doubleknits to show him he's got nothing over on me. "Get me her policy info," he says. "I'll set her up with dependable personal transportation."

"You mean it?"

"I'll expedite the claim." He grabs a brochure from the counter and staples his business card to it.

I take the brochure. The emotion washing over me as Stan breaks into a Hallmark moment smile is such honest gratitude—it's all I can do to not bow down to it.

Ten Things We Say When Emmie Picks Me Up for Up the Wazoo's Show

"Wearing bridal lace isn't fly for this gig!"

"I better go home and change."

"This whole house is yours?"

"Once it's furnished, it'll be homey."

"Your closet's ginormous."

"How does this jacket look?"

"Can I borrow these hot shoes?"

"What if I redo your hair and makeup?"

"You're making me look like a Gap ad."

"It's a good look on you."

Whoever Can Dig It

"Live! One night only at Mariner Hall!" I call to Bridgit and Tess, on-stage with the gear. "Chavez Productions presents *Loosen The Noose*, a punk rock festival featuring the lamby pies of riot grrrl rock—Uuuup The Wazooooooo!"

Bridgit smiles at my huckster enthusiasm. She and Tess both wear lavender tops.

"What's with the shirts?" I say. "Hijacking The Donnas' color-coordinated look?"

"Just a coincidence," Bridgit says.

"Another big night for us!" I say.

Scampering tech dudes connect pre-amps to amps, other amps to bi-amps. There's wire to tape down, mike stands to drag out, razz to matazz. The first three bands' equipment is being set up all together to keep intermissions short. UTW opens the show. Our gear's up front.

"How's your dad, Tess?" I remember Stoney's news about her visit home. "Was he really sick?"

"He had a stroke."

"Sorry."

Tess stacks the Budda on top of the bass amp. "He's walking and talking a bit."

"That's good. I know from experience what it's like to not be able to walk or talk."

Tess connects the Budda cable. "When you're drunk?"

"No, I've been laying off the booze." I hate being thought of like my ma. "I have a seriously sick friend I take care of."

The tech guys hook up the vocal mikes, running the lines back to the inputs.

"The in-house mikes are Shure 58s," Tess says. "Best sound set-up we've ever had."

"When'd you get back?"

"Boop," Bridgit says, "the floor tom's still in the van. Can you get it?"

"Three days ago," Tess says.

"Did you practice for this gig?" I ask.

"We ran through some songs this afternoon," Bridgit says. "Will you go get the floor tom or not?"

"And no one called me." My tone sounds accusatory, even when I add, "You should've practiced more."

"It's lucky I made it at all," Tess says.

"Glad you did," I say, running a Supportive Manager flag up the pole to see if anyone salutes. The Goober Goes Here drummer wanders by, wood drumstick in one hand and chicken drumstick in the other. "Where's Stoney?"

"Around." Tess checks the Budda's settings.

Bridgit peeks from behind her tom-toms. "What vampy shoes, Boop."

"These old things?"

She locks the nut on her high-hat stand. With her suede boots and V-neck lavender top, *she's* the vamp.

I stick out one foot in Emmie's spikeheel slingback. Party shoes for this gig.

"Sexy," Tess says.

"Your hair's nice, Boopy-Dupe," Bridgit says. She fishes her keys from her bag on the floor.

I pat the hair spray Emmie lacquered on. "Where's Angie?"

"Around," Tess says.

I wonder if Angie's getting "around" with Stoney? He should see my feet and hair.

Bridgit holds out the keys to me. I must still be the band's manager. No one's kicking me out, and I'm being asked to retrieve equipment.

"You got here late," Tess says.

"Door guy gave me a hard time for bringing a 'plus one' who's not on the guest list."

Bridgit and Tess aren't interested, but I go on. "My friend paid admission, but they gave her a backstage pass."

"The van's parked on Minna," Bridgit says. "Use the stage entrance, and hurry."

I don't appreciate being ordered like a go-fer, but I take her pom-pom keyring and whirl on one heel, my billowing dress flashing gam like I'm Marilyn Mon-fucking-roe.

"Sex-SAY!" Tess says as I stiletto away.

"Don't encourage her," Bridgit says.

If I was a comic strip character, the cell that showed me toting Bridgit's drum up First Street in Emmie's fuck-me-Chucky shoes would have this thought balloon—*Beauty sucks wind.* Clasping the drum's slippery shell isn't easy. My arms burn. The rim bangs my chin when I use my shoulder to brush hair out of my eyes.

Suffering for the band's success.

The door guard waves me through to the restricted zone.

Ha! A big drum appears to be a sure-fire "All Areas" pass. Next time Nine Inch Nails play S.F., I should shanghai a snare—and these shoes—and waylay Trent Reznor.

Stoney is chatting up a cortege of backstage could-be's. When he sees me teetering with this payload of drum, he dashes to my rescue.

"Que pasa?" He lifts the instrument out of my grasp. He's wearing his black vest.

I shake out my arms. "Grassy ass, Señor."

"De nada, Boopito."

"Roadies should NOT wear spiked heels like these."

He's too busy negotiating the pokey drum legs through backstage rumpus to notice my splashy footwear. I tag behind him through a short hall.

We pass a girl with distinctive red hair—Cinder Block—whose band is headlining. I have half a mind to stop and say it's a thrill to open for Tilt, but with everyone so blasé, I don't wanna come off like a teenybopper.

Out on the stage right boards, Bridgit points at the snare. I slide it and make room for Stoney to place the tom.

"Thanks, Stoney," she says. "And Boopy."

The black curtain creaks closed on its runners. The drapery edges meet with a plop and release umber puffs of soot. Under the floodlights, the stage feels incubator warm. A sound guy sets a mike in the kick and hangs another under the snare. A female stagehand taps the head of Angie's vocal mike. "Test, test, the west is the best," she says. "One, two, buckle my shoe."

"Three, four, kick down the door," I say.

"Drummer!" a crew guy says. "Gimmie a level check."

Bridgit drums a ruffle from "Green Piss."

"Boop," Stoney says, "your check's upstairs in the office."

"I get all this spunk-rock excitement and filthy lucre, too?"

"Only your twenty dollar cut of lucre," Angie says, striding out from the wings.

Twenty dollars toward the wheelchair deductible. Angie has no idea what anything means to me. "You can sweeten my kitty anytime, dawg," I tell Stoney.

Angie plants a territorial hand on his ass. Not wearing lavender is her one positive attribute. Her black hoody makes her look like a vampire. Her white vinyl skirt is torn. "Who's that?" she says, pointing with her elbow. "Daisy Fuentes?"

Standing in the wings with orange drinks in both hands, wearing her cropped red jacket and a Colgate smile, Emmie could also be mistaken for a stewardess.

"My missing-in-action friend." I wave my arm. "Hey, Emmie!"

Emmie hands me a Tequila Sunrise and mumbles a shy hi to Angie.

"Where were you?" I say. The ice cubes are melted to slivers, the fluid diluted up to the rim.

"Talking to the bartender."

I slurp from the glass and—no big surprise—catch Stoney eyeballing man-bait Emmie.

"This is Stoney," I say. "And Up The Wazoo. Tess, Bridgit and . . . ." I kiss the air at Angie. "What's your name again, Sugar Bean?"

Angie parts her lips. Her teeth seem like a grandfather's dentures. The stage lights dim, as if snuffed by the chill molting off her.

"Time to open the doors." Stoney strides off the stage. "You're on in 30."

The equipment's power bulbs on the dark stage twinkle like Christmas lights. Tonight's the holiday I've been impatient for.

———

In the "artists' lounge," Bridgit and Angie veto my help with writing the set list. Tess props her Fender against a chair and disappears, probably to shoot insulin. Emmie is seated on a scabby Naugahyde couch. I join her to finish my drink. The bartender made it strong, no doubt hoping she'd get tipsy and give him her phone number.

"Were the Sunrises free?" I say. "After all that flirting?"

"Who says I was flirting?"

"Whoa, Sheba. We don't get drink credits at this shoestring production, so I thought if the bartender liked you, he'd ply us with complimentary cocktails."

"I paid for the drinks."

"I haven't been drinking much lately." I set my empty on the floor. "I wouldn't want to get polluted and end up breaking six of the ten steps by hunting down some one-night punk love."

"I'd stop you from doing that," she says. "And it's twelve steps, not ten."

Seventeen minutes to show time. We chat about bands—she favors Gypsy Kings and Counting Crows. I declare that another round of Sunrises won't compromise anyone's morals, so Emmie revisits the bar. Much as I'd like to find Stoney to claim my check, he's probably up to his earlobes in pre-show hassles. I'll collect my pay later while we're celebrating a job well done. I play air guitar and think about Stan's promise to come through on the wheelchair.

Emmie returns and hands me a full glass. "That was fast," I say.

"Drinks were free." There's a twinkle in her eyes.

"To a master seductress," I toast. This Sunrise is sweeter and redder than the last. "Don't deny it."

Emmie swallows some drink. "Bad habit."

"No offense meant, but if I was about to become Mrs. Wifey, I wouldn't waste time at a downbeat recovery group. If I was you, I'd work my assets and get my last licks in."

"You're naughty."

"But nice. Right?"

"My mother used to complain about 'Wifely Duties.'" Emmie takes another sip and giggles. "Her version of sex ed, when I was little, was to tell me my brother had a 'peanut' and I had a 'giant.'"

"Moth-ers," I slur. "Can't live with them, can't get born without 'em."

"It didn't make sense. My brother's five years older. He was the giant."

"You must've been a sexy little shaver as a kid."

"Not really."

"Your brother live near here? Has he got some hot skillet buddies to introduce me to?"

She puts down her drink and stands, looking seasick. "Where's the bathroom?"

"Off the hall. You okay?"

She strides off with her Daisy Fuentes mystique.

Alone on the Naugahyde, I park my elbows on my knees and laugh about the giant between my legs. I close my eyes and feel it rumble.

A couple of minutes later, wandering the hall and trying not to spill my drink, I see Tess.

"I met your friend in the bathroom," she says. "She said you met at church?"

"So?"

"You're religious?"

"I go to AA at St. Henry's." I gulp some Sunrise.

"Should you be drinking?"

"Not that kind of AA." I salute Tess with my drink. "To Up The Wazoo's big night."

"Speaking of which," Tess says, walking on, "I need to get the song list."

"It's a special AA for sex and love," I call after her. "That I go to."

Sex and love and rock and roll, she sings back.

"Good evening," Stoney's voice bilges from the P.A. speakers in the concert hall's lucious darkness. "Thanks for coming out to the second annual *Loosen The Noose Festival*. Join me in welcoming the East Bay's Up The Wazoo."

The spots click light on the stage. Stray hoots rise from the floor. Seeing the act I nurtured—the girls I whupped into shape and wrote lyrics for—stalk to the mikes is almost too much for a manager to bear. Bridgit's drumstick counts down to the virgin guitar lick. For whoever can dig it—right here, right now, is as über alles as life gets.

G-Force and G-Spot At Last

Waiting in the sidestage shadows with Emmie, I cross my fingers for luck. The names of my heroes—Danita, Dee, Selene, Corin, Theo—from the tuffest babe groups ever—Bikini Kill, Babes In Toyland, 7 Year Bitch, Lunachicks, Sleater-Kinney, L7—burst like firecrackers in my head. In a blink of the eye, Angie, Tess, and Bridgit will become the underground world's newest sensations.

Sure, we're rookies compared to gold standards like Lunachicks, but we're walking in their sacred cow footsteps. I'm so stoked to be a speck of punk history, my brain will probably aneurysm.

Angie rips into the stadium-rock chords of "Heartslayer."

"Their second worst song!" I wail.

"It's a kick," Emmie says.

I grind my teeth and await a segue to the band's trademark indie riffs. When the kids smoking outside hear the good stuff, they'll buy tickets and rush the front, converted to adoring fans. If only I was calling the shots.

Angie has her hoodie cinched at the chin like a nun's wimple. Under her old Stratocaster, her legs look like Tinker Toys. Being a skinny little bitch isn't her problem. Her skinny little voice is. She's hoarse and using the mike like a rank amateur, losing half her words. I can't see past the footlights into the pit to tell what kind of snot-core audience is out there and if anyone likes this song.

"Insulin Shock" starts, hopefully to redeem the band. At our gig at The Frontline, Tess made faces and pretended to be slipping into diabetic shock while singing back-up on this number. Tonight she's skipping the monkeyshines. The band delivers the song bare bones and underwhelms even me.

"These greenhorns are not on tonight," I complain into Emmie's ear.

"They're cute!"

They'd be cuter putting more oomph into the performance. But I bag my thumbs-down expression and fake a rapt smile. Because if your own manager isn't into you, who will be?

Angie generates heat belting out "While You're Twisting, I'm Still Breathing." Tess goes into a lather on the bass lead, nailing notes all over the place. At the "push me, push me, I don't care" lyric, I sing along. This's what I'm talking about!

The cover finishes, and instead of claps or cheers, a phlegmy cough and half-hearted whistle from onlookers are the only responses. Pros like The Gits and 7 Year Bitch must have had warm-up gigs that left showgoers cold. That's part of paying your dues, riding the learning curve. I coached these Wazoos over the first hurdles. It's up to them to generate sparks now.

Angie muffs the words to "Shove It Up Your Morass," our best song! My pseudo-smile stays put. "Their lack of practice shows," I say. Emmie shrugs.

I'm grateful she drove me here. Only a birdbrain would fail to appreciate a life-sized Barbie for a friend. Still, how tight would it be if Corin or Danita was in her place? Someone in the punk know, a tremendous talent who'd tell me, 'Things'll be okay,' and things *would* be. Someone who'd remind me riot grrrls kick gluteus.

Emmie's ass sways to the music like a Dixie Chick. She likes this version of "Shove It Up Your Morass."

The set flies sloppily by. Tess honks through the disgraceful "Did You Ever Stop To Wonder." Angie's playing is shameful, her singing soulless. Just weeks ago, the Frontline appearance spawned legit buzz. This follow-up is going belly-up. Bridgit looks as miserable as I feel.

These shoes aren't getting more comfortable, either. My second drink went to my stomach instead of my head. "Loosen The Noose" is nowhere near the triumph it was supposed to be.

During "Green Piss," the spotlights catch seven or eight spectators bouncing on their toes. Nothing wild and woolly, but building energy. With Up finally showing what they can do, given half a chance and one-twentieth of a crowd, I grin at Emmie.

Angie picks this moment to bollix a chord. Her fingers tangle while breaking to the chorus. Ticked off, she uses the error as a selfish excuse to unplug her guitar and stomp off the stage, the opposite direction from me. Tess and Bridgit play on. But Angie doesn't come back out, so before the next verse they follow-the-leader. The people in the hall boo at the emptied stage.

Fuck me with a spoon. They don't come back out. They're trashing this opportunity. Stoney will read me the riot act about the band not meeting its obligations. They had 30 minutes to fill. They were on for 20. Where's Stoney *been* the whole time?

"Rocky finish?" Emmie says in my ear.

I uncross my fingers and groan, "Bush-league."

The curtain closes by some invisible hand.

Backstage, Tess sits on the Naugahyde sofa, her cheeks haggard. A stage hand tells us Angie "has left the building." Bridgit's supposed to move her drum kit off-stage, but she's smoking and acting aloof. Stoney hasn't resurfaced. The Goober Goes Here guys are sharing a pre-set doobie. I pace past them, hoping to be offered a toke, but they keep their scooby snack to themselves. Foot pain makes me pant. Every exhale tastes like harsh tequila mixed with gaggy red syrup. Recorded music pipes through the P.A.—that Blink 182 radio hit that's been played to death. Emmie hovers close, wanting to be helpful. At least she's turned off her whale of a smile, now that the gig's so wack.

"I like what I heard," she says.

She doesn't know the difference between a concert that blows people away and one that blows chunks. "It choked," I say.

"They'll do better next time."

I march to Bridgit, who drops her cigarette stub in a Pepsi can. "What was that?" I ask. "Stage fright?"

"Not really."

"Angie shows up looking subnormal then spoils the show. What drug is she on?"

"We've gotta off-load my kit. Get Tess. We'll talk later." Bridgit stalks to the stage-access door.

Tess looks shell-shocked, her bass across her lap. "C'mon," I say. "Help with the drums."

"Naw," she says, rubbing her eyes with the back of her hand.

"You and Angie need hands-on managing. I'm more into this band than you are."

"Rooty-toot-toot for you."

"Tess, you don't get many shots at living out your dreams."

She stares at the pick-up on her bass.

I tap my left sling-back shoe against one of her Maryjanes. "Gotta make the most of the chances you get."

"I don't need a lecture."

"I think you do." Tess has always been a nose-to-the-grindstone college kid, with the band as a hobby. "Show me commitment," I say, "and I'll give my life for you. Now get off your ass."

"I'll get off my ass when I'm ready."

I remember how blown away I was seeing Bikini Kill live during the *Pussy Whipped* era. Kathleen and the band were all blistering, revolutionary spitfire. Out in the audience, I was so wanting some of that. Bikini Kill got past these kinds of nights. They overcame the obstacles. They had ideals. They had a following. God, I wish Angie and Tess were more like them. I repeat what Little-Miss-Positive-Attitude Emmie said, "You'll do better next time, right?"

Tess crosses her eyes at me. "What next time?"

Enlisted personnel being scarce, Emmie chips in muscle power to dismantle Bridgit's kit. Each harrowing step in these punishing heels makes me fume about Angie and Tess not helping.

The toms, snare, and cymbal get stowed in the equipment room until intermission when there'll be more time to transfer them to the van. As Bridge and Emmie carry the bass drum, I absorb a final moment of Mariner limelight. It was swell for a few minutes. The crew and handlers chase me off stage. I find a spot to park my rump on a pile of guitar cases. Nevermind tonight's setback. There's future glory to map out.

Stoney shows up during my Enterprising Manager moment, accompanied by a gabbing, thin-haired guy. Quick as a lick, a primal hankering to sexually defile Mr. Thin Hair hits me since Stoney alleges to be off-limits. Pork-and-beaning a convenient stranger isn't what people go to their graves remembering with pride, but it can be one hell of a consolation prize on a shit-happening night like tonight. I need a shred of comfort.

Like a life-sized reminder of 12 Step *semper fidelis*, Emmie appears behind the men. If I was her, I could get Stoney to want me in seconds. What a waste that's she's in SLAA. The lust-buster routine makes sense for me, who's gotten no pleasure from being a sex addict in recent memory. Emmie's a different kettle of fish.

"Next band's up," Stoney says.

The curtain parts on Round 2's punkabaloo fivesome, Goober Goes Here. Me and my friend join the sixty-person rabble rushing the stage. Where were they when Up The Wazoo played?

For us, it's not that Goober's a bad-ass band. It's more that in our unspoken, Tequila Sunrise-fueled urgency, me and Emmie are hell-bent on losing ourselves in the rollick. Sex addict energy has to get channeled somewhere.

I bust a move to Goober's hucklefuck licks to keep my toes, crammed in hot-girl shoes, from getting trampled. When the thrash escalates, I scream at my mosh pit newbie pal, "Steer clear of the brute force, okay?"

But over the banjo power chords and herky-jerky screeching, no one can hear squat. And Emmie doesn't seem to mind the elbows bayoneting her.

A hardcore song gets a phalanx of young toughs boiling. Jampacted in front of the stage, I smell skunky BO and taste salt seeping from people's pores. The fact that my feet are bloody pulp in sling-backs almost slips my mind.

Emmie propulses to ground zero of the melee as my friend Spaceman Steve crashes toward me. "Steve!" I grab his shoulder.

We grin like monkeys across a fruit basket. I haven't seen Steve, The Beam-Me-Ups' drummer, in months. He's all bone and cotton in my hand. I want to ask if he saw Up blow their set but doubt he'll hear me. A hand I hope is his gropes one of my tits, a turn-on I dig until Emmie slam-dances back, her presence reminding me—no cheap erotic kicks allowed. I hop clear of Steve's grasp.

"Who's your friend?" he booms, staring at Miss Push-And-Shove-With-Glee. Who would have guessed Emmie had so much punk cheek? Maybe she's been pent up from too much psychotherapy, wedding plans, or secrets kept from the future groom. Without warning or permission, Steve hoists her into the air. Other hands grab her Victoria's Secret body, and she's off and crowd-surfing whether she likes it or not, windmilling her arms and whooping like a thunderstruck flamingo. Standing on tiptoes, I watch her being handed along overhead.

Being levitated and touched all over at the mercy of strangers, while disorienting at first, can—I know from experience—be the ride of a lifetime. G-force and G-spot together at last, yielding to a gusto that's bigger than your throbbing little self. If Emmie wanted to forget her issues and have a classic punk exploit, this is it. The thrills of the mosh pit!

And the chills. Getting your pubes probed, your clothes ripped, your hair pulled, your skin gouged, your wallet stolen, your shoes lost, your rotator cuffs wrenched, your eyes poked, and your spine disjointed—all of which have happened to me—as you tack a sea of heads and shoulders in the name of good, clean escapism.

Raised hands by the dozens relay Emmie toward a runty punkette who's holding her ground at the fringe of the slammers. This girl must not want some groovy chick's decorative ass landing on her, because—and this happens almost too fast to see, let alone prevent—instead of bearing Emmie aloft like a cooperative mosher should, this purple polyester jellyfish steps out of rank and lets my homegirl plummet. And that's the suckiest part of crowd-surfing—going down.

I battle my way to the crash site, scared of what I'll find. Emmie's prone on the floor, the mob avoiding her. One positive sign of crisis averted is her leg drawn compactly to her chest instead of hanging limply like an unconscious person's limb.

I push past a spiked-necklace skinhead standing between me and my friend. Instead of making way, the brickhouse gink shoves me so hard I hit the deck near Emmie and end up sprawled, legs akimbo, in the clearing with her. I don't believe this is even slightly symbolic. Yet the only thing it appears I've busted is the strap of one sling-back. "Are you okay?" I say.

"I'm hurt," she says, but with a laugh.

So I smile. Another half hour survived with neither of us acting out. And we're only slightly scathed to show for it.

"I might have broken my back," she says.

Spaceman Steve escorts us to the car, me mincing barefoot, Emmie clutching the shoulder she now thinks could be dislocated. We can't help tote Bridgit's kit to the van. This emergency is valid.

In the past, when me and Steve crossed paths, he was hammered on tranqs, but tonight he's high functioning. He helps Emmie into the Mercedes Benz and lopes off to argue his way back into the hall to see Tilt, even though a sign up front says "No Ins and Outs."

Emmie asks to be taken home, not to the hospital for X-rays. I get behind the wheel, start the engine, and go.

In the rear view mirror, San Francisco's glass towers shine. If my punk Muses were to catch sight of this yuppie auto, I'd have to throw myself over the Bay Bridge guard rail to preserve my reckless image. We pass the spot where a section of the deck collapsed in the '89 quake and killed a driver—goes to show that at any moment, the ground under you can give way.

"Damn," I say.

Emmie leans toward me. "What now?"

"I never picked up my cut of the proceeds from Stoney."

"Have him mail it."

"I wanted to collect in person. Wouldn't you love to take a bite of that guy's ass?"

She settles back in her seat with a grunt of pain. "You keep trying to get me in trouble."

"Sorry. Any time I'm upset, the automatic first thing I think is, *Who can I screw?*"

"What're you upset about?"

"My band just blew off the biggest show of their careers. You were there for the crash and burn."

"I was there for the crash."

"The thing about head surfing is you gotta be ready to land on your feet."

"Now you tell me."

My hands tighten around the leather steering wheel. "I almost zuked, watching you take that spill."

"It already hurts less. I'll be okay."

Soon we breeze off the 580, into posh Piedmont, and onto Seaview Avenue where Emmie's stone and wood behemoth sits on its half-acre. I stop the car under a tony, ornate streetlamp. "Here you are," I say, unfastening my seatbelt. "Only problem is, here I am."

"You should have dropped yourself off first."

"It crossed my mind, but you would've had to drive home."

Emmie rubs her neck. "Spend the night. Tom's away on business."

I picture us romping through the mansion—when Tom's away, the kitties play. We should have invited Steve to join us. Except Emmie's hurt. And we're trying to be good ex-addicts.

"We're short on furniture but long on hospitality, "Emmie says. "I'll loan you a nightie."

I picture white chiffon with feather trim. "It all sounds tempting. But that next door lady I take care of? I have to look in on her before bed."

Emmie being all heart, I end up the overnight owner of her hot rod. My first thought, peeling from the curb, is to gun it back to The Mariner, find Steve, watch the show, help Bridgit, collect my check, invite Stoney for a ride. One look at this dream machine car, and he might be less busy.

A nightcap at The Graduate's another option. Or a drive up Mountain Boulevard to some tucked-away grove where I can howl at the moon like a she-wolf.

I've disturbed enough peace in my time. Straight to Sada I go.

She's not asleep yet. "A fellow called after you l-left," she says. "He needed my Medi-Cal n-number."

"Was his name Stan?"

The smile on her face when I carry her to the bathroom makes up for Stan ruining the wheelchair surprise.

Come morning, there are tasks to carry out before returning the car. I pile everything that sleeping Sada needs at the foot of the bed. My boots are at Emmie's house—I forgot them last night when I borrowed the spiked heels. I'll be Miss Barefoot Manager, kicking the necessary booty.

Liz, Bridgit's roommate, says our drummer left for Ashland within the hour.

I stamp my foot. "How does Bridgit expect Up The Wazoo to make it if she disappears to Oregon?"

Liz stares wordlessly at me.

"How long is she gone for?" I sound desperate, even to myself.

"She didn't say." Liz shuts the door.

I don't know where in Albany Angie moved or where Stoney lives these days, so I drive to Tess's and hope she's gotten over last night's funk.

She leads me to her kitchen where her coffee maker burbles. She's wearing a Power Rangers shirt and pink slippers.

I try to hide my dirty, bare feet under the cabinet. "I'm gonna kill Bridgit when she gets back."

"From where?"

"Ashland. So it's not just me she left in the dark. You, too, and it's pissy she's gone 'cause there's ten indie record labels I wanna send a demo to, but we need to make it."

Tess pours a mug of joe for me. "You need to bag that plan."

"No way."

Mr. Coffee drips, hissing, onto the hot plate. "Angie doesn't want to be in the band anymore," Tess says.

"Since when?"

"She came back to the Mariner last night and quit."

"I don't believe you."

"Where were you?"

"Dealing with a sudden emergency."

Tess frowns, presuming my emergency was getting louied by whoever I could pick up. She doesn't know the nympho me is pretty much extinct.

The coffee smells garlicky and tastes charcoaly. I park the mug on the wood block counter. "All you Wazoos need is a guiding light."

"We disbanded."

"Don't say that."

Tess pours herself coffee and replaces the pot under the filter mount. "It's over, Boop."

"I won't let it be. There's too much talent to throw away. Everyone's frayed emotions just need a little smoothing. I'll talk to Angie. No more spitting, I promise. No more whisky. My whole focus will be making this band succeed."

"This isn't about you."

"Sure it is."

"Then get another group to manage. We're over." She sips from her mug.

What disloyal rat-dick clients.

"Wait," I say, crafting a quick new plan. "We get a new guitarist. I come in as singer."

"I don't have time to be in a band. I'm still catching up on the nine days of college I missed."

"When she gets back, Bridgit might want to start a band with me."

"Sure. I've got a class." Tess puts her mug on the counter. "You need to go."

"Did anyone tell Stoney the band's breaking up?"

"Angie did."

"What'd he say?"

"I don't know. I have to leave soon."

"You're not just trying to get rid of me?"

"Yah, I'm trying to get rid of you. To get to campus."

———————————

I sit listening to the Mercedes rev and wail. That saying about whatever doesn't kill you makes you stronger—it isn't true. What doesn't kill you all the way kills you part way. It kills your fighting spirit. Maybe it's asking too much from fate to be a Babe in Toyland. Some people see their dreams become reality. Not me. Goodbye Bikini Kill. Goodbye Super Babyfat.

I sit in Emmie's luxury ride, barefoot, dismissed from duty, blasting the heater, teeth chattering, mouthing a silent goodbye to Up The Wazoo. We could have been rock stars with cred. A little tribute candle in my future just blew out.

I sniff back some mucous and notice a custardy smell in the car. Either the upholstery's osmosing chemicals, or Emmie left a hint of perfume behind. The least I can do is return her property without further delay. And not go find a wall to drive full-speed, head-on into.

A Naughty Fantasy Where I Get To Be Stoney

That chica with the perfect bon-bons makes my cojones burn. I don't remember her name, but if she's hanging with Boop, she must be freaky. Those two bebés looked hot at the show. I was busy as diabolo, chasing down pizza, keeping cast and crew in line. It's tough for a gato to stay chido and show off his chops to a fox when there's one screw-up after another. The bar okaying dozens of fake IDs. Angie, the singer I've been doing, having a meltdown. The lighting tech almost electrocuting himself when a followspot shorted out. None of that was pretty.

But Boop's amiga was. I searched for her when I had a spare second, but she and Boop must have left after Up The Wazoo's swan song. All the sweat and blood I put into that gig, and the first half flopped.

I still can't get Boop's gringa Daisy Fuentes friend out of my head.

Mother of God, the muchacha I've been thinking about just called me. She got my number from Boop. Gave me her casa's address and said it's now or never.

Speeding illegally in the Nimitz carpool lane, I tingle with deseo. What's on this panocho's mind?

Her digs sit on a swank street. All the houses have flagstone paths and leaded glass windows. Emmie opens the tall, blue door on the last toll of her three-tone doorbell. As I enter, she leans against the paneled foyer wall, showing off her supernatural tetas. Her fiancé, she says, is out of town.

You'd expect such a girl to be spoken for. It's still heady 411 to hear that her esposo's out of the picture. What she means is obvious. A handout from Lady Luck to me.

Her gauzy blouse pulls my eyes to it. "Appreciate the invite," I say.

"Let's skip further talk." She scales the carpeted staircase off the entry.

She likes the silent type? I'm her gaucho, ascending two stairs behind her calabazo.

As a rule, I get my share—white babes, Latinas, black sisters, Asians, punk girls, and not-so-punk girls. But being led by this mamey toward her bedroom—oye! It's not your everyday chocho. This is come-to-Jesus time. This buzz is muy electrico. I'm predicting a booty call with this pepita that beats any others. And the no-talking condition? Any tia who knows when to keep her mouth shut, I'll pay back the favor.

We cross the upstairs landing to a bedroom with French doors and Persian rugs. Everything real whipped cream, not artificial topping. She's not the whitest Anglo I've ever done but definitely the elitest. Boop's hanging with classier acts. She herself looked caliente la otre noche.

But no one can vie with this jackpot—Emmie—who for reasons unknown leads me not to the four-poster bed but to the window. I owe Boop big time for this puta. Her supermodel fingers slide my vest off. I unzip my pants and undo the pearly buttons of her top. I step from the black denim pools at my ankles. Emmie's blouse drops to the carpet. Her pink lace bra is so sheer my throat squeaks. This mango's got it all over Angie, who's a bigger problema every day, and who doesn't have half as much to show for herself once *her* skirt and bra come off. Desnuda, Emmie could make a man weep.

But rather than crying, this ese's going to make her forget whoever bought this bombollero house. The taste of her skin when I lick her shoulder is melted butter on warm tortilla. Her body wiggles like a chihuahua in heat. But I don't touch her. I make her wait. She grabs my morrongo. When it's close to exploding, I finger her crica. I was born for this.

"Nena," I say.

"No talk. Just do it."

"Si, coño."

"No Spanish."

My nabo in her hand, she walks me to the bed.

Angie can fuck herself. I'm getting mine right now. All the little angels in heaven are smiling on this house and whispering that me and this encantadora should do what comes natural—engulf my pinga in her nido.

She presses me down onto a soft sheet. She wants to take charge? Be on top? My ego can handle it. I close my ojos and await the advent of bliss. The room is as holy as una iglesia.

I dismiss a distracting shuffling sound as the flow of blood in my ears. A faint brisa raises goose flesh on my flanks. We are meant to be.

The mattress sags abruptly. Sensing trouble, I open my eyes to a naked white guy with long hair and a mean tan line about to board our tren de amor.

Chingalo! I shield my falo with my hand. "You said your esposo was away!" I cry.

"I'm the pool guy," the intruder says.

"No talking!" Emmie says.

I should punch this perverso's lights out. I'd like to know what the hell these deviant linksluts have planned. I should collect my duds, clear out, act sensible. Before I make a move, Emmie slides my verga up in her bacalao. Dios!

Not to be left out, the pool boy slaps himself onto Emmie's back and pumps and thrusts with energia I can't tune out. It's a good thing I'm not the one on top with this cabron up my virgin backside. Emmie is digging her double whammy, a real chucha cuerera. It doesn't say a lot for my machismo, but maybe it takes more than one man to satisfy this tonto's almeja. I shut my eyes again and try to ignore the pool man, but the hairs on his legs brush mine. I was raised Catholic. Kinky sex is sinful. But my cabeza's not bueno, not thinking straight with my bloated cipote pushed so deep in raja it feels a foot long. I'm a man, not a santo. There's no stopping now.

At each of five rip-roaring cum squirts, I violate the code of silence with cardiac screams—

"Si!

Cusca!

Mamacita!

Yo lo amo!

Boopito!"

Untranslatable Slanguage

What death rattle windbags we are. I mouth breathe. Sada fights to pull air into her lungs.

Night approaches. I switch the lamp on.

If Sada was a psychic or telepath, my three-way daydream about Emmie and Stoney would gross her out. She'd rethink sharing her blankie with me. The last thing she needs by her side is a trollop spinning homoerotic ethnic fabulisms while passing herself off as normal.

Not that Sada's the epitome of normal. Spotlit under the lamp, she's strange fruit collaged onto a drab apartment.

Hugging a pillow, I'm the invisible mooncalf on the dark side of her bed. If Sada *could* read my mind, she'd know my Stoney obsession isn't as over as I claim. If she saw me touch myself or caught wind of the slurry between my legs, she'd understand what I'm up against—my body demanding that I Do it, Do it, Do it all the time, even when my head tells me no.

But Sada won't notice squat, 'cause she's zonked. Curved like a fetus, she's resting up from more than her share of medical melt-downs.

Which leaves me free to indulge in harmless fantasies. I'm not gonna really do anything to upset her. We've hoed that row already. These days, I'm walking the mellow brick road. My imagination's the only thing running wild—it's my addiction's sole outlet.

Sada's breathing sounds more labored than ever. Her doc just renews prescriptions when I beg for help. He's done all he can—his belief. My prayers at St. Henry of Uppsala go unanswered. Stan the Man says the wheelchair deal will take a month. The best us shut-ins can hope for is a holding pattern.

Sada's face is guileless as a child's. When feeding or diapering her, I often picture my wasted mother and think Ma must've taken care of cuddly infant me, at least minimally. I'd have starved or drowned in baby shit without basic tending.

Sada would be up shit creek without me. Her husband divorced her prior to her illness. A car crash killed their only child before he supplied grandkids. Not a single friend has called or visited to see how she's faring. We're the two most alone people I know.

My head hurts. So does my heart. I help myself to a pain tablet from her pharmaceutical stash and swallow it dry.

A scrap of blanket lint flutters on her cheek. As I brush it away, Sada's eyelids flick open like dolls' retractible eyes. Her contracting pupils find me. "What's wrong?"

My face burns. Did she see me take the pill? "Nothing's wrong."

"There's a l-look . . . ."

I don't want to be a heartache glum bum. No need divulging I was M-ing in her bed, either. "Just thinking about stuff," I say.

"What stuff?"

"The Spanish language, for one thing."

"Are you fluent?"

"Nothing from school stuck. But through the years, I updated my Spanspeak a bit. Got a crash course from two hermanos on a Reno trip a few years ago. Jorgé and Luis were the brothers' names, and they didn't speak much English."

"Say something. It's a . . . ." She gags like a turtle spewing its dried-fly dinner. "L-lyrical language," she croaks.

I stare at Sada's wax-museum mano, bundled in excess red skin. Her other hand's the same. When she sleeps, I sometimes read her *Living With Diffuse Scleroderma* booklet. The misshapen hands are sclerodactyly, which sounds and looks like a duck disease. I squeeze her fingers. "Can't think up any Spanish."

"You said you . . . ." Swallow, swallow, swallow.

"It's hard to produce foreign language on command."

Her legs shift under the blanket. "What time is it?"

"Que hora es?"

"There. Spanish. But I want to know the time." She pulls her hand from mine and taps a forefinger on her wrist, as if on a watch.

I twist to view the clock, just readable at the edge of the orange lamplight. "Coming up on eight."

"A.M.?"

"P.M. Woman, your bio-rhythms are screwy."

"Did I eat?"

"No. Want some organic applesauce?"

She pushes two fingers against her thumb, twice, and shakes her head. Swallowing is hard. Wasting away is easy. I won't let her starve, though. "When you're fiendin' for a nibble, lemmie know," I say.

"You eat. You're . . . kuh . . . too thin."

Me, thin? My duds have gotten a shave looser, but I'll never be heroin-chic thin, punk-sexy thin, like Angie. "I'll eat if you eat," I say, resorting to blackmail.

She taps her mouth and grinds out words. "Speak—more—Spanish."

I wrack my memory and finally say, "Here's a phrase that comes to mind—Ella tiene furor uterino."

"Kuh—"

"Don't ask what it means, 'cause I don't remember," I lie. It means 'she's got a hot pussy.' Jorgé said it to Luis when they had me blindfolded on the Reno hotel floor. In that position, a girl listens. "Just some untranslatable slanguage," I say.

"I—" Sada's words get burked off by pops in her throat that sound like "cut, cut, cut." It's a pattern I've noted with alarm. We talk, saliva collects in her mouth 'cause swallowing is hard, and the surplus overwhelms her.

"Shhh," I say.

'Dysphagia: difficulty swallowing, stiffness of the throat' is also listed in the information booklet and checked off by someone—not me—in black ink.

"Kuh—" Her fingers make distorted shapes in the air.

"Can you breathe?"

She tilts her head and gasps, "Buh—"

I pat her head, like a dog. The gesture soothes us both. We're okay, pat pat. We're okay.

We're not, though. Any dumbass can see she's getting sicker. I may play a stupid nit in the cable movie of my life, but in real life I can read the writing on the wall. It says I better get used to her hitting the skids. In exchange for ending my years of no-great-shakes man-prowling, I get to watch Sada's life decrapulate. As a diversion from my misfortunes, hers suck.

"We have all night to talk," I lie. She should drop back to sleep—there's a lot less choking when she shuts down like a power failure. "Everything's gonna work out."

If she *could* talk, she might be pointing to the progress I've made. Sex, drinking—both way down. Ditto for smoking. Vitamin-taking, up. I hardly know myself. I'm a has-been, a rudderless ship. Though compared to Sada, I'm a plush specimen with lungs that sound nothing like sawdust sucked up a straw.

I drag her higher up her pillow. Maybe her windpipe will unsnarl if she's more upright. I fingercomb silky hairstrands behind her jagged ear. Her hands curl into funny shapes, and she opens her mouth to say, "Boo, I, kuh—"

"Once the wheelchair's delivered," I interrupt, "first thing we'll do is roll down to the pier. Get pixelated on sea breeze."

Face pinched as a prune, one eyebrow arched with the strain, the other pressed down in judgment, Sada sputters three words before I stop her—"I speak Spanish."

The combers in the bay, the southwesters . . . my nautical mirage vanishes. "Ay, caray," I curse.

Something Transcendental

It wasn't just the Spanish phrase that Sada understood. I saw in her eyes two tiny snapshots of Hot Pussy Boop. Without me having to supply sordid details, she knew the Luis and Jorgé junket wasn't my finest hour. Mortified, I reeled out to the porch to collect myself.

The full moon's face glows, a pale punk with black-rimmed eyes. The sight tempts me to believe something bigger than human will calls our shots. Maybe gravity pulled Sada and me together like the tide to the shore, like rock to roll, like bigfucking to deal. If it wasn't for Sada, I'd have fallen apart by now. Even autoimmuned half to death, she keeps me on the up and up. She called me her guardian angel when we met, but she had that backward. She's mine.

When I was young, my ma was into the occult—astral forecasts, scorpio rising, Age of Aquarius, you name it. Even so, the life she's led has been sorry enough to make anyone doubt the heavenly bodies' positive impact on people. The stars above seem meaningless as spilled sugar.

But this moon! It's converting me into a lunar worshiper. With my venus stuck in retrograde, what else have I got to swear by?

"That's a red zone," I say from the darkness under the eave. About to go inside, I saw Bridgit's van pull up and illegally park. She walks toward me in floppy zories, smoking a cigarette. Maybe she came back to make up.

"Hey, Boop," she says.

"I thought you were in Ashland?"

"I was."

"You and Jeremy broke up?"

"No. I came to get my stuff. I'm moving in with him."

"For real?" I cave against the lobby door, feeling K-O'd. "Up there?"

"Uh-huh." A long drag on her cigarette flares the tip like a red taillight.

"Good for you, girlfriend," I say, without conviction. Another worst case scenario is playing out—Bridgit skipping town, leaving no chance for the band to regroup and fulfill my cherished dream.

Her head bobs impatiently. It's true I haven't been the bestest bud. But unlike her, I don't leave the area code. I don't move beyond stateline. I assumed we'd get close again, against all odds. But she's obviously still at odds with me. It just goes to show that right when I think the time has come to fix the mayhem of my life, there's no time left, no chance, and it's sayonara baby, cut your losses, screw off. I'm out in the cold, no matter what I try or how much I change. No one's asking me what I want, what's good for me, but damn it, Bridgit should.

"Everything I own is in the van," she says.

I shoot a hostile glance at the van. "Where *is* Prince Jeremy? Not helping you move?"

"He couldn't miss his classes."

"Your boy and Tess are a pair of college Smartacuses the rest of us have to tiptoe around."

"You went to college."

"One year. Community college."

"More than I had."

"Have you thought this Oregon thing out? What's there for you besides sex with Jeremiah? What will you do with yourself?"

She shrugs. "Get another job at Starbucks?"

"Starbucks? What happened to Royal Pie?"

"They fired me. Remember?"

Right. She got caught ripping off turkey pot pies for me. I bite my tongue.

"I changed jobs ten months ago," she reminds me. Smoke trickles from her nostrils.

"You still mad at me for getting you axed?"

"No." She fiddles with the metal buttons on her denim jacket.

I should tie her down, prevent her from going. She could have contributed to the world's treasure trove of alt-rock and done something A-1 with her life, but she'd rather serve lattés in a way-north greenbelt. She'd rather squander her potential on a boyfriend who's too white bread to be worth running after. She'd rather give up her bestest friend. "Taking your drums with you, I assume?"

"Yep." Her arm motions toward the street, the van, the interstate highway, and the northwest adventure awaiting her landfall.

"Guess I have to recruit new clients. Maybe Spaceman Steve has some leads, if I can find him."

"He lives near the Outback. A mechanic shop converted to a music squat."

Nostalgic peckerhead that I am, I'd rather have Up the Wazoo stay the same. We had something transcendental. "Someone's got to keep the punk fire burning," I say.

"You were a great manager. Landing our first gig and all."

"Funny, I didn't think you noticed."

"Funny, but I did." She coughs out a ball of smoke, like a kid learning to inhale. When she recovers, she looks me over. "You're thin."

I stand up straighter, pleased she noticed. "I gave up junk food and binge drinking. All abstinence, all the time—that's the life for me."

The cigarette butt she tosses away spins and makes orange squiggles on the dark ground before disappearing. She coughs. "I need to stop smoking."

"Living in the woods will inspire you to quit. Everyone up there wears Timberland boots and hugs trees. I hope the move works out." Actually, I hope Bridgit goes out of her mind with boredom in the Cascades and returns to California. "We're not friends anymore, so do what you gotta do."

"What's that supposed to mean?"

"You never called about the band. When we did talk, you told me I'm a loser."

"That night with those guys on the freeway?"

A train blows its horn down by the bay. The woo-woos race up the flats to us, sounding homesick. My lower lip twitches. "Just so you know—that nutsy phase I was in is over. I made some new friends. Ones who stick by me."

She's silent, maybe weighing whether or not to call me on my bad behavior one last time. Or she's thinking about her future as a gleeful Oregonian.

"Speaking of friends," I say, exhausted by this long goodbye, "one's waiting for me inside, so . . . ."

"Want my TV? I came to give it to you."

"You don't need it?"

"Jeremy's is better. I'm overloaded as it is."

"Sure. Fine. TV me."

As we wrastle the luggage, boxes, and hangers to extract the RCA from the back of the van, I picture Bridgit and Jeremy in bed, watching stupid pet tricks on Letterman, like me and her used to.

We portage the TV up the walkway. "Hauling shit together again," I pant, "just like when we roadied our gigs."

"And the times I helped you move," she says, not mentioning my evictions. "That white TV you used to have looked like a washing machine."

I grunt. One blotto night, I knocked the TV over, and it broke. "It was hella lighter than this one," I say, shouldering my half of the RCA to dig keys from my pocket. "By the way, did you find out why Angie went bitchcakes at the Mariner?"

"It doesn't matter."

"To me, it does." We back through the lobby and rest at the mouth of the hallway. "Did she ruin the show to spite me?"

"No."

"I think she did."

"She was upset 'cause she found out she had an STD."

"Really? Something she got from Stoney?"

"Dunno."

"Not HIV, I hope?"

"No."

"Then I wasn't the only unregistered sex offender." I roll my head to pop the vertebrae at the base of my neck.

"Let's finish moving this."

We enter my apartment and lower the TV to the floor beside the big fork. My shoulder stabs as I straighten up. I don't even need this dumb television set. I can watch Sada's any time. Is this Bridgit's idea of a consolation prize for not being friends any more?

She looks my place over, surprised. Everything put away and clean.

"Wanna poke next door?" I say. "Check on my friend?"

"I better not. Got a long drive."

"It'll only take a sec. Come see."

"Why?"

"Nevermind. Just thought it'd be nice."

"Okay, alright. Can we make it fast?"

Sada is sacked out, her breathing notably obstructed. Bridgit looks as if she can't believe anyone so leathery, pustuly, and fleshless can be alive. At least the sheets are clean.

"What's wrong with her?" Bridgit whispers.

"A rare disease we shouldn't discuss now."

"Anything I can do?"

"Like what, when you're so eager to leave? She's got me. I don't jump ship on friends."

"Jump ship? Boop, I wanted to live with Jeremy this whole year but stayed down here 'cause of the band and you. I stuck it out as long as I could."

"Stuck it out? You got to play in two amazing clubs."

"Yah. Some cool things happened."

"And some uncool things, right? Don't candy-coat the truth. I know I let cock rule my life. I know I dragged you into narfy situtations."

"So, you realize."

"I'm sorry, too."

"Okay."

"I'm not the bakebrain I used to be."

"That's good, Boop. I'm glad."

Now is when, in a perfect world, she changes her mind about splitting. But she turns toward Sada's door.

"You're lucky to be leaving." I lead her out. "This music scene's tanking. Clubs out of business. Unaffordable practice space." I open the door. "You should join a band up there."

"There's more music in Portland than Ashland."

"I just wish Up The Wazoo ended on a higher note."

"I've got an all night drive." She hovers in the doorway like a delusion.

"Travel safe."

"I will."

Down the hall she flip-flops toward her fairy tale with King Jeremy. No looking back.

I carry my desolate self to the bed, crawl over my sleeping friend's legs, and stretch beside her like the next sardine in the tin.

"You believe Bridgit asking if there's anything she can do?" I say, though Sada's deaf to my disappointment. "She's so busy breaking up the band . . . . There isn't a thing she can do for anyone except some Ashland resident feening for frappucino. Honestly? I'm glad she's gone. When I apologized for being bad, did she say she was sorry for how *she* acted? If I wanna discuss how I'm not a goddam nympho anymore, I've got 12 Step. I don't need Bridgit spouting bunkeroni about friendship. Let her go work as a jizzmopper at Fourbucks the rest of her life."

I roll onto my back and cram my fists against my churning stomach. "God, I hate when someone who claims to be my friend is a fake who doesn't care a hang about me."

Sada murmurs in her sleep. I stroke her back with the tips of my fingers. My green nail polish from months ago is almost all chipped off.

"Like she'd be any help," I say. "What could self-important Bridgit do for us?"

I turn on my side and stare at the window, trying to banish Bridgit from my mind. In her sleep, Sada nestles against my back.

"I don't need a goddam thing from that fluckerhead."

A knock pulls me off the bed. I open the door. Bridgit's in the hall, eyes filled with tears. She silently hands me the RCA remote control. Then she leaves me all over again.

Cable Movie of My Life

Act 4, Making the Scene

EXT. BERKELEY MUSIC STORE – DAY – 1995

Street nomads and college urchins congregate on free-form Telegraph Avenue. Jewelry and incense vendors make the sidewalk look like a Middle East bazaar.

BOOP, 23, voluptuously braless in a black lace sweater, loiters with PUNK BACKPACKER COUPLE, young vagabonds in tattered jackets.

                    BOOP
          The place is abandoned?

                    BACKPACKER GIRL
          We've crashed three nights. No one's come by.

                    BACKPACKER BOY
          We're throwing a party tomorrow. You should come.

                    BACKPACKER GIRL
          Bring beer. We're broke.

                    BOOP
          So am I.

                    BACKPACKER BOY
          Wear that sweater. Your tits are hella fine in it.

                    BOOP
          Keep your monkey in its cage, chief. 'Til the party.

                    BACKPACKER GIRL
                    (to Boop)
          Fuck you.

INT. DILAPIDATED OFFICE – NIGHT – PARTY

Candles in jars illuminate bedrolls and backpacks on the floor. Hippie punks suck face or mosh to lo-fi rhythms.

INT. NEXT OFFICE OVER

BOOP stands in her underwear, surrounded by PUNK BACKPACKER BOY, CHINESE DUDE, and HEAVILY-INKED GUY, in various stages of undress.

Green streetlight flows through a single window. Siouxsie and the Banshee's song "Happy House" pipes from a boombox held by Heavily-inked Guy.

                    BOOP
          Come 'n' get it, boys.

INT. DILAPIDATED MAIN OFFICE – PARTY

The candles are burned down. BRIDGIT picks her way through shadowy, naked pair-ups, flicking on her cigarette lighter to see where she's going.

INT. SMALLER ROOM – BOOP'S PRIVATE PARTY

Bridgit's small flame illumines Boop in a body knot with the three males, revealing surprising contortionist talent for a chubby girl.

Boop turns her head toward the light, but, pinned by flesh, she can't signal to her ashen-faced friend.

If Boop realized then what she does now—that multi-partner porno fantasies blow goats—she'd extract herself from the pile and leave with her friend.

The lighter flicks off. Bridgit exits. "Happy House" replays on the boombox.

Hope

Almost all is lost. Up The Wazoo disbanded. Bridgit decamped to the north. I'm wallowing in chastity, lacing my boots in my apartment. Any given day, all I do is mop, sweep, de-scum, launder, feed, medicate, diaper, and hide from the world. It's hard to know prezactly what there is to be hopeful about.

Yet this tummy twitter might be what hope feels like. Because a person can withdraw from human contact only so much and doubt herself so much and blow people off so much before she decides, as a last resort, to revisit the sex addict hootenanny and see where that gets her. Even though little of the 12-prong cure has sunk in or had much effect on me thus far, I have been contemplating not just my navel but my entire addict history and where I went wrong. Maybe the other 12 Steppers would like to hear some of it?

Like how, since the age of 14, I've jumped at every chance I had to get poonjed. Like how religiously poncing around and having rip-snorting orgasms at the drop of a hat didn't, in retrospect, make me happy. Adrenalin surges fizzle fast. The more pud pie I got, the more I had to get. The never-ending frustration of it! I was incapable of feeling anything other than hunger for more.

It's taken time to understand and to want to say this in public. The last ten years could have gone different. Fewer bad choices. Less time wasted. But being a love junkie could have been worse. I could've gotten hurt a lot worse.

Which makes me think someone *has* been watching out for me—the Higher Power or the Dukes of Hazard or the Great Dalmuti or Sada Pollard or the moon goddess. I've had dumb luck for someone who acted so dumb. Only a fool would press it further. I'm ready to take the plunge and speak at a meeting. A big step for me. A sign of hope.

While Sada naps I haul myself over to Transports Shoes to buy some Reebok Gratifys, 'cause my boots are not made for walking anymore.

UNTHINKABLE BUGABOOS

A squatty nurse in Crayola-pink scrubs identifies herself as "Sloopy Delizio, county healt" and steamrolls into the apartment—stethoscope around her neck, plastic bin in arm. Today is the first time I'm present for Sada's monthly yogurt delivery, light housekeeping, and home visit checkup.

I power off the bleating TV as the nurse deposits the supplies on the floor and lifts Sada's limp forearm. Joining her at bedside, I watch her press the sickling's wrist pulse point. Sada sleeps through it all, the handling, the snap of chewing gum while the nurse studies her digital watch, the booming voice, demanding, "Lady alway in bed?"

I nod, though weeks ago my neighbor walked well enough for a field trip to St. Henry of Uppsala Church. It was unfathomable *then* that *now* I'd be looking back fondly at the grief workshop.

The nurse inserts her stethoscope earbits and lifts the chest ring to Sada's breast. Her eyes swivel and strain to focus, as if she's misplaced her glasses. "Condition is worse?" she hollers.

"The pain in her legs is." I mimic a pillow shape with pressed-together hands and pretend my head's asleep on it. Pointing at Sada, I say, "Lower your voice?"

Nurse Delizio slits her eyes as if that helps her hear the pulsations rising from the slumbering body to her ears. Our visitor could be legally blind for all I care. It's still a relief to have her monitor Sada's vitals. Sclerosis is a mad dog I don't know how to kick down. I'm just a neighbor, a friend—not someone equipped to deal with a disorder that doctors call incurable. I'm no healer. I'm a punk rocker.

The physical exam wraps up as quickly as it started. The nurse confirms the afflicted is still alive and in need of public health services. The bin is retrieved from the floor. "I bring to eat, is good," Sloopy says.

It's me who gallivants around town, scrounging up groceries and supplements to entice nourishment down Sada's stiff throat. This payrolled caretaker whizzes in, pro tem, and assumes I'm not providing? That's screwed up. "I fix a lot of smoothies," I say.

"Smoothie? Ah, ha ho." Again she puts the crate on the floor. She draws Sada's blanket down. "Change de sheet."

"I put on fresh bedding this morning."

Her palm brushes over the bed linen as if determining the cleanliness by feel. "Is change," she declares. She leans down, googly eyes getting bigger. The stethoscope ring dangles near Sada's nose, unnoticed by Sloopy.

"Something wrong?" I say.

This nurse's slantindicular vision might be a defense mechanism to spare herself the sight of wrack and ruin, and who could blame her. "Is bad, de skin." She finally restrains the instrument's swinging tubes.

"I rub aloe vera gel on it."

"Ah, ha ho. Aloe." She re-hoists the supplies and walks them to the kitchenette.

"I'm not joking." I tag behind her. "It's a natural liniment."

As she loads Martinelli bottles and shrink-wrapped Yoplaits into the 'fridge, I find myself wishing the cuplet rations included berry yogurt, instead of lemon, which Sada dislikes. But I doubt any declared preferences would get communicated to the supply chain.

Nurse Delizio seizes the sponge mop leaning against the sinkstand. The floor's had a recent encounter with Mr. Clean, my main man these days, but if our handy helper wants to go back over it, atta girl. She pinches a corner of the damp sponge panel and glances at the floor. "Is you mop?"

Last night I sang "Real Wild Child" and swabbed the decks, stopping now and then to frug-dance à la Iggy Pop to make Sada laugh. If I was this rotational nurse, I'd be thinking who *is* this yahtzee doing such a bang-up job taking care of Sada Pollard? "I is mop," I say, smiling.

"Okay. Is done."

"Coffee? I can make some quick."

"No, tanks. I busy."

She's not busy here. The place was borderline antiseptic before her arrival. Even so, I'm pacified by her presence.

I follow her back to the bed. She covers Sada's mangled nut of a body and mis-aims a smile at the overturned box that serves as a night stand. The eight or nine outpatient cases this nurse must handle each day, multiplied by five days a week, add up to unthinkable bugaboos. Hell of a job she's taken on.

"Thank you for coming," I say. "We appreciate it."

"Bye for you, lady," she softly tells Sada. "You in good hand."

Vindicated to pieces by her words, I wish this oompa-loompa could stick around and not race off. A little company to break the monotony. A chance to ask what more can be done to ease Sada's plight. But Sloopy's immigrant English might not stand up to in-depth exchanges of info. Besides, she's halfway to the door.

"Do I pay you?" I say, catching up.

"Is pay Alameda healt department."

"Next month, I'll save the mopping for you." We glance back at Sada, and I know what she's thinking. But I'm thinking, Hang on, Sloopy. There's still a chance Sada will rally from this setback.

"Ah, ha ho." She looks me in the eye for the first time. "Get de power of a tore knee."

"De what?"

"Make easy, de hospital, every ting. De power of attorney. You get. Is good?"

"I guess, yah." My emotions roller-coaster down a headlong plunge I wasn't ready to take.

The nurse removes a small item from the waist pocket of her medical scrubs top and presses it into my hand. A packet of Chiclets gum. Am I to give her some token gratuity in return? There's nothing here to give. And what is this gum—a sympathy offering? Delizio darts to the hall and out into the community to lend assistance elsewhere. I linger at the open door, guarding against a future that's not welcome at this house.

The six remaining squares of shiny white gum tumble from the packet into my palm. I toss them into my bazoo and grind out a speedball sugar rush.

Is good—for fugitive seconds.

Dear Bay Area Legal Aid

Please send forms to grant my caregiver Power of Attorney over my financial and medical affairs.

Sincerely,
[forged]
Sada Pollard

Earn My Chit, Sleep With A Pod

Here it is—Save My Soul Day, Earn My Chit Day, Spill My Guts Day, Sleep With a Pod Day, Admit I'm Powerless Day—and I log barely six blocks in the brand-new Miss Jock Reeboks before my toes and heels grow a set of screaming blisters.

I glare at the sky, look around me. There's no posted route stop nearby. I wave down a 12 bus that comes gnashing by. The driver takes pity on me and stops in the middle of the street, the coach trembling like a cold elephant as I board. I feed every coin on me into the fare box and stagger to a seat.

Under one peeled-down sock, three red bullas on my heel are fat with fluid. I ease the cotton back over the blisters and dangle my stinging feet while the bus chuffs on.

Add to Shopping List

—bandaids

I hum random bits of songs and try to think outside the socks. Halfway to St. Henry's, a burning asbestos smell fills the bus interior. We roll to the Telegraph Avenue intersection and, apparently brakeless, sled through it against the red light. It's no 35-millimeter, popcorn-fueled suspense ride, like *Speed* starring Keanu Reeves—the nearest cross-traffic is a quarter-mile off—but it's not normal commuting, either.

Trumpeting cuss words, the driver cranks on the parking brake, levering with his full strength. The appreciative riders among us applaud when the bus squeals to a stop.

The driver jumps out and tosses a hazard cone on the asphalt to our rear. Ping-ponging back up the step well, he crouches on one knee and radios word of our mechanical failure to Transit Headquarters. Apologizing for the service disruption, he waves us off-board and promises the arrival of another bus in ten minutes.

There's time, and more than enough blisters, for me to wait. All of us leaving the decommissioned rig find ourselves in front of a slumpy apartment building. The name *Bahia Shore* is calligraphied in wood on a wall painted a flesh-tan color that was trendy fifty years ago.

Broke-down in mock Brazil and no one to samba with—story of my life.

The passengers form a loose posse on the sidewalk, twitching like rabbits in a hutch. I zip my sweatshirt and burrow my chin down in it. Minutes pass. Holding my feet dead still makes the pain subside. I glance at a pacing man's watch and see I'm late for my meeting. Drat. My on-time record was perfect 'til today.

Reverting to Plan A—pounding the pavement to St. Henry's—seems my best tactic. Better late than never. "Hasta lambada, bus buddies," I say under my breath, taking some first steps.

Of course, the Reebok friction flares up instantly, the blisters stinging like wasps. I try pulling my toes in and pressing my heels into the non-rubbing middle of my shoes, but a person can't really walk that way. Could the bus breaking down be divine intervention? Its replacement never arrived. The blisters are spreading like flesh-eating bacteria. Are these warnings to skip my intended 12 Step spiel?

A force must be testing my will, tricking me up, making me second-guess myself. "Jesus have-your-way-with-me Christ! Can't a girl get a break?"

I stick out my thumb to catch a ride, stay faithful to the plan. Get me to the church on time, as Ma used to sing.

No car picks me up. I plod on, panting at the pain. Hee-hee, hoo-hoo, focused breaths as if I'm birthing a papoose. I wonder if Gita's still pregnant. I hope so. As I tread on, the blisters pop or deflate or callous over. Story of my life—lapsed pain. I speed along.

One block shy of the church, a striped bus rumbles by. I backognize the heads of some riders. "Hey!" I call as the coach streams toward the horizon. I fetch up at Redemption Central in time for the last part of the meeting.

"If this was a test, I pass." I glance at the sky. "Jesus have-my-way-with-you Christ."

Emmie and Roxanne sit shoulder-to-shoulder, listening to a speaker, as I enter Room 3. Wrapped around Emmie's neck is a thick, white truss.

I sit directly behind her, shocked she's still injured bad enough to require whiplash support. She must have seen a chiropractor or neck doc. Maybe she'll sue The Mariner for permitting crowd surfing. I want to apologize, ask if she's okay, but Fred is in the process of explaining his sins to the group.

". . . need to make amends to the dispatcher from the Hayward trucking office."

Besides beating me to the soapbox, hump-head Fred is stealing the step I decided on my trek down here to talk about. Making amends, redeeming myself to people I've wronged.

"... told her not to take what happened at her sister's place personally," he says, "because I'd slipped into some kind of fugue state. Nothing seemed real. Even when she fell down the stairs. Pushing her wasn't a premeditated—"

"Fugue state?" I blurt.

Emmie about-faces and blinks big, brown gims at me. In her tawny blouse and white neck band, she looks like a deer in the forest. "Shhh," she says.

Fred levels a hate stare my way. "The court psychologist called it that."

"Go on working your step," Jonathan says.

Fred gnaws one of his thumbnails, like a dingo with a thorn in its paw. "We were arguing," he says, dropping the hand. "She wouldn't take her car to my mechanic friend. Wanted to go to the dealer and pay double for the same work. My buddy even offered a discount on her repair. Me and him were in the Guard. We have each other's backs. *She* had to be difficult. Someone crosses me, I forget, um, what-do-they-call-'ems. Consequences. I don't worry about breaking a law or a lamp, even a bone, when I get heated like that. I just lash out."

I wish memories of being lashed out at weren't trapped in my cells like radiation.

Fred says, "My head felt like it was gonna explode."

I wish his head *would* explode. Something needs to shut Fred up. Where's the accountability at these meetings?

"Last year, a Chili's waitress I was seeing got a concussion when I found out she was married. I pushed her away from me, and her head hit the car window. Again, not something I intended. She didn't want her old man finding out about me, so I wasn't charged."

He should have been indicted, incarcerated, electrocuted. "Not personal?" I blurt. "When you ram her head through a window?"

"We observe turn-taking rules here," Jonathan says.

"How about decency rules?!" I jump up and grab my ears by the lobes. "Does anyone hear what he's saying?" I turn from drop-mouthed Jonathan to clench-fisted Fred. "After making these hollow token amends, you think you're basking in the love of the higher power? Think again, Whamakus! You're a bully. You're assaulting women!"

My knees shake. If Fred's forgiven, the power is *lower* not higher.

"You'd better calm down," Jonathan says.

"Fred doesn't calm down when he's supposed to!"

"Please, Boop," Emmie whispers. "Respect the process."

"Assholes like him don't respect us." I turn to Fred. "Do you, asshole?"

"Don't swear at me," Fred snarls.

"Don't *look* at me!" I kick my chair aside and long-jump to the door.

The white-haired coffee peddlers stationed in the hall watch me whip past their klatsch, my shoelaces untied and dragging.

"Where's the fire?" Salami-Head says.

I don't stop to say it's inside me.

Two blocks from the church, on a street of dilapidated rooming houses, Roxanne catches up with me.

"I'm not going back," I say. Sidewalk mica blinks in the foggy morning light. "I've had men like Fred. They violated me."

"You're upset," Roxanne says. "It's okay to not go back."

"Are you alright?" Emmie calls, bringing up the rear with the lumpy albatross around her neck.

"Are you still injured?" I cry.

She un-velcros the supporter and takes it off. "It's just to keep my neck steady. What about you?"

"I wish—Oh, man. Remember at The Hollyhock, when I told that wanker we were a chapter of Nymphomaniacs Anonymous?"

Emmie looks perplexed.

"Why *can't* we form our own group? Forget Fred and Dales. Have it be just us three girls. Is that in the realm of conceivability?"

"Maybe this once," Emmie says. She turns to Roxanne. "What about going to that bakery again?"

Roxanne looks doubtful. "Now?"

"I didn't mean to screw up that last breakfast we had there," I say.

Roxanne bugs her eyes at me. "Just so we're clear . . . . You dated men like Fred?"

BALLYHOO

"Yes," I say to Roxanne. We're settled at a Hollyhock table. She and Emmie expect some sort of confession. I'm ready. "I've done my share of Freddish jerks." I gaze at the crock of raspberry preserves on the table. "Some of these dudes beat me down. But that's over. The money question is why I sank so low to begin with."

Roxanne unfolds her paper napkin. "What's the money answer?"

My eyes flash at her. "Are you going to come up with complicated theories?"

"No. Go on with your own explanation."

I scratch the back of my neck. "The truth is that for a while, in the past, I was getting dieseled so much that, to keep it crunky, I went looking for blood-on-fire spooge."

"Can you say that in plain English?" Emmie says.

"Like the hit song?" I sing the line I have in mind, "*'I like pleasure spiked with pain . . . .'*"

Roxanne shakes her head.

"By the Chili Peppers! A huge band! Nevermind. Can we just admit there's a payoff to being some sport's anything-goes girl? To pushing the limits?" My eyes fall back on the jam jar. "Though, admittedly, during my little danger games, a line got crossed. I didn't much like the degradation. So I finally bowed out. Dumb, huh?"

Emmie pats my fingers. "Sad. Not dumb."

The warm contact of her fingers encourages me to explain further. "This last cocksucker—I pretty much begged him to whomp on me. And he was all *get lost, bitch, or I'll hose you*, which I guess, in retrospect, was good. If he hadn't shut me down, I would've met Fred at S and L and thought, *Here's another live one*. Could've gotten my brain bashed, like whoever Fred was talking about in the tribe. It shows everything happens for a reason. Oh man, now they've got me spewing poky 12 Step sayings."

"You shouldn't let SLAA rile you up," Roxanne says.

"Fred's phony excuses ticked me off! He's so fucking proud of how he pounds on his snooks. That sucks—I know from experience. Just talking about it gives me post-traumatic stress."

A waitress drops off menus. Me and Emmie ask for coffee.

"Fred's in pain, too," Roxanne says quietly.

"From whacking women's heads? Whose side are you on?"

Roxanne crosses her arms. "I'm speaking broadly. Addicts make bad decisions. Fred, Sameula, all of us. I convinced myself the affairs I was having were soulful adventures when it was cheating on Ronn, plain as day." She looks at Emmie. "Far be it from a sexual predator like me to claim the moral high ground over Fred."

I pick up my knife and gesture with it. "Us acting PC does not make Fred less of a shit stick."

The waitress delivers our coffees, glancing warily at the knife in my hand.

Roxanne opens her red plastic menu. "Addicts confuse insecurity, love, and anger. That isn't PC, it's reality." She scans the menu and looks up again. "What you described with *your* lovers could be sexual aggression turned against yourself."

I pretend to threaten her with the butter knife. "Don't headshrink me, you."

She pushes my wrist away. "Maybe you lack compassion for other addicts because you can't forgive your own behavior."

Emmie takes the knife out of my hand. "Can I say something, Boop?"

I grab my coffee mug handle. "No more psycho-twaddle, please."

"I've seen you start to believe in yourself," Emmie says. "Psychology may not be your thing, but my therapist says self-respect has to be the addict's touchstone."

"Like *you* need to work on self-respect." I tear open a sugar pack but decide against dumping the contents in my coffee. "Look in a mirror."

"I do, every day. And there's a woman looking back at me who's scared of getting hurt."

"By who?" I ask, surprised.

"Doesn't matter. Let's stick to talking about you."

I mindlessly stir my black coffee with a spoon. "There wasn't much *to* me 'til Derek Frick popped my fig. After that, I got popular. Helled around in the neighbor boys' yards. Middle of the night, my stepdad would check my bed, and ha-ha, no Boop. Made that dickass crazy, me getting all that nookie. Ma was drunk. I could do what I wanted."

"Where was your real father?" Emmie says.

"He busted a jig when I was little." I take a gulp from my mug. Too hot. "Boo hoo—never saw him again." The coffee sizzles in my empty stomach like venom.

"Mine left when I was thirteen," Roxanne tells me.

"Sooo," Emmie says, as if we're getting somewhere, "you two have absent fathers in common!"

"Mine moved to Canada," Roxanne says. "The divorce wasn't enough. He needed a new country. My mother was bereft and made me promise to hold on to my husband forever." She rubs her nose. "Unfortunately, I didn't keep the promise."

Emmie presses her lips together, gears whirling in her brain. "Maybe you both used sex to compensate for losing your fathers?"

My stomach growls. This talk makes me jumpy. "You sound like an expert," I say to Emmie. "Did your pa desert, too? Is that what caused *your* case of the hot to trots?"

"No."

"Then what was that 'scared in the mirror' stuff?" I ask. "Was it about your father?"

"It's not what you think." Her face transforms, lovely to tortured, in no time.

"What do I think?" I slowly say.

"Not my father." Emmie's voice thins, barely audible. "My brother."

The peanut. She mentioned him at Up the Wazoo's gig. "What'd he do?"

"Stop!" Roxanne snaps. "She's upset. Look!"

"It wasn't my brother," Emmie whispers.

Roxanne gives Emmie's shoulder a soothing rub. "You're not obligated to tell us anything."

"But you *can*," I say. "Maybe you *should*."

Roxanne looks at me crossly. "You're egging her on out of flagrant curiosity."

"I am not. We're friends."

"It was my brother's friends," Emmie blurts. "When I was eleven."

"What'd *they* do?" I say.

The waitress returns with her order pad. "Just the coffee for now," I say.

"And a mint tea," Roxanne says.

The waitress slaps the pad into her apron pocket and leaves.

Emmie's eyes follow the waitress. "It seemed so innocent at first."

"That sounds bad," I say. "Then what?"

Emmie fiddles with a lock of her hair. "One day, my brother said his friend liked me."

"How old were they?" Roxanne asks.

"Sixteen. I thought Skip was teasing me, as usual. But a couple days later, Adam Lazlo invited me to a movie."

"Adam Uh-oh." The knife is somehow back in my hand. I squeeze it tight.

Emmie sniffs. "I kept our plan secret so my parents couldn't say no."

I nod. "I snuck out with older dudes plenty of times."

"The night of our date, I met him at 7-11. He showed up with JT Velch, who had a car. We held hands in the backseat. Tina Turner was on the radio. I was wearing a pink sundress."

"Okay, you were in the car . . ." I say.

"Instead of picking up a date for himself, JT drove out behind the sewage treatment plant. To watch the sunset, they said. When they muscled me to the ground, it seemed pre-planned."

"Oh, God," Roxanne says, "you were raped."

"They pulled off my panties and said don't scream or they'd hit me. If I thrashed, dirt got in my eyes, so I stayed still. The sewage chemicals smelled like Pine-Sol."

"Rat bastards!" I bang the bottom of the knife on the table. "Were you crying?"

"Not even when dirt got in my vagina. The sun sank behind the hill like a blood clot. When JT finished, I put my underwear on, and we drove back to 7-11. I crossed the street and sat in my dirty dress at Willy's Washette for a couple hours until a man in a fishnet shirt asked if I needed help. I ran home, showered, threw my bloody underwear and stained dress in the garbage. My first date. Eleven years old."

Roxanne's face has turned a horrified shade of white. "Did your brother know?"

Emmie's eyes seem faraway. "They might have bragged to him. Maybe he was in on it all along. We never talked about it."

I drop the knife on the tabletop. "Skip the Drip. I hate him."

"Did you tell anyone?" Roxanne gently asks.

"My mother," Emmie meekly answers. "She said to keep it to myself. Don't tell my father. Don't tell my teacher. She saw I was hurting, and it didn't matter. She protected Skip."

"Omigod, same with me!" The words break out of me as if I'm someone else. "Ma didn't care!"

Roxanne snaps her head around. "About what now?"

My mouth hangs open. Blurry snapshots and ugly words bombard my mind. "I don't believe this." I feel sick down to my dugout. "I think I got raped, too."

Emmie slides her chair closer. "Keep breathing. You're alright."

Roxanne stares. "By one of the boys you snuck out with?"

"No," I say. "Holy crap. My father. I remember. Oh, shit."

"Gravity check, Boop," Roxanne says. "What're you saying?"

"This can't be." I shake my head. "Forget it."

"Let it out," Emmie says. She takes my wrist in her hands.

"I can't think." But a scene focuses in my memory, and I start to recite. "One day, Ma came home early from work. This was ages ago. She had one of her backaches."

"Uh-huh," Roxanne says.

"The popster had picked me up from school. I was naked. Ma went ape shit."

"Was your father naked?" Roxanne asks.

I try to picture it. "I don't know."

Emmie presses my wrist. "That's okay."

Swooping in to set a mug of tea in front of Roxanne, the waitress takes one look at our faces and flees.

"That was the day he split." My voice shakes. "The last time I saw him."

"This must hurt," Emmie says.

I nod absently. "Ma was punching him in the head. He tumbleweeded out of the house with his shoes in one hand and a carton of smokes in the other."

"Then she did care," Emmie says. "About you. She was hitting him."

"I guess."

Roxanne glances from her steaming mug to me. "What happened before she got home?"

I take a breath and shake my head. "Drawing a blank."

"It's okay," Emmie says.

"Some time after that I woke up from a bad dream one night and called for Ma. She comes into my bedroom and sees me holding my crotch. Gives me the same rap you got, Emmie. No one did nothing. Don't be a dirty little girl. Shut my stupid mouth. She'd stopped caring by then, if I'm remembering right."

Roxanne taps her lip. "How can you not remember whether your father molested you?"

"I was small," I whimper. "What did I know? Ma called me a sick little twit, and I believed her. Up 'til now I didn't realize what was buried in my head."

Emmie nods. "Not something you want to keep reliving."

"My recall's not total, going back twenty years." I turn to Emmie. "And half that time I was trashing my neurons with tequila and drugs."

"My story triggered your memory," she says.

"Be glad you *know* what happened to you." My cold fingers grip the corner of the table. "Instead of this dodgy memory jam."

"Could this all be ballyhoo," Roxanne says, lowering her eyes at me, "to get attention?"

"Thank you for the vote of confidence. That's just great. Did I accuse you of inventing that bit about your father deserting after I said that mine ran off?"

"Stop," Emmie says, "both of you. Undercutting each other is not the way to deal with this."

"You're right." Roxanne stands. "I should get going. If *my* mother is kept waiting, I'll hear about it for weeks." She throws a few dollars on the table. "You two stay."

"I'll call you," Emmie tells her.

"Ta-ta," I say glumly as Roxanne moves off.

Emmie reaches for her menu. "We're not rushing to visit our mothers. Why don't we eat something, talk a little more?"

"I wasn't lying!"

"I never thought you were."

"I remember Ma's expression that day." My eyes close. "She was seething. Something wrong went down."

"There's a link between abuse and addiction. I've read research on what we've been through."

I open my eyes, push my menu away. "Not hungry."

"Me, neither," Emmie says. "Know what my therapist says sex addiction is? A 'juggernaut.' It's from eastern religion. A force that's overwhelming."

"How are we supposed to stop something that's overwhelming?"

"It only *seems* overwhelming. It's a metaphor for our struggle."

I clutch my hair that's grown too long to gel into spikes. "We need anti-bi-addict drugs. Medicate the juggernaut away. Then we can quit going to meetings."

"12 Step's not all bad. It brought me closer to Tom. And I met you at a meeting." Emmie smiles. "Everything has its reason. As a wise person once said."

"Your shrink?"

"You! Five minutes ago."

I smack my forehead. "I told you my brain is fried. Didn't I?"

Dear California Medical Association

Enclosed is my Advance Health Care Directive form giving Power of Attorney over my medical care and finances to my trustee Dickinson Park.

Sincerely yours,
(forged)
Sada Pollard

I VANT TO BE ALONE

Like dot famous voman vonce said.

I vant to vatch Comedy Central in bed, volf down microvave popcorn and svill vhisky. Get vasted, do vhat I vish, vidout dumb vindbags or vicked fadders anyvhere near me. Vidout vackos squirting der jizz vhile not caring one vhit about my vants.

No more being treated like I'm vorthless.

CHEWYLICIOUS JUGGERNAUTS

Emmie linked this addiction we're ditching to a religious idea, a juggernaut, something that human will can't resist. The word sounds more like a candy bar to me. TV commercials hawking this confection would toot, "Chewylicious Juggernauts—kids love 'em!"

Or juggernauts could be the name of plastic wine jug stoppers, those dealies that are too stiff to recork, so instead of letting the leftover vino go to waste, you polish it off and get liver-lubed.

Or the pegs that fasten hubcaps to car wheels—aren't those juggernauts?

During Sada's nap, I'll tote myself to the library and look the term up. See if any juggers are there or naut.

A librarian named Zephyr wanders past the lectern where I flip Webster's New World skin-thin pages. I used to be a regular at this branch, dropping by to read music 'zines or poke through the piss-ass Cassettes-For-Borrow section. I stopped in recently to read about scleroderma. The building's exterior is generic office glass and cement, but inside, the library features southern-exposure windows, noise-muffling ply carpet, and thousands of books that smell like dusty cookies. I've read every Vonnegut in circulation.

Juggernaut: incarnation of the god Vishnu, whose idol excited worshipers so much, as it was hauled on a cart during religious rites, that they threw themselves under the wheels and were crushed; thus, whatever exacts blind devotion or sacrifice; a terrible, irresistible force.

Lifting my eyes from the minuscule print, I imagine this charismatic higher power, this incarnation of a god, spreading havoc through a crowd like in a kaleidoscopic scene from *The Arabian Nights*. Vishnu must be mighty strong magic if just a statue of him causes such a flap. I head to the reference section and pull the H volume of the encyclopedia off the shelf. I find a comfy warren in the stacks where I plop myself down to read up on Hinduism.

"In a former life I must have been a Hindu," I tell Emmie when she pops up at my crib during my break from working with Sada. Emmie has come bearing a bouquet of spirally red peonies in a plastic water vase.

I've just showered. My hair hangs in wet shocks on my black polyester shoulders.

The caramel-colored, twilly fabric of Emmie's outfit shimmers when she sits and crosses her legs. The creepy neck brace is gone.

"If anyone ever worshipped phallus," I say, two-handing the vase and peeking at my friend over the tops of the flowers, "and lived by the kama sutra, it's me, right? And you."

"Our phallus-chasing days are over." Emmie cups her keys in her hand like a mass of shrapnel. "Remember?"

"How could I forget?" I set the vase on my shelf and perch beside my friend on the sofa.

According to Emmie's Swiss wristwatch, *The Price Is Right*, a ritual amusement for me and Sada, is starting. The other day, I heroically swapped Bridgit's TV for Sada's, lugging each of them on my own power. I hope I left the remote control within Sada's reach.

Emmie looks pigeon-toed in her suede sandals, a slight imperfection that doesn't subtract from her 10-ness. I'd trade fifty of my lovemonkey conquests for one of hers, to feel what it's like to be a bona fide erotic maestra. These days, with marriage on the near horizon, she's supposed to funnel all her carnal knowledge to one lucky recipient, which might turn out good since her intended's got lots of snaps, and money's the ultimate macrodesiac in our culture.

I knock my knee against hers. "You're getting all the ground rations you want from trusty Tom, aren't you? I'd hardly call that suffering from penile-deprivation."

Emmie rises to her feet, steps over the giant fork, and gazes out my window. The North Oakland view is a patchwork of downsloping rooftops injected with vents and jerry-rigged antennas. "The excitement's always been the chase." She shrugs. "That part is gone."

The chase. I know it well. The hormo-eroto-emo hunt that once was oh-so-mouth-watering but now leaves me down in the mouth. The same must be true for Emmie. Why else would she cast her lot with monogamy and 12 Step?

I stand and park myself by her. "Lucky you, with your stamp-of-approvaled beau to supply orgasmic services."

Dust on the outer window surface has formed a driblet pattern. The inside glass is filmed with grease. When spick-and-spanning my apartment, I managed to miss this accumulated window ugh-liness. But even immaculately housekeeped, my crash pad would be a cesspit compared to where Miss Top Drawer lives. Emmie has everything a girl could want.

"I've never had an orgasm," she says.

"Right. And I've never polished off a box of Bagel Dogs."

She faces me straight-on. "You're the only one besides me who knows. Not even my therapist." She grips her ribs as if they might fly apart.

"Holy moly." Her secrets immediately unspool in my head as if they're my own. Like how, after her brother's friends raped her, a hidden core of fury must have ignited. She soldiered on in the love trenches all these years by being a power hottie, constantly guarding her emotional safety. *Don't enjoy this* must be the message her brain sent her hurt-girl clit. Frigidity turned into ammunition against vulnerability.

My poor friend. I take her hand. If I hadn't veered the opposite direction without once thinking my options over, it could have gone the same for me—self-protection over self-destruction. Me and Emmie are the flip sides of one coin. We're the beast with two backs, both fucked.

"But how could you spread your legs for jillions of hunks," I say, bouncing her hand in mine, "and be faking it?"

She pulls her hand away. "You'd be surprised how easy that's been."

Considering how well the male ego deludes itself, I'm not that surprised. "But girlfriend, what's in it for you if you're faking? Especially with the hubby-to-be? Sure, after screwing sex up real bad, who am I to expect a successful relationship? But you . . . ." I glance out the window, then back at her, a new tune welling up in me. "You have the chance of a lifetime to live happily ever after. Don't destroy it. Enjoy it. You need to tell Tom the truth. He'll understand. Together, you two can go to mating paradise. I guaran-damn-tee you."

She laughs. "It's good one of us knows so much about love."

"Me? *You* are the femme fatale. Or so I thought." I hop over the giant fork and sniff the scentless peonies. "I've never gotten flowers before. Isn't that sad? Not once. I've never had a real boyfriend." I turn. "You must've gotten fieldsful of roses from your multiplude of admirers."

Emmie comes to me and fluffs my damp hair with her beauty-savvy fingers. "Bringing flowers was my excuse to see how you're doing."

After dropping my bombshell about my popster violating my tiny loins, she means. "I'm alright. You have your own stuff to deal with."

"My therapist said you had a recovered memory."

"You talked to your therapist about me?"

"A little. You're part of my rehabilitation. I hope I'm part of yours."

"Rehab? What are we, criminals?"

"Of course not."

"We *are* a pair of outlaws."

"No, we're not."

"I'm the outlaw. You're the in-law—to-be."

Emmie smiles and scrunches the other side of my hair. "Tom's going to be shocked to hear I haven't ever climaxed with him."

"He'll get over it." My mind revisits my first glorious Derek Frick bang, that maybe I've spent my life trying to duplicate. "You'll thank me for this, girlfriend."

Emmie presses a hug on me. "You're better than my psychologist, you know that?"

Hamhandedly returning the hug, I feel like a baby chimp who's not used to affection, whose mother got killed by poachers. Emmie's molasses-y perfume reminds me of graham crackers. I pull away and rub my nose. "I gotta get back to my other patient." I lead my bestest friend to the door. "It means a lot to me that you checked in."

"We never decided about next week. Are we attending 12 Step—or forming another group?"

"Talking at The Hollyhock's been hecka better than the Jerkoholics meetings, don't you think? For dredging up emotional stuff?"

"Yes . . . ."

"Nymphos Anonymous forever!"

"But it's not official."

"So?"

"We hardly know what we're doing."

"We're doing alright," I say.

"We should find out what everyone wants."

"What Roxanne wants, you mean. Sure. Let's ask her at the church, okay? I can be flexible. Reasonable R Us. Good as your shrink. Isn't that what you said?"

"I said you're better."

———————⋆———————

Sada is asleep on her back. Her chest lifts with each cloggy breath, then collapses like a sand tunnel. The remote control is welded to her hand. Our TV show plays on the screen.

"Betsy Vulcani, come on down!" says Rod Roddy, the gonzo announcer.

The camera pans a live audience hepped on dreams of fab prizes, or perhaps they're just aping enthusiasm for the dumb fun of it. A contestant descends the studio risers.

On the sound stage set stands Bob Barker, who has emceed this show my whole life. Framed by fluorescent white hair, his face has the starkly contoured cheeks of a made-up geisha girl. His smile can't disguise a not-all-here look in the eyes. It's possible he doesn't give a rat's ass who will guess the cost of a Proctor Silex Food Dehyrator without going over the MSRP.

Neither do I.

I pry the flicker-flacker from Sada's grasp and zap the TV power off. In the absence of the television's blare, the next cut on the soundtrack to the cable movie of my life becomes audible—Sada's lo-flo breathing. When her sawbones doc returned my call to his office, he said it's as if cement is slowly solidifying in her lungs.

The rhythmic snores are strangely tranquilizing in the aftermath of my Chatty-Cathy visit with Emmie. I forgot to tell her about reincarnation—how it can be a step up, like from grocery bagger to Maxim model or petty grifter to federal judge. Me and Emmie should convert to Hinduism. In her next life, she could be the most sexually satisfied woman in Oakland who has a big greasy orgasm when her boo just whispers in her ear. And my few kind deeds might jack my restless soul up the karmic ladder, too.

As I dislodge my underwear out of my butt crack, Sada chokes in her sleep. Apnea—another complication predicted by the doctor. I hold a finger under her nose, prepared to administer CPR in the event of air flow loss. If Sada was Hindu, she'd be made. For being a friend when I least deserved it, she's entitled to rebirth as a Wheaties-box athlete in her next go-round. And her incompetent physicians, and Skip's rapist friends, and Emmie's mother, and my mother, and my father, and Gordon, and Fred, and Hippie Bob can all be pubic lice in their next lives.

I stare out the window at the thick, green bush. Samsara doesn't work this way, but I feel reborn already. I've morphed from compulsive sex fiend into Sada's protector. I became the confidant of a fellow addict who's pretty as a news anchor and nicer than Mr. Rogers. For the first time in my life, I feel something akin to faith—in myself, in others, in something beyond humanity—even if Vishnu sounds more like a sneeze than a god.

". . . ving."

I turn from the window. Sada has awakened and said something. "What'd you say?"

"Starving!"

I grin my way to the kitchen to whip up the best smoothie ever.

Yes, we have one banana—loaded with potassium. We have "Vanilla Rice Dream" and "Soy Protein Isolate." I drag out of the cupboard the experimental dietary supplements obtained during my health food store runs. What superfood might ramp up immunity and vitality?

"Standardized Black Cohosh Root Extract" smells foul. "Super Lycopene" comes in pills I can't grind fine enough to clear Sada's gullet. "Propolis Drops" must be made by, or out of, bees, considering the label's illustration, but when I draw out the dipstick, the resin goozing off the tip does not look like a good buzz.

I push these products aside and let my thoughts stray to Emmie. So she isn't the perfect It Girl I assumed she was. Hippie Bob used to say, "When you assume, you make an ass out of you and me." His chiding infuriated me, though in this case he wouldn't be off base. Assuming Emmie was a hot, happy hussy was wrong. Getting raped fusterclucked her entire sex life. 'Til 12 Step came along, and maybe a little help from me.

I pick up a jar of "Chlorophyll-Rich Spirulina Powder," edible algae with the legendary power to repair body cells. Too bad it's hell's bells to digest—I know from experience. Supposedly "Supplemental Lecithin," this next jar, calms spirulina so its benefits can be enjoyed. I break the seal and unscrew the top. The granules have no smell, and, licked from my palm, no taste. I load the blender with some of each, trying to build a wonder-working elixir, because, talk about juggernauts— try scleroderma for a force no one can whup. It'll stiffen you up, starve you out, scab you over, and leave you terrified. Some Hindus say the material world is illusion, so let it be. But in my shoes, even practicing Hindus would pray for a way to keep their friend's material body alive.

The finished blender concoction is chlorophyl-green, like pond sludge, and the consistency of runny oatmeal. This must be what Nurse Delizio pictured when I bragged about making smoothies.

I carry the hideous manna out, and, bless her sclerotic soul, Sada drinks it down.

Steps

St. Henry of Uppsala, 1,902 steps from home.

First Nature Health Foods, 2,144 steps.

Spring Fever Flowers, 998 steps. Sada's favorite: white tulips.

Payless Drugs, 2,473 steps, eight medicine prescriptions to refill.

Safeway, 392 steps. Charmin', Tide, Clorox, Brawny, Depends, Snuggle.

Cal-Fed, 1,622 steps. Disability checks, forged and unforged.

My couch to Sada's bed, 17 steps. 12 x/day.

Boycott Away

People who stand up their pals at meetings give addicts a bad name. Emmie checked the community room. I checked the WC and coffee stand. No Roxanne. We're cooling our heels out front 'til she appears.

Dastardly Dales and Screwy Samuela show up. A battalion from Mothers Against Drunk Driving arrives. St. Henry's worshippers flock in for coffee, dressed to the fives instead of the nines, due to poverty. Everyone but Roxanne is in attendance.

I don't like churches or support groups, but here I am, in case our third Nympho wants to schmooze with omelets and danish and Emmie and me. "Wanna bet she's drinking mint tea at The Hollyhock?" I say.

"I don't think she'd go to the café on her own," Emmie says.

"Let's go see."

"Go, if you want. I'll stay."

Even if Roxanne is already there, by the time I walk or bus over, our little spoilsport will be gone. "I thought we'd talk about our traumatic experiences today."

Emmie fixes my flipped-under jacket lapel. "Still can. Let's reconnect later."

"Sada's catching her death of everything," I say. "I can't stay out very long."

"Take care of her, then. That's best. I'll call you tomorrow."

The second I leave, Roxanne will show up and whisk Emmie out to breakfast. "I can wait a little more."

Jonathan dweebles toward us in a green and yellow baseball cap. "Morning," he says to Emmie. "Coming in?"

"Couple minutes," she says.

He frowns at his watch. Our meeting starts in less than that.

"Actually, I'll walk in with you," she says.

With Elegant Em at his side, Jonathan walks tall. She's coyly colluding, opening her little heart up to him. Forget me, left on the sidewalk like a dog that rolled in its own doo. Poxy Roxy is ruining my morning.

Emmie and Jonathan's conversation at the door is so scintillating that they linger, the meeting slipping from his mind. Without his leadership, the Room 3 people might group-backslide into a rowdy orgy with Fred and Dales and Samuela winning the grand prize for grossest sex acts ever committed on church grounds.

Emmie's cheesing at Jonathan. There is a faint scrim of lead-wolf allure to him, and if Emmie's not completely sold on holy matrimony, she may not be able to stop flirting with whoever's momentarily alpha. And Jonathan's a sex addict, isn't he? Gazing at her in that come-hither way? She's a honeydip in those platform shoes, indigo denim, and ponytail hair—like a rural beauty queen. For all I know, they're saying to each other, "Nevermind sobriety, let's get a room."

Or not. They're probably threshing out the finer points of what it means for addicts to make a fearless inventory of their wrongs, and it's disgusting of me to think otherwise. I'm just pissed because Fisty Fred, my least favorite sexhead, just walked by, wearing his gladiator sandals and looking bloodthirsty. To think his ilk used to baste my meat locker.

Jonathan follows Fred into the bowels of St. Henry's, and Emmie rushes back to me, reaching the same conclusion, I hope—that our barely-hatched but potentially incredible Nympho chick collective is the smart alternative to him, them, that.

"The meeting's starting, and I need to attend," she says breathlessly, "but if you want to bow out, I understand."

"Did you see Fred's obscene suck-me look? We should boycott meetings with that sick fuck in them."

"Ignore him."

"Why should I?"

"Then don't. Boycott away."

"You, too! C'mon! Forget Jonathan."

"Don't be mad, but I was telling him 'my friend' had a recovered memory about her abusive father."

"Just now you were talking about *me*?"

"Not by name. I lied and said it was someone from another 12 Step group I go to."

"You lied to protect me?"

"Boop, Jonathan thinks you should ask your mother what happened, and so do I. Find out the truth and move on."

"Ma can't remember that far back. Even if she could, she doesn't give a damn about truth."

"What have you got to lose by trying?"

"I don't know."

"What if I drive you to her house? Be your moral support?"

"You'd do that?"

"I'll pick you up tomorrow at eleven. We'll have our talk then." Her index finger taps the air as punctuation. "Let her know you're coming, okay?"

I smile, say, "Shit," but it's meant it in the nicest possible sense because Emmie's my friend. A friend is someone who reverses your expectations in a good way. Unlike Roxanne. "Can we go out there now?"

"I'm not ready to quit 12 Step."

"I get it. See you tomorrow."

"Hope your neighbor's okay." Emmie rushes to the door to salvation. She disappears into St. Henry's, leaving me good-to-go.

But there's still that chance Roxanne will show up to friendnap Emmie. I'm staying on the lookout, and if she appears, we can go be the Three Nymphos and make solid progress. Why would Emmie prefer the meeting circus over that?

I scan the street in both directions. Roxanne is obviously not coming. Either she's cured, or she no longer wants to affiliate with me.

Glued to this spot, I'm like a girl in a movie, the camera zooming up and away, revealing how empty the world can be, how alone she is—loser in love, abandoned by friends, needing to change except it doesn't happen fast enough. The ground spins under the girl, a special effect that makes her hermitude cinematic.

Cut to the next scene, can we? Where I get some grub and shake off the vertigo.

At One-Stop Liquors, I filch a pack of mini-donuts. I haven't boosted merchandise since my teenage malt liquor shoplifting days. The counter help is asleep at the switch. I saunter outside with my five-finger discount, tear away the cellophane, and stuff the first powdered-sugar sinker between my teeth. The dense donut is hardly worth snarfing.

As I chew, a rat under a newspaper stand catches my eye. Something dark hangs from its mouth. Its rodent body convulses. The One-Stop counter kid appears in the doorway, cigarette burning, looking at the swag in my mitt. I scramoodle away before being asked to explain.

I wend down Sacramento Street—away from, not toward, home—and lose the donuts in a dumpster outside a building. Roxanne would never jay junk food and drug herself with a carbo load outside a rat-infested bottle shop.

Sada once said that rats can't throw up because they lack a gag reflex. The One-Stop rat might beg to differ. I hope the zoological facts Sada loves to regale me with aren't all false.

Animal Fun Facts

A honeybee has two stomachs, one for honey, one for food.

If you cut off a cockroach's head, it can still live for weeks.

More bugs live in one mile of wild land than the total people on earth.

Mosquitoes prefer blondes to brunettes.

Aphids are born pregnant without having had sex.

All clams start out male; some decide to become female later.

The bottom of a horse's hoof is called a frog.

Cat urine glows under a black light.

Swans are the only birds that have penises.

A female ferret in heat dies if it can't find a mate.

THE VICE-SHEDDING FAD
I'M ALL ABOARD

My nose hasn't lost its knack for sniffing out a lark. While thinking about ferrets and strolling from One-Stop Liquors to Sacramento Street, I home onto what must be Spaceman Steve's crib. The Outback store that Bridgit said he lives by is down the block, and this building has a mechanic shop entrance. It's built wide for cars to drive through, facaded with rolled-down chain metal, and padlocked shut. A fairy castle entrance to adventure.

A person-sized door lies just beyond this gate. I knock until the door opens, releasing warm, petroliferous air. Steve appears behind the weather-stripping.

"Hey, Space!" My greeting doesn't draw the glad reaction a visitor hopes for. "I was at this thing in your hood," I say ("thing" meaning addict meeting), "and while walking home" (roundaboutly), "I remembered you moved to a chop shop on this street." (Actual events didn't follow this exact logic).

Steve peers out in drowsy silence. Everything below his chin is lost to shadow. "Hey," he finally says.

"I'm glad you're up."

"I wasn't, 'til you pounded on the door."

I scratch my ass, hoping his panties aren't all in a wad. Those donuts I rustled earlier would have come in handy right about now. Breakfast delivered, nummy-nums. Stupid, stupid, stupid to have discarded them so fast. *Waste not, want not*, Ma used to preach the rare nights she put food on the table, macrobiotic goulashes she claimed were wholesome—parsnip mash, millet gruel, lima stew that I dumped, untasted, into the trash. I was a stringy, ankle-biter who'd rather starve than choke down the silage she cooked.

I suck in my gut which, even after dropping a full size, still packs some sumo wrestler excess. "Last time we saw each other was Loosen The Noose. My friend almost broke her neck." It hurts to talk while clenching my entrails, but that doesn't stop me. "What a galahad you were that night, dude. You ever need a favor, just ask. I mean it. Anything. Ya think I could come in?"

"Uh, I'm not dressed."

"Psshh. I'm not looking. I swore off men, in case you haven't heard."

"Another time."

"Okay. Whatever's clever." A school bell trills somewhere in Steve's neighborhood. "It's just . . . . Earlier, I was flashing back on your flat on Dwight Way. Remember me dancing naked as a squirrel over there?"

"Naw."

"Small wonder. You'd dropped 'Ludes someone brought back from India. You could barely sit up. It was like Weekend at Bernie's."

"Yah, well, I'm off coffins. Mandrax, Xanax, Special K. All that. You ever kittyflip?"

"I might've done a bump or two."

"Don't. Honestly. A few months ago, I was in a K-hole for hours. Hospital said I could have died. Be careful around that shit, Boop."

I smile. Isn't this buttah, Steve wanting to save me from some narcoleptic coma? He's one of the good guys. "Smart advice." I undo my jacket's top button. "We're not young and resilient anymore."

"Got that right."

"Guess I'm not the only one who's had to give up some vices."

"Guess not."

"How 'bout I come inside?"

"What for?"

To use the plumbing is one what-for, though instead I say, "I have a business proposition."

"If you're looking for drugs, I'm not slanging."

"Steve! We're both saying we graduated from druggy life. Why would I ask if you're holding? I never even had a baby habit to kick, let alone showing up begging for a fix."

"I stand corrected."

I take a breath and wish we were chillaxing inside. "You still in your band?"

"We split up."

"How come?"

"Artistic differences."

"Up The Wazoo just went blooey, too. Same sort of thing."

"Up The Wazoo? They're hella cool."

"*Were* hella cool. It's been a comedownance for me. You should start a new band. You're the best drummer since DJ Bonebrake. Or maybe you could resurrect

The Beam Me Ups, with new band mates. Remember that party where we threw our shoes out the window during your cow song?"

"'Fuck Leather'?"

"Exactly. Harry Slesser's Doc Marten got run over in the street, and he bawled like a spanking baby. And I found your green hightop in a bush."

Steve draws the door open a whiff farther. "What a memory," he says.

"That was what, three years ago?"

"Four. Or more."

I lean against the doorframe. "I miss the old punk revival thing."

"The what?"

"You know! Bands breaking down barriers like the first wave of punk did. Our anti-multinational rebellion. Not just the mohawks and spikes and superficial anarchy, like today. We were asking questions that needed asking, like who needs NAFTA? Real activism's dead."

"People stopped giving a shit."

"We lost the best part of ourselves."

"Hang on, okay? I'll find my robe and let you in."

"Okie doke."

He shuts the door. I stare at the peeling sepia paint and think, *Not okie doke.* What if I get in there, and Steve's warm and naked under his bathrobe? What if desire proves irresistible? We'll be Jack and Jill Hook-up, whether I like it or not, and there go my 12 Step pledges.

My body feels wet with sweat, saliva, nose-run, pussyslick. Deep inside, adrenaline, stomach acid, and estrogen produce their own slippery-tenterhooks sensations.

I could play it safe and leave, as if some errand can't wait. But what kind of friend splits without a toodle-oo, especially when we're tripping down memory lane? Steve deserves better. And I could use a friend. One who's not moving to another state or marrying herself off to Mr. Bankroll or fixing to die. No law or step says I can't befriend a dude. I just have to avoid stupid moves.

"Hey." Steve swings the door open.

I dry my sweaty forehead on my jacket sleeve and swallow a cheekful of cold spit as I enter what once must have been the shop office. The rectangular space is lit by a single overhead bulb. A red sleeping pad lies on industrial flooring. A metal staircase spirals to mysterious darkness above. The plate window opens onto a ghost town garage, empty except for Steve's drumkit, dwarfed in a corner. The space is silent as a hazmat site and smells like a hundred lube jobs.

Steve looks dapper as a Euro-spy in his striped robe. Insert a pipe and martini, and he'd be James Bond. He kicks a Taco Bell bag aside and says, "What do you mean you swore off men?"

Light-headed, I sit on the lowest metal stair. If only I had those donuts to raise my blood sugar. Maybe one of the doors across from me leads to a kitchen. Maybe the john's the other door. "I don't wanna disappoint anyone," I say, winking and ignoring my pee's little voice coming from beneath my belly button, "but I'm in a self-imposed cooling-off period."

He tucks a strand of hair behind his ear and shifts on his feet. The strand falls back on his face and sticks to the damp corner of his mouth.

"It's part of the vice-shedding fad that I'm all aboard." I see stars from the strain of holding my stomach flat. "I'm test driving the road to self-improvement."

"Whatever you're doing, it's working. You clean up pretty nice."

Hearing these words is like finding a Hershey's Kiss in my pocket—wish it was Good 'N' Plenty. "Thanks." I touch the thickly-applied lipgloss Emmie gave me. Emmie's as sex addicted as me, and she cohabitates pre-maritally. The S & L rule seems to be that if who you have sex with is your steady, if he's half-nice and not instantly regrettable, then conditions are kosher, and you're cleared for takeoff. Not even Rigid Roxy raised objections to Emmie having a resident valentino at her beck and call.

If me and Steve teamed up, we'd be just as 'licit, 'cause he's definitely half-nice. Inviting me in. Cheering me up. Pretty nice-ing me.

I smile and catch myself getting ahead of myself in my dunderhead way, mindframing Steve as my next mistake. "I'm so ironic," I say. "Losing weight and cleaning myself up right when I'm self-purifying. Of course, I don't plan to be celibate forever. Only as long as it takes . . . ."

"For what?"

Good question. I gaze through the glass at the garage. There's not even a pneumatic jack in there. I turn and see Steve rubbing his eyebrows. Why I brought up recovering from addiction, I don't know. All of a sudden, I'm honest to a fault?

A ringing phone saves me from having to explain. Steve digs a clunky wireless phone from under a pile of clothes and turns away to talk—"Sure, I'm available. Uh-huh. See ya soon."

I'm jealous of the "ya" he's seeing soon, when I'm here! "You need a modern cell phone," I say when he pushes the antenna in. "Fits in the palm of your hand."

"Gotta do some work with my stepbrother."

"On Sunday?" Hooray—it wasn't a girlfriend calling. "What sort of work?"

"Hauling and dumping."

The old me, given this setup, would come back with a flirty crack about balling and humping. New me lamely says, "But you're not dressed."

"I better change. He's on his way over." He pulls me to my feet and chaperones me to the door, looking into my eyes in a tame-wolverine way that's as foreign to me as Romanian. Who'd've thought *not* getting a swerve on could feel so sweet? "Take it easy, Boop." He plants a tiny wet one on my cheek.

As the regular-sized door closes, I stare at the garage's portcullis entrance to my left. I'd love to label Steve's kiss on my cheek as one of life's princess moments, but it's best to nip that romantic habit in the bud. Like some wit once said, *A hair of a difference makes all the difference in the world.* So I hop, skip, and jump my fine line home. I need to pee something fierce.

Fat Loss Crash Diet

Breakfast
Black coffee

Snack
Altoid

Lunch
Celery.

Snack
Diet Sprite

Dinner
Cucumber

Bedtime Snack
Cigarettes

In Which I Imagine Emmie's Take on Our Visit To Ma

Most of the paint on the tacky ranchette's porch is eroded. In case of sinkholes, I climb the wood stairs with caution. At the top, Boop clomps ahead.

Loose hasps and hinges barely hold the splintered door to the splintered jamb. Where the doorbell button should be, a red and white two-ply wire dangles.

Boop knocks and tries the metal knob. The door is locked, yet she insists her mother is home. We descend the steps and pick our way along the side of the house, through thigh-high quack grass and tamped-down trash. The ruffle-edge shingle siding would look retro chic if it wasn't so in need of a sand-blasting.

The unlatched back door leads to a bare pantry and a kitchen with laminate counters, brass hardware, and a yellow 'fridge, all in bad repair. I step over a ruptured teabag and glistening spill, snatch a black banana peel off the floor and chuck it into the sink loaded with smelly dishes.

I have only myself to blame for being here. I pressed Boop to visit and deputized myself her moral reinforcement. *Something* better come of this.

Boop's mother, the forty-something mistress of Park Place, sits in a shuttered den, barefoot, across from a turned-off console TV. She grips a rustic mug, looking as "swacked" as Boop predicted, though she smiles at the sight of her daughter accessorized in dress flats and a silk shawl on loan from me. The room smells grapey and varnishy.

Boop stations herself alongside a helter-skelter bookcase, standing as motionless and tongue-tied as a lizard camouflaged on a rock. Our whole ride out here, she shrugged off questions and repeatedly checked her face in the visor mirror. A case of nerves, I assumed. Observing what a sorceress her mother seems to be, I understand why Boop might clam up in her presence.

I take the initiative and say, "Hi, I'm Emmie, Boop's friend?"

Mrs. Park's muddy-water eyes scrutinize me.

"Ma," Boop manages. "Say hey to my friend."

With her pinky nail, "Ma" scrapes a shard of something off a yellow tooth. "Should've told me you were coming. I'd have cooked supper."

"You didn't phone ahead?" I say.

"Even if I had, she'd have forgot."

"But—"

"Trust me," Boop says. "You don't want supper."

Mrs. Park grabs a green bottle from near her feet and pours beet-red wine into her mug. "You never call."

"When I do, Bob badmouths me and won't put you on."

"But you're here now," I remind Boop.

Boop pulls the shawl up her neck. "Yah." The TV is supported by short peg legs, like a hippo. Boop gazes at the lightless screen and rubs her stomach.

"Boop?" I cue.

She turns to face her mother. "We oughta talk, Ma."

The woman lowers the mug. "Ya look good, kid. Give ya that." Her head tilts toward me. "Who'd you say the Day-Glo cheerleader is?"

My face flushes. I should have worn something more modest than a yellow jumpsuit.

"Emmie. She gave me a lift."

Wisely, Boop doesn't explain how we know each other. Her mother, no fake Betty Crocker like my mother, would probably ridicule support groups.

"Care for a drink, Femmie?" Mrs. Park says.

"Bit early for me, Ma'am."

"Grab a mug in the kitchen," she tells Boop. "I'll pour you the rest."

"I quit drinking, Ma."

"Who you trying to fool?"

"I'm not selling you a ticket. I really quit. You ought to try it."

"I quit trying to quit." Her chortle touches off a coughing jag that jerks her whole body in repeated spasms. She caps her free palm over the mug to keep the wine from splashing.

Boop stares at the Ferragamos I loaned her, mauve ballet flats with bows at their throats, bought in a Waikiki boutique. Her feet look stuffed into them.

"Can I get you some water?" I ask Mrs. Park.

"Don't bother." Boop turns to her mother. "Can we get on with this?"

The woman barks, "Get on with what?"

Boop shrinks from the question and wrings her hands. "Nothing. Nevermind."

"Don't back down," I say. Her mother was accurate about me being a cheerleader. In high school, I did splits and herkies, shook my poms and cheered,

Goooo, 'Cudas! to stir up the crowd. How can I persuade Boop to do what she came for? I can't pep call, "Gimmie an N, Gimmie an O, Gimmie an F-E-A-R!"

Her mother sets her mug down. "If this gingerbread girl chauffered you here to cadge a handout, you're wasting your breath on that bunco. The well's run dry. You already owe Bob three hundred bucks."

Boop reaches down her shirt and digs a nugget of folded money out of her bra that she tosses at her mother's feet. "There's twenty."

Mrs. Park's bare toes rake the bills towards her. Fishing them up, she nearly nosedives out of her seat. "Bob said we'd never see a dime of this."

I could write a check and dispense with Boop's IOU. She works hard for her neighbor and deserves a bailout. $280 means nothing to me. Being a friend means plenty. But clearing Boop's debt should be agreed to ahead of time.

Boop glances warily through the doorway. "Where is that prick Bob?"

"Day job at the new Costco."

"Good. I don't want to run into that cocksucker."

"You've got a fresh mouth," her mother says. "What's Bob ever done besides keep you in line? Which ain't easy."

"You've seen that shitstain run his eyes all over me!"

"He does not. Don't be tetchy."

"Saying I'm good-for-nothing—you've heard him. When I was little," Boop says to me, "he sprayed his pressure washer on me. Another time he packed me a sandwich for school—a wad of duct tape on stale bread. Paying me back for not eating some tripe he'd over-microwaved the night before. Why do you stay with that toss-pot?" she asks her mother. "Always going around like he's got something over on me."

"What would Bob have over on you?"

Boop glances at my shoes on her feet. "He knows something," she stammers.

Her mother chuckles. "Not that I've noticed."

"He knows what my father did! Doesn't he?"

Good for Boop, playing her hand, not acting like a lily-liver after all. I side-slide quietly toward the window to give my friend space, not rope.

"And Bob is penny ante if you compare what my father did," Boop pushes on. "I was so freaking young, Ma!"

Yes—setting it out like a landmine for her mother to step on. I hope there's relief in this for Boop.

Her mother hunches over her wine.

"That's why you kicked him out, isn't it?" Boop says. "I know what happened. So does Emmie."

Her mother glances accusingly at me. With her frizzy hair and acne-mauled face, she resembles a witch about to cast a world-of-black spell. "You know nothing," she tells me, then turns to Boop. "Where do you come up with this piffle?"

"Bob's been hinting for years. He thinks I'm a slut that asked for it."

"You always had a problem imagination."

"Then tell me what went down. Just once, Ma. The nitty gritty."

Her mother's face quavers like a snail showered with salt. Checkered light from the shutters behind me falls on her hair.

"It damn sure helps explain your past twenty-odd hammered years," Boop says.

"Ma" aligns her lips to chug more drink. "You don't know what you're talking about," she says, unaware that wine is trickling down her chin. "Back off if you know what's good for you."

What Boop said yesterday—about our mothers being in denial—was spot-on. They hide the truth and have no right. I would never treat a daughter so bad.

"You know what you're doing, Ma?" Boop paces a couple of steps and pivots back. "You're saying what he did's okay. Not worth remembering. Even if it's had a hellacious effect on me—which it has—you don't care. I told Emmie we'd never get acknowledgement from you. You condone what he did with your selective forgetting."

"Better than your selective *bellyaching*."

"You're supposed to defend *me* against Bob's battery acid put-downs and my pa's . . . ." Boop wheezes, catches her breath. "I'm your kid, for Christ's sake. The only goddam one you've got."

Except for the only-child part, Boop could be speaking for my family, blasting at the same injustice. I'm thrilled for her, for us, for this breakthrough.

"Like hell, I haven't defended you," her mother says. "Who bailed you out of the pokey? And got you qualified for disability? Who handed over doleouts when you were down to your last nickel? Bob and me wore ourselves out saving you from yourself. Now you come and torment me with cock and bull."

"It's not bull. I have a memory."

"You have shit for memory."

"Then tell her the truth," I say.

They both glare at me. "Should I wait outside?" I ask.

"Yes"—from her mother.

"No"—from Boop.

The windowsill I back into gnaws my tailbone. The shutter louvers smell yeasty.

"Stay as a witness," Boop says.

"Witness!" her mother hoots. She points her elbow at me. "If your friend here's known you more than a day, she's witnessed enough to know you're not 'Of Sound Mind', quote unquote. Bob had no trouble registering her as mentally disabled for SDI benefits—did you know *that*, Femmie?" She pours out the last of the drink.

"Don't lie!" Boop rushes the chair and cuffs the refilled mug out of her mother's hand. The wine arcs out and hits her mother's flowered blouse like spatter from a bloody throat-slit. The mug pinwheels down and shatters. "I didn't have a breakdown," Boop says, grabbing her blouse. "Bob dreamed up the wackaloon scam, and you know it."

Off-guard and plastered, Mrs. Park lets Boop lift her out of the chair. Locked fist to cloth, daughter and mother hiss like badgers in a turf war. My shawl slides to the floor, just missing a pool of wine.

I watch in horror. We've opened Pandora's box. Out flew insanity, abuse, and welfare fraud, along with the molestation we came to ask about. Boop is liable to add murdering her slop-jawed mother to the list. I yank her away. She doesn't resist.

"Easy does it," I say, putting into service a 12 Step chestnut we've heard at meetings.

The older woman drops to her knees and swats at her shirt's wine blotches. "Should've put that son-of-a-bitch man in jail when I had the chance," she mumbles.

Boop Kung Fu whirls herself back around to kick her mother's shoulder. The flimsy Ferragamo shoe inflicts no damage, but Ma springs up in self-defense. She claws Boop's chin before I can get between them and take a couple of scratches for the team.

Mrs. Park backs away, her mouth foaming with wordless sounds.

Boop dabs her chin and makes noise of her own that sounds like, "Fuck, fuck."

I pick up the shawl and gather it against my chest.

"Why'd you come and start all this?" Boop's mother says.

"I needed to hear the truth," Boop says.

Her mother staggers toward her chair. "I don't know what truth you think you heard."

"You just said it—my father should've gone to the brig for the perverted things he did to me."

"Wrong, as usual. That isn't what I said." The woman cowers over the chair back like a vulture on a wind-swept bluff. "I meant what happened to your brother."

"Who?" Boop says.

I step closer, in case of I'm not sure what.

Ma peers defiantly at the empty space between us. "Either of you got a cigarette?" Boop flashes me a look—doubtful and freaked. I answer with a brave smile while lighting a Doral for Mrs. Park. Exhaling, she closes her eyes and says to Boop in a storm-gathering voice, "I got pregnant with you when the baby was four months old."

Boop shakes her head.

Mrs. Park deflates into the chair like a punctured ball. "Three months later, he was dead."

"How?" I say.

"Talk about imagination run amok!" Boop says. "You'd trump up any corker to duck the truth."

"You asked for the truth—here it is."

"Horseshit. What'd this bundle of joy baby brother do, starve to death? It was me that went hungry half my life. Remember? Jesus Bullshit Christ. How could I never have heard about a sibling?"

"You weren't born yet. Thank your lucky stars. Those were *not* the days. Not for me." Ma removes the cigarette from her lips. "Morning sickness so bad I got laid off for taking too much time off. Aunt Arliss, who babysat for me, was diagnosed with emphysema. She'd ignored the symptoms 'til it was too late. I had to get to Highland Hospital to see her. I left the baby with that bastard for a couple hours tops. What'd Vic do? Brought the kid to his tootsie's place."

"Vic the Prick," Boop mutters.

Mrs. Park turns to me. "There I was, puking every thirty minutes, trying to hire on at the Del Monte plant, the aunt that raised me on her death bed—and a fry cook named Loralee Drackle was more important to Vic than his own baby son." She drags on her cigarette. "They left the tyke on the living room rug and went to fool around in the bedroom. Loralee's Doberman hadn't been fed, I found out later. My cheesedick husband claimed he didn't hear any crying—too busy banging that slut. The body the EMTs brought to the morgue had a crushed skull and chawed innards."

My eyes well with tears. "Oh, my God."

"Animal Control put the dog down. For all the good that did."

"A dog ate my brother?" Boop says. "Isn't that a version of the homework excuse?"

"Hush," I say.

"This's what she does," Boop insists. "Changes the subject, plays you for a fool. Can't you see? It's a ploy to psyche me out!"

"What if it's not?"

Mrs. Park shakes like hot milk. "You force me to talk about Ezra's death, then you reject the—"

"What kind of name is Ezra?!" Boop's face is red. "You're so full of it!"

If I was Boop, I might not believe the story either. But maybe I'm here to believe it *for* her. "Try to reserve judgment."

"Ezra?" Boop repeats.

"He was named after a poet," Ma says. "Just like you."

"Like crap," Boop says. She waves her arm at me. "Got another cigarette?"

I light Dorals for both of us. Our exhaled smoke fills the room. Boop's eyes narrow. "Okay, alright," she says to her mother. "Supposing this tabloid yarn is true. Why *didn't* you throw the son of a bitch in jail?"

"I had reasons." Mrs. Park pats her stomach, which once incubated Boop. Her cigarette smoke slants up from her midsection, as if a puffing fetus vents smoke out her belly button. "Right when I lost my job, Vic got something in construction. I was pregnant with you. We had to get by."

Boop rests her hand on her own stomach, unthinkingly mimicking her mother. "But, Ma," she cries.

"Taking him back wasn't the smartest decision," her mother says to me. "But how was I supposed to know what else he'd do? I told the brass that investigated the dog mauling that it was all a tragic mistake. They dropped the criminal charge. I pretended to forgive him."

"How could you live with him after that?" I ask.

"By never letting the SOB back in my bed. I cut him off. Too bad I didn't cut *it* off."

"I'm gonna be sick," Boop says, shuffling out of the room.

I glance at her mother, then follow Boop out. As I go, the woman comments from her chair, "That toe-rag daughter of mine thinks *everything's* about her."

On the silent ride home, I wonder if Boop overheard her mother's parting barb.

"Sorry to put you through that," Boop says.

"I'm sorry, too."

Her fingertip explores her scratched chin.

"I was scared you and your mother would hurt each other," I say, not mentioning my own scratches. I switch the car fan on.

"Crazy bitch."

High noon sunlight bears down. Boop positions her face in front of the vent. We pass a dead raccoon on the road shoulder.

"She made a stupid crack on my way out," I say.

Boop fiddles with the shawl folded on her knees. "I heard. About me being full of myself?"

"Your mother doesn't know the you I know."

Boop chuckles bitterly. "Which me is that?"

"The one who gets in a friend's skin and tries to help."

"But doesn't succeed."

I bite my lip. Now's not the time to get into it, but my boyfriend rose to the challenge. I did what Boop recommended—explained my trouble with getting aroused—and overnight it stopped being a problem. Boop might know without being told. She must sense that I understand what she and Roxanne almost wrecked their lives chasing after. I'm lucky—my life is far from wrecked. I can marry Tom. Even Boop thinks I should. But would *she* want to be married? We need to discuss these matters. But at some better time.

The car leaves the tract housing behind and climbs a grassy hill that slopes to a patch of woodland along the artery road, San Pablo Dam.

"Are *you* alright?" Boop eyes me.

"You're a good friend, Boop."

"So are you. Sticking by me through that gothic nightmare. You're like my bestest friend, so shut up."

I concentrate on driving. Cars coming the opposite direction exceed the speed limit. "How 'bout we stop and grab some salads?"

"You mind just dropping me home? I'm tired."

"You really want to be alone?"

"I'll be with Sada."

"*That's* the Boop I'm talking about. Committed to taking care of someone else when . . . ." I trail off rather than going back over it. Bluish evergreens line the reservoir on our left. Questions bounce in my head. I pick one to ask. "Was your stepfather that much of an asshole?"

"Yep. He was, and he is."

"How old were you when your mother—"

"Shacked up with him? Seven or eight. They only tied the knot a few years ago. Took Ma that long to divorce Vic. Bob didn't let me attend their dumb Casino Pablo wedding."

"Why not? You and he haven't ever—?"

"Done the nasty? Noooo. He pretends I'm beneath him. Then acts all hot for me behind her back."

"Leave it at that."

"Did Ma say she kicked my father out of the house? Between the lines, wasn't that her story?"

I try to remember.

"Which she did to protect me," Boop says, "even if she won't admit it."

"Maybe you'll never know the full story. At least you found out about your brother."

"There'd be a birth certificate if he existed, right? Or a death certificate? Not that it matters anymore."

"I can take you to the county clerk's if you want to confirm."

A utility transmission station looms up on the left, a glomeration of silver pillars hung with shining capacitators.

"Ezra," Boop says. "What a name to saddle a kid with."

"What poet was named Boop?"

"Huh?"

The shopping village appears, the cue to watch for the freeway marker. The Orinda Books sign flies by. "She said you both were named after poets."

"Boop's a stage name. Didn't I tell you my nickname growing up was Dick?"

"Dick? For a girl?"

"Short for Dickinson."

"You're named after Emily Dickinson?"

"Sounds familiar. Who's she?"

"The poet I'm named after, too."

"Really? This is huge! Just think—Ma's tales from the crypt led to us finding this out."

"Another connection!"

"Everything in my past used to seem random. Now it's the opposite."

Beside a stand of oleander bushes lies a young, dead deer on its flank. "More road kill," I remark.

"Typical along this stretch, though usually not so close to town."

I drive up the narrow ramp to Highway 24. "Sometimes I wish the past stayed in the past."

"Worrying about what's over is so five minutes ago," Boop says. "My new motto is *let the past take care of itself.* And you, Miss Emily, need to get on with your yummy life with Steve."

"You mean Tom?"

"Right."

I merge into traffic, convinced Boop knows about the sex. But where'd she come up with *Steve?*

"I didn't know you smoke," Boop says.

"Tom wants me to quit."

"They don't expect us to totally give up our vices, do they?"

My shawl is twisted into a thick twine in Boop's hands. "Who?" I ask.

"Whoever. Tom." She sees me glance at the shawl. She smoothes it out.

"Not immediately." She needs to keep the shawl. Even her mother noticed how pretty it looks on her—only positive thing either of them said. I'd be just as hostile confronting my mother. She protected Skip and his friends at my expense. If I ever drop my defiance bomb on her, I want Boop along for tactical support.

We enter the Caldicott Tunnel, a diesely culvert. I switch on the headlights. While Boop was sick in the bathroom, her mother followed me outside and led me across the street to her Chevy Nova. The old shrew wanted me to breathe into a court-ordered interlock on the ignition, a dirty, plastic mouthpiece with a digital meter box wired under the steering wheel—meant to prevent her from driving drunk. It made me wonder if some kind of chast-o-meter rig wired to me could have stopped me from bedding down with a hundred handsome-heads.

I almost gave the "Breathalyzer" a blow so Boop's mother could go buy more wine. It seemed the least I could do after bringing Boop there to open old wounds. But that would have been enabling another addict. Luckily, Boop came outside and told her mother to leave me alone, and we left.

Boop stares at the circle of light at the tunnel's end. "Hard to imagine Bianca as a poetry lover."

"That's your mother?"

"Yep. We've all got the fancy names. Dickinson, Ezra, Arliss, Loralee, Bianca. And we're all fucked up."

Traffic lanes funnel from the tube's end like spreading lava flows. "Let the past take care of itself," I say, repeating her advice. "But you're okay now?"

"Okay enough." Boop stretches her legs into a band of sunlight refracted off the asphalt.

"Talk to me. What are you thinking?"

She sighs and adjusts her electric seat farther back. "Just wondering what that brother-eating hound was named."

The $100,000 Question

Once I pick up the pieces, where do I put them?

Writing and Wronging

A guy with a shaved head knocks on my door and—just like in movies—hand-delivers a plain, padded envelope. Inside the envelope is a book of poems. I start to read the introduction.

No wonder me and my sex addict friend are named after Emily Dickinson! Whoever wrote this preface says the poet had it bad for a holy man. A married minister no less, that naughty lass. So the world famous writer and inspiration to thousands wasn't just a lady of letters. Heavens, no. Trapped in the reclusive spinster the public knew was a closeted lusty wench. I can hardly wait to talk to Emmie about our namesake's true nature. She probably already knows. After all, she's the one who sent me this book.

The scholar who wrote the intro says we should note the "pulse," "heat," and "bite" in the masterpieces. My take on the first poems I glance at? Puzzling. Icy. Toothless. Anyone seeking heat, stick with the biographical facts.

If she lived in *our* day, Emily D. might sidestep restraint and end up at 12 Step in St. Henry of Uppsala. Or the poet could join my unofficial spin-off, Nymphomaniacs Anonymous. We could use her "pulse" to keep the group ticking. I seem to be the only one committed to the cause.

If *we'd* lived in *Dickinson's* era, social strictures might have stopped us from being addicts. We might have become celeb authors instead, channeling our ids into writing instead of wronging. Having nymphets named after us three generations later.

A beautiful book. Silver-embossed. No note enclosed. None needed.

No one's given me a present my whole crappy life. Not even on birthdays or Christmas. Which is why this gift means so much, especially after the theater of the absurd Emmie got treated to at Ma's house. We drove there with the hopes of hearing whether my father molested me or not. All we got were Ma's liquored-up fables and evasions.

For Emmie to be named after a poet isn't far-fetched. Her mother wouldn't win a Parent Of The Year award any more than mine would, yet she could be a literature buff. All *my* ma reads are Chianti price tags.

Though she did spell Dickinson right when naming me. And there were books in our house while I grew up.

Now Ma claims her baby, "Ezra," the brother I never knew, was named after another Very Important Poet before getting dog-bit to death. Maybe Ma was a poetry hound. If *she's* read these starchy little stanzas, I sure as hell can. I've got the time.

And good reason. Me and M-Dick share more than a name. We're lone wolf types, the two of us, with checked-out mommies and Daddy Dearests who drove us bazonkers. We're both prone to smittenenza—E.D. was love-sick for a Mr. Charley Wadsworth, and me, lately, for Spaceman Steve, who I'm not supposed to think about *that* way while "in recovery."

Losing friends—me and the poet both experienced that. Friends who relocated or gave us up for worthless or got sick and died.

Emily Dickinson croaked at 56. I always expected to burn out, not fade away, though the healthy new habits might extend my lifespan. Even Ma's only ten years shy of 5-6, though she already looks 6-0. All the old soak's ever done for me besides not aborting me at the fetal phase is to gimmie fucked family fodder to chew on. If I was *more* like Emily Dickinson, I'd ride that material to fame.

The problem is, I'm no poet. Can't even write a song to save my life. But I compose scenes in my head. If I could get them organized, I might be some kind of author. Dickinson Park, cable movie writer. Big on the small screen.

Dear Showtime Production Veep

Enclosed is Act I of my true story. "Nymphomaniacs Anonymous" is not your mother's sexaholic saga. It hasn't been sanitized or common denominatored into a network weepie. It's the real mccoy about a riot grrrl's raging hormones—from her carefree days of coitus-on-the-run to Death Valley of Debasement later on.

If the enclosed sample leaves you panting for more, I'll forward the next installments of my script-in-progress. Act 5 will be where our flawed-but-gutsy heroine has her dreams come true. I'll be damned if the movie of my life doesn't have a happy ending.

Dickinson Park
Oakland, CA

<u>Nymphomaniacs Anonymous Act I</u>

EXT. PUBLIC SCHOOL BOOP GOES TO KINDY-GARDEN AT – DAY

A pick-up truck peels from a red curb in front of a mission-style
school building.

INT. TRUCK

Boop's DADDY, VIC, mans the wheel like a pirate ship captain, hair
whipping in the wind, testosterone to spare. VIC is 24 or 30, heavy
or medium-set. Since no one remembers, he'll match the description
of whoever gets cast in his role.

His motivation is also tough to pin down as he pets his daughter's
little head.

                    DADDY
          How's my little bug?

BOOP, known as Little Dick then, is a bundle of 6-year old kinetics.
Un-belted, she bounces on the seat and sings:

                    BOOP
          I got a gold star from teacher!

INT. OUR APARTMENT – LATER THAT DAY

My bed has a blue blanket. A Skipper doll sits on the pillow.

My father is naked. Did his clothes get dirty at work? Is he about to
take a shower? I have run from his bedroom to mine. He comes after
me. Does he force me to do something? What naughty thing does Ma
see when she gets home?

I don't know what to write. I wouldn't even be able to ID Vic in a line-
up. My memory's the barest bones:

He picked me up at school. He got naked. I got a gold star.
Ma got home early and went limbic.

I can't complete the scene beyond that. Someone else make it up. I'm
not able.

 DÉJA BOO-BOO

I nab a barstool and catch Tiny's eye. If the opportunity presents itself, I'll explain how the bed-head I caretake ordered me out of the house. Take a powder, Sada said. I balked at leaving. But stinger missiles of light shot from the gun-bore pupils of her eyes. If I disobeyed, she'd just nag me to "g-g-go" and gag herself to death. I made her promise to stay in bed during my absence.

Tiny of all people would agree that The Graduate's a swell place to wet one's whistle and clear one's head. Sada's right about needing a change of scenery. My good old watering hole. I'll be back home in under thirty minutes.

Six strangers are dotted around the establishment. Tiny moseys toward me from the end of the bar, wearing his *Mountain Water* t-shirt, slowing down for every motherhumping distraction—the occupied tables, the goblet rack, the house flies looping overhead. A neutral observer might read his dallying as reluctance to serve me. He has no legal grounds to refuse. I've got a shirt and shoes on. Maybe he's waiting for me to holler, "The usual!"

It's only been a month of Sundays since I last dropped by. In that short a time, Tiny can't have forgotten the mucho grief I've given him. Unrattled by our past, I snap my fingers and order soda water. Giving up inebriating substances has been easy-breezy, especially since visiting Ma.

If the switcheroo from my regular beverage surprises Tiny, he doesn't let on while dispensing my selection. The glass fills with ice and wet fizz. The Tine-ster deposits the tinkling tall one on a coaster without conveying any recognition of me.

Two can play the cool game. Let him walk off, drying his chapped hands on his soggy rag. See if I care.

I do care, though, because of what I decided on the walk over here to accomplish, as part of my 12 Step process.

Watching for my opening, I lift my drink. A shopping list item jumps to mind—cordless phone for Sada to have 911 at her fingertips. If I was worth my salt, I'd be at Payless Drugs buying a phone instead of hemming and hawing here.

Before resuming practical duties, I intend to run rule number 9 by Tiny—"make amends to those I've harmed," "those" meaning him. There's no one else to play the atonement card on. Bridgit's AWOL. Angie and Tess, the other members of the band, would snub me if I approached. Sada is exempt. Ma is stagnating in la-la land and would never make amends, so why make any to her? To hell with my stepdad, too. Since I've stayed on best behavior with Emmie, no amends to speak of are called for there. As a bartender, Tiny's a professional sounding board. Customers regularly unbosom their woes to his willing ear.

I push back my hair. One word voiced by me lets Tiny edge me out in this cool contest we're in, yet that's copacetic. If the gyrating brawl of life has taught me any lesson, it's that few games are worth winning.

My lime wedge bobs and sinks as I suck the straw. What also sucks is Tiny tarrying in Butt Fucking Egypt at the far end of the bar with a mulletted, trucker-looking dude drinking a Rob Roy. My heart's lodged at the base of my throat. It's almost time to start for home. I'm anxious to say my piece.

I twirl the straw through the wasting ice cubes and debate signaling Tiny for another round. For months, he's demanded legal tender before decanting my tequila shots, a rule he doesn't enforce with anyone else, not even first-time customers or homeless draggletails that wander in—just me. Tonight, though, I'm getting the long-due respect a regular patron deserves, being trusted to settle my tab when I'm ready. Of course, fizzy water costs two bucks, which isn't much for Tiny to be out if I *was* to ditch paying.

Some frau is gabbling to her husband about a spinning class. Whoever belongs to the orphaned beer two stools over must be taking a dump in the can and hasn't footed his bill yet, either. The beer's foamy head of tiny bubbles exhales the lathery musk of hops. The smell doesn't tempt me. Get alcohol of any type in me, and soon I'm doing something I regret or regretting something I don't get to do.

That nonsense is so over.

Which is sort of what I want to tell Tiny—that I confuckulated every chance of us being pals by gypping him on tips so I could buy more felony juice or by hitting on him or getting so wired to the tits that I turned myself into a dragger. I never thanked him for driving me home at closing time the night I lost my booze compass. Worse, I thundered in here days later and made a calamatious scene about him having his way with me in his car. No one believed me—that's how obviously false my accusation was. What Tiny doesn't know is I wished he *had* forced himself on me, to prove I was slightly irresistible.

Back then, the compulsion to screw screw screw whoever I could could could, even under the least ideal conditions, blitzed my judgement. Friends, common sense, self-respect . . . they all got fed to the monkey on my back. I was a drunk, betrayer, flop, tramp, and the rottenest customer a bartender could have. Tiny knows most of this already but hasn't heard my penance. After all that's gone down, it's not likely me and him will be friends like me and Emmie, but maybe we'll bury the hatchet.

"So, Tiny," I call.

"So, Boop," he calls, winning the game by speaking only after being spoken to. Yet proving he knows me.

"Can you come here?"

He ignores my summons. If I holler my planned message, anyone in earshot will hear my private apology. I inhale down to my navel to work up the moxie to call, "You're not still exercised about me grabbing your ass last time, are you?"

It's a dumb opening and barely out of my mouth, let alone Tiny getting a chance to answer, before the moment's wrecked by a lout in leather reclaiming the stranded beer on the bar. "Wanna grab *my* ass?" the guy says, installing the a-hole in question on his stool.

It's Gordon. Was Tiny dreading his return from the washroom this whole time? Anticipating a raucous reunion between us? No wonder I got the cool reception.

"I know you," Gordon says between swallows.

I smooth down my hair, clipped with Sada's cuticle scissors. Only a little orange dye remains on the tips. My body's trimmed down, too, compared to the last time Gordon saw me. My clothes are clean. His gawking makes me feel cheaply alluring.

Tiny keeps close watch. He doesn't want any argy-bargy in here, and he's not gonna get any.

"Sorry," I tell Gordon, "you're not what I'm here for." I tuck my peeking bra strap under my top.

"You live with that cripple," he says. "Hell. Now that freak's in my head again."

I bite my tongue. Any reply would dignify his stupidity. And because of the oath I silently swore, to cause no argy-bargy, I resist what every fiber in me wants to do—smack Gordo's mouth off his face.

"Where'd you dig that fossil up from?" he says, weakening my commitment to pacifism. My left hand trembles like a human liver I once saw bathed in chilled plasma on TV, awaiting transplantation. My other hand fastens over it, creating a ten-fingered wrecking ball that jerks up as if it's possessed and knocks my empty drink over.

"Sorry, Tiny," I whisper. The glass cracked. So has my enthusiasm for step number whatever brought me here.

A departing glance at Gordon's pit-viper head kindles a déja boo-boo in my mind—the image of me and him trawling each other to the exit that night we met, a pair of bulletproof rakes. Get-hot Gordon stopped short of the door, as if second-thinking the whole pick-up thing. I was dicknotized, so up for my fix there wasn't a chance I'd let Tiny and Jimmy the Gardener and everyone else who was schlitzing in here that night see me get shafted by a semi-repellent barney. I was gonna do whatever it took to be danced out of this place. I landed a square slap on Gordon's ass that hurt me more than him. Assault always gets a man's attention. Ergo, Gordon grabbed me by the neck. "I thought we were skiddooing?" I choked. Tiny probably noticed how well my plan of attack worked as Gordon squired me out to his truck.

And so on, except since that night, I got myself invested in a face-saving version of what happened. In my revision, I wasn't the hostile girl with no self-esteem who goaded Gordon into hitting her. I was the innocent victim coming afoul of a hatchet man who knocked me around for kicks. More accurately, I struck the first blow. I as good as said to Gordon, *Rough is how I want it.* Hippie Bob claims you create your own reality, and with Gordon, I got what I asked for.

Tonight, I'm better than that and asking for nothing. "Good for me," I whisper, sliding off my stool.

Not a drop of booze in me, but I'm drunk on stark truth. The floor feels piggly-wiggly under foot, like bayfill land liquefying when a big quake strikes.

"Buy you a drink, Good Lookin'?" Gordon says.

Mack Daddy wants me again? Apparently, I'm not gross anymore. Here's a chance, if I want it, to go another round with this twat-angler.

I don't want it. And Gordon must be as dumb as I used to be, to wanna frag someone with a proven record of bringing out the worst in him.

"No, thanks. Though I do wanna say—you know how it got kind of ugly between us? Sorry about that."

He slurps down his tapper and waves the empty mug like a conquerering Hun's axe. "You should be sorry," he says.

Let him have the last word. Apologizing to him was spur of the moment, not in the plan. I glance at Tiny, who's staring at the salty grin on the Rob Roy drinker's spackle-complexioned face.

Gordon laughs for his own coarse reasons. "Almost crapped my pants at the sight of your tombmeat roommate."

He thinks my apology was about Sada. The scratching, biting, kissing, stripping, shoving, screwing, and slugging with me—all of that's good as forgotten. So be it. I can still cross Admitting-Wrongdoing-With-Gordon off my itemized list of AA scutwork. No step says the apologizee has to comprehend the apology.

"Tiny! What's my damage?"

"I thought you were gonna show me how sorry you are." Gordon belches. "About that *Night of the Living Dead* we spent together."

It's true Sada's appearance is hard to forget. It's her suffering Gordon doesn't grok. He's missing the humanity gene. Even if I had been nicer to him from the start, there's no evidence he'd have been a kinder fuck buddy. No use in me taking *all* the blame when he's a hellhound in his own right.

Tiny arrives, swinging his arms like a grogzilla on a TV beer ad, unaware of the emotional knots I'm untying.

"Two bucks?" I pat my hips and butt for pockets. This skirt has none. I left home without money. Or ID. Someone could stab my back on the way home, and crime scene forensics would have to figure out my identity from dental records— if Tiny doesn't behead me for swindling him.

Gordon grabs the fingers I've carelessly left on the bar. His grip feels like lockjaw.

"Let go," I say.

He doesn't let go.

"Hands off the lady," Tiny says.

The lady—gotta love it.

"Or what?" Gordon says.

Tiny glares. "You owe sixteen-fifty, buddy. Settle your bill and hit the road, or you'll see what."

Gordon releases my fingers. I tuck my smarting hand in my armpit. Gordon tosses out a twenty. "Leave my change," he says, tramping off to the john again.

Tiny dispatches his mug into the sink and says, "S.O.B."

I nod, grateful for his grizzly bear willingness to help. "I didn't get to apologize to you."

"For what?"

"A long list of stuff."

"Huh?"

"I can't pay you, for one thing. Forgot my wallet."

"Don't sweat it. You're a steady customer."

I'd love to linger to relish this bar love, but I want to beat Gordon out of here. I've stayed overlong. The look in Sada's eyes as I left was off the charts, that determination to send me out, like she had to be alone. Omigod. Could she be overdosing on painkillers while I'm dickering with a red-blooded nonentity in this watering hole? Taking her life while she still can? Choosing a dignified end? It makes terrible sense.

I run to the door. "Catch you next time!" Tiny calls. I slam out and Reebok away, "next time" echoing.

Block after block, I plunge toward home—enduring cold, exertion, fright—'til our apartment house leaps to view, familiar but strange, the way buildings look when someone you love dies in them.

The lobby is locked. I have no keys. I jab every call button on the panel. Some tenant has to be home to answer. But no one does. Don't these door chimes work?

Through the glass brick, a resident finally appears at the far end of the lobby. Hyperventilating, I bang the buzzer buttons furiously, watching this blobby individual approach the door excruciatingly slow. "Let me in, damn you!" I scream.

JANE COWPOKE

The lobby door wedges open. Sada stands in the gap.

"You can walk?" I gasp.

She has broken her promise to stay in bed, but this disobedience is welcome. I take it as the start of better days ahead at the OK Corral!

As this thought improves my mood, Sada pulls a header. I have to act fast and leap the threshold to catch her before she hits the floor.

Alright, okay—this bundle of limbs and hide in my arms is, at the moment, helpless as a just-born calf. When push came to shove, though, she rose to her feet and made herself mobile. I'm all yippee-ki-yo-ki-yay that I got home to see this rad development instead of the last round-up I was fearing.

"You heard me buzz the door," I say, staggering under what's left of her weight in my arms. My call-button panic seems forgivable, considering Sada's steep deterioration in recent days.

"Too much buzzing."

I nod. Less droll and less forgivable is how I imagined her, dead on my arrival. She's got inner strength that I should never underestimate.

My throat burns as I huff and puff across the lobby. There hasn't been any occasion to run so all-out fast since I went chasing after a skater boy in my hometown for miles at age sixteen. I caught up to him where Santa Rita Road inclines uphill. He kicked up his skateboard platform and said, "You sure worked up a sweat." Me and him worked up a whole lot more of one on a parched grassplot in Lamoine Park.

I clutch Sada tighter and let that teen memory fade. Sada taps a finger against her other hand. "I heard . . . you call . . . me, too."

I humor her with a smile even though I didn't call to her. Why would I try to drum up help from someone who I thought couldn't walk or stand? Maybe she sensed my hair-trigger hysteria through a nonverbal vibe. A paranormal who recently appeared on the Leeza Gibbons Show explained that people who spend a lot of time together tap into ways of communicating via extrasensory power.

Something even stronger than ESP could have architected me vacating Tiny's bar like batgirl out of hell. Destiny might be working its magic, returning Sada to the land of the living. Karma in action. Gotta love it.

I back my way into her apartment, careful to not bang anyone's elbows. The bed sheets enfold Sada like mummy linen. It pains me to watch her lapse back into a circumvegetation stupor. To keep her awake, I ask in a cheerfully loud voice, "What did you do while I was gone?"

She opens her eyes. For the second time tonight, there's phenomenal play of light in these eyes—bright radar dots signaling *alive, alive, alive.*

"I danced," she kids me.

The joke makes me feel like doing a two-step of my own. "How about tomorrow, we get our jig on together?"

Her eyes re-close.

I sink to my knees. "Or just take a short walk, you and me. Like, to the bathroom? What do you say?"

"Okay," she whispers, to please me. Or to shut me up. I won't be quieted, though. This connection . . . the way we lift each other up . . . I need to reassure her and give her strength. I'm not the tequila-swilling, looking-to-get-poked, car-thiefing, lying-through-her-teeth, nihilistic fate-meat she first met. She needs to know she doesn't have to worry herself sick over me any more. If only I could open my head and show her the jumbled regrets, realizations, and smarter decisions that would take a season of Showtime episodes to dramatize.

Since issuing Sada a total-access pass to my brain isn't possible, I drag the chair to the bed and talk while unlacing my shoes. "Believe it or not, I've been reading about how Hindus view life. Basically they see it as a balancing act between thinking, being, and bliss."

A popping at Sada's mouth sounds like surprise.

I remove one striped sock. "Hindu bliss is oneness between self and world. Not the fast and loose doinky that for a decade I thought was bliss when it's been anything but." I take off my other shoe and sock, stare at my wiggling toes, and take a shot at explaining my state of mind, scared to look her in the face as I speak. "So, Sada, at least the idiodyssey that I've been on for way too long has opened doors to a better place. I'm out of the woods. I'm gonna be okay. I want you to know. And no matter what, I've got adorable feet to fall back on, right?"

I turn to Sada. She looks peaceful, floating in the Land of Nod. I've either set her mind to rest or bored her to sleep.

I shrug. "Unless in my next life, I come back as a mollusk."

MY LUKECOLD LIFE

I push the headset off as the last note of Hüsker Dü's "59 Times the Pain" fades in my ears. The metal band encircles my jugulars. The foam disks settle like bug-eye necklace charms against my collarbone.

The first time I heard this song's searing manifesto of desperation, it instantly became a three-minute refuge that helped me face my own lukecold life. Listening to iconoclantastic recordings used to make me feel like a plane crash survivor or a kid with a triple-chocolate sundae. Rock and roll supplied essential relief and joy.

Not today. Not when Sada lies burrowed under the covers like dead weight. She promised to take a walk. That was a lie. Now everything feels like a lie. Even my favorite music.

Making it to the lobby on her own steam the other night was a fluke. A last hurrah. All she's been capable of since then is practicing the art of nonexistence.

"What are you trying to do," I say, "make me drag you out of bed?"

She has decarnated—from woman to hibernating toad.

"I wanted to go see whether Spaceman Steve is hauling and dumping today. But I'm waiting for you to get your second wind instead. I've got a book of poems to read. See? And there's laundry to keep me busy if I get tired of reading."

She ignores everything I say, but that doesn't stop my monologue. "I'm not going anywhere, Sada. Once that other stuff's done, there's letters I can write."

I get a pen and paper to prove my point.

To Whom It May Concern

I am writing . . .

. . . to renew my State of California disability benefits . . .

. . . to reinstate a suspended driver's license . . .

. . . to check the status of wheelchair order R724-01 . . .

. . . to inform you that the Dickinson Park Talent Company is expanding its client list . . .

. . . to extend Worker Compensation benefits for Sada Pollard . . .

. . . to request a "Money Back Guarantee" refund for Bio-Soy Lecithin Granules . . .

. . . to exercise Power of Attorney over the estate of my terminally-ill ward . . .

PUTRANK

"Good morning, good morning, the best to you each morning," I melodize, adhering to a new *Fake It 'Til You Make It* motto. "Up and at 'em, girl!"

Sada lies in bed, immovable and mute.

If me and her had bonded pre-disease, we could have sat down each a.m. to neighborly Kellogg's corn flakes and been semi-normal. I kick her half-empty bag of size L Huggies. Depends don't come small enough for her shriveling buttocks.

"Diaper service is hereby suspended. Disposables pollute the earth. You need to get up. Ally-oop to the powder room to make a wee. You wanna be eco-friendly, don't ya? . . . .

"Your sheet's getting wet . . . .

"You'll be swimming in Lake Pee Pee soon . . . .

"Please? . . . ."

I grind my teeth. Sada's no fool. She pissed her bed all putrank the morning I went to Gordon's. She knows I won't let *that* happen again.

"For crying out loud," I say, yanking a fresh Huggie out of the bag.

A Qualified Practitioner

Folks don't often knock on Sada's door. A Fed Ex guy once confused Apartment G for J, but that doesn't count. The pipsqueak nurse, Sloopy, counted, for being in the right place. I've waited for her to come back, to tell her I got Power of Attorney. But today, *Fred* Nightingale has arrived instead—official clipboard and June care package in hand. "Where's the Latina from last time?" I peer at his big arms.

"Taking a personal business day."

"I must have scared her away." I glance down at my slobenly attire.

"Nurses don't scare easily."

I snort. It's true I'm harmless. Also true is that I'm keeping it real, the best I can. Shouldn't a home nurse, especially one with a laid-waste caseload, keep it real on her end, too, and not allow personal biz to conflict with making her rounds? A qualified practitioner should act like Sada matters.

I sure would, if I was on this case. The patient spirals to the end of her mortal coil, and the county sends a replacement nurse who looks like a plumber in coveralls. Even with the food and forms as his credentials, I have misgivings. His hair's too long. The outline's not right.

"No worries," he says. "I'm a trained professional, like the other gal." He shifts the clipboard to the top of the yogurt party-pack. Pinned to the left of his solar plexus is a plastic ID badge—Abel VanTurk, LCPN.

"What's LCPN?"

"Life care planning nurse. May I bring in these perishables?"

I step aside. A peanut butter smell trails after Abel VanTurk. "The convalescent's in bed." I point. "Give her the best life care plan you've got."

Once Nurse VanTurk finishes stowing the provisions in the kitchen, we deploy in lockstep to the bed. I switch the floor lamp on. Its cone of light helps him read Sada's case notes.

All briefed, he smiles at the bedclothes. "Hello, Ms. Pollard. How are you?" True to form, Sada doesn't emerge from the covers or utter a peep.

"Some apartment you've got."

"This pit?" I say.

"Quality touches all around," he says to the blanket. "Original crown molding." His eyes 180 downward. "Oak flooring."

While he goes agog over the floorboards, I take a gander at the scar across the bridge of his nose, a pale bulge offset by a crudely-stitched crater. Some hair-raising long and short of it must explain that facial souvenir.

"Wonderful glass brick in the lobby," he says. "This building is a find."

With his made-for-fame name and theatrical looks, this guy could be one hell of a character actor. He should read the auto-bio tele-pic I'm writing. He can play himself.

"One thing this apartment has going for it," I say, as he coochie-coos at the casement window, "is cleanliness."

"You're in charge here?"

"Yowzah." Saying so makes me proud.

He jots a note with the pen attached to the clipboard by a spiral cord. "Relation and name?"

"Next door neighbor. Dickinson Park. I-n-s-o-n. Like the poet? My studio's pretty much the same as this one."

"A little stripping and staining," he says while writing, "and this apartment could be an architectural gem."

Any off-color buzz I get from "stripping and staining" jiffy-morphs into my gaydar pinging at "architectural gem."

"A World Monument site," I quip, looking him over for outfit giveaways. Though not up on fashionista trends, I'd wager that janitorial coveralls aren't the gladdest rags in the queer nation. "Are you really a nurse?" I say, "or a home contractor prospecting for clients?"

"A nurse that lives in blah Concord and wants to move closer in."

"Closer to Friskytown, right?"

He peruses Sada's pharmaceutical smorsgabord and doesn't reply. Not that confirmation's needed. Any back-porch buddy would want to live in San Fran-swish-co over straight-laced, cultural wastepot Concord. If Abel is able to revive our patient, I'll help him find a place in the Castro District.

"Be polite to the sweet new nurse" I say to the bed lump. "He speaks good English and loves our building. Lift your head out of the sand."

Sada stirs, faint as a lake ripple. One Fourth of July, Hippie Bob dragged me and Ma to Lake Berryessa to sit in dorky swimsuits on a dirt beach littered with pine needles. Them two drank Colt 45 all afternoon, while all I got was dehydrated. When I griped about my deadly thirst, Bob said to go jump in the lake. I almost did—to wreck Ma's day by drowning. We all came home with second-degree sunburns.

"Motivation problem here," I say, snapping back to present time. "Days ago, this woman actually walked to that lobby you love with the glass brick. On her own, mind you."

"Yah?"

"Goes to show what she's capable of. How 'bout you help me get her up?"

He looks at the protuberance under the blanket. "Would you like to get up?"

"Tuh! Give her a choice, you can lay money on a no answer," I say. "Old 'fraidy cat has to use it, so she don't lose it. Where's being stubborn gonna get her? I know from experience—nowhere." My eyes lock on VanTurk's. "If you'd been trying to talk her off her back day after day, this apartment wouldn't look so dandy. Please, use your professional craft to galvanate her."

"It's not my policy to force—"

"If it's for her own good?" I bend toward the bed. "Let's lift her. Come on."

He softly brushes my arms away. "Let's slow down. I just got here."

"News flash, Florence—this isn't about *you.*" I gesture at the blanket. "Ask her if she walked. I dare her to deny it. We need to parlay each step into a next one."

VanTurk's dark eyes flash with what looks like fright. "Parlay's a betting term. I don't gamble with a patient's well-being."

"Walking to the toilet's a risk? Getting out for coffee? Or fresh air? Oh, please."

"Why don't you step out? Take advantage of my being here."

I cross my arms. "This isn't about me, either."

"It *is* about you. Caregivers have a tough job."

"I'm not grumbling."

"I know you're not." He moves a half-step closer. "I'm just saying, here's a chance to recharge. Go get some coffee."

What big eager-to-get-rid-of-me he has. Can I trust him? Sada's not used to him. "No, thanks," I say.

He retrieves a water bottle from the floor. "Just taking a drive can be a good break."

A recent crime bulletin jumps to mind—a necromaniacal nurse with a poison hypodermic needle dispensed untimely ends to a dozen and a half patients up north near Bridgit. Of course, the statistical chance of this nurse also being bent on harm is tweakingly small. His thumb caresses the plastic bottle's neck. My gut says don't be leery of him.

Yet taking a drive is not in the cards. "Look, Ma, no car!" I spread my empty arms wide.

Here's Sada's chance to speak up and offer her auto. I know she's listening. Haven't I proved deserving?

VanTurk digs a leather keyfob from his coverall pocket. "Use mine."

Talk about being careful what I wish for. "Such a generous gesture. Unfortunately, I don't—"

"Black Jetta, parked this side of the street . . . ." His brain crunches points of reference.

"I don't have a current—"

"That way," he talks over me, pointing a finger south.

I step back. Can't this nurse see I'm all no, no, no on his idea? Car keys are a sore subject in this household. Let alone my suspended driver's license.

He presses his fob into my hand. "Can you drive a stick?"

I glance at the bed. "Whoa, Pants." Tipping my head at the eyes peeking over the satiny blanket piping, I say, "How about the three of us take a ride?"

"We don't remove patients from their residence, except in a crisis. Which, happily, this isn't."

Sada's forehead inches back under the covers. If this nurse thinks stagnating in bed is happy-time, he's tripping. Though, if wills must clash, I'll let him take his turn clashing with Sada. "Fine. I'll beat it. Sassy Fras," I say to Sada. "County Nurse is here to help. Let him, okay?"

No reply. I pause at the open door and tell the nurse, "It's not like I never get out, you know. I go to the store. The bank. Most weeks, I get to my meetings . . . ."

He acknowledges with a knowing head dip. "I'll do my best to make her more comfortable while you're gone."

"Good luck. Nothing I ever do helps."

He steps closer yet and lowers his voice. "Don't blame yourself."

"I can't help it. I've been sick, too, in my dumb way, and damn it, the better I get, the worse she gets."

"That sounds like survivor guilt." He draws me out of the apartment by the arm and shuts the door behind us. "Your neighbor's condition is degenerative. If anything, your help is extending her functionality."

I hang my head. "I doubt that."

"Trust me." He uses a finger to lift my chin. "It's time to start letting go, however. Give yourself permission to grieve, if you haven't yet."

"But she's had days of good—"

"Think of her pain coming to an end."

"I'm supposed to celebrate that?"

"Conflicted feelings are natural. You've done everything in your power."

"If I had any power, she'd eat something!"

He glances at his watch. "Come back in twenty-five minutes. I'll show you a feeding technique. You mustn't neglect your own needs. Your friend will want you to jump back into life."

"What life?"

He laughs. "You seem full of life. Go get 'em, tiger."

"Ha, I'll get right on that. Raaaarrrr! You're good, ya know that? You're funny."

He pushes the door open. "So are you."

Considering VanTurk's long commute between home base in Concord and points west, where the action is, his Jetta, parked where he said it would be, barely looks the worse for the mileage. If not for some fried egg shaped spots of corroded paint, it'd be a shwank ride.

I won't be adding any damage or odometer uptick, won't repeat my snafu with Sada's Don't Drive Me-mobile. Sitting in VanTurk's car will be the extent of this encounter. My DMV appointment isn't for three weeks. Only a nerf-head would jeopardize getting her license back by driving without one. The kind of luck I have, Peace Officer Prettyman would flash his lightbar at me within two blocks and send me packing up the river.

I key the ignition. The clock LED activates. In twenty-three minutes, I'll boomerang back to Sada's. Someone else's parcel of juice and yogurt waits on the backseat in glazy high-test shrinkwrap. I button the radio on.

"Serbian forces began withdrawing from Kosovo," a news reader says. "Ethnic Albanians in gutted towns along convoy routes celebrated the end of Serb atrocities . . . ."

I key the car off. Foreign war updates are no use to me. My butt rash needs ointment. My eyeliner needs reapplying. If I tiptoe, Sada and Abel won't know I'm stealth-hygienisizing next door. I can even eavesdrop on them through our mutual wall.

As I reach for the door handle, a toad-green Dodge swings into the closest driveway and parks. Two dudes get out. The bigger one's neck and bald scalp hang in fatty bunches, like a Shar-Pei dog's coat. The other man is a sawed-off, tuberculotic hobbler right out of a *Midnight Cowboy* scene. He has to cock his head way back to look up into his beefy mac's face. They plant themselves at the footpath to a brown building I've never much noticed. They're blocking my only route back. The big dawg with the neckfurters throws jokester air punches at everything the waggy pup says. Their hijinks piss me off.

I bat down the window visor. The tiny mirror automatically lights up. My nose, like Abel's—though not half as bad—appears mangled, thanks to Gordon's Serbish handiwork. I used to think of any little breaks and pains I got as love trophies. Combat scars are more like it. Commander-In-Chief Clinton should Purple Heart me for courageously putting myself in harm's way. My theme song ought to be "Blitzkrieg Boop." What a hypocrite, claiming Ma's old *Make Love, Not War* motto as my own, when again and again I've picked fights and been a careless, angry girl.

And I'm still fighting—but this time *for* Sada. A justifiable battle. I don't care if Abel thinks I'm in the "denial" phase of grief. He should be going to the mat to win Sada more time. The mourn-and-move-on phase is not yet upon us.

I key on the engine power again. " . . . traffic brought to you by Lasik America, the vision leader," a female radio voice says. The clock shows 10:59. "Over the Sunol Grade you're looking at stop-and-go, and the 101-South has a stall in the number two lane. Lasik America has six Bay Area locations. See what you're missing. The K-NEW's forecast. Clear tonight, clouds tomorrow. S.F. temp, fifty-eight."

It feels warmer than fifty-eight degrees in the car here in Oakland. "1-800-22-WENDY!" a weight loss jingle sings. Fat—another opponent I'm fighting. The starvation pains from my water fast have finally gone away. I'm waiting for the psilocybinish high that's supposed to hit on Day Three of no solid foods.

I stretch my legs and unsuccessfully try to picture The Sunol Grade. My mind is full of information gaps. What my father did that afternoon won't come into focus, either. Have I been trespassed? Despite not eating for three days, I feel heavy. Weighted down in the soul.

My eyes blink. The clock says 11:36. I must have fallen asleep and lost track of the time. Good grief. I get out of the Jetta and scramble past the saggy skin guy and his peewee chum, still horsing around like boys on the sidewalk. The old days, I'd have been on this pair of good timers like a skeeter on a *No Pest* strip. It's me no one loves, the expelled friendasaurus who even blows the easy job of frittering away twenty minutes. Sada's probably lying in bed, wracked with visions of me crashing her nurse's car, and no mad skilz the nurse has can calm her down.

VanTurk is combing Sada's wet hair when I enter, a neato surprise, since her last bath was two weeks ago and not a graceful operation. She wags her fingers at the nurse like shadow puppets.

"I'm late," I announce myself and hand his car keys to him.

"Just in time for lunch," he says, passing me the comb. "Can you style her up?"

He goes to the kitchenette. I part Sada's hair to the side. A giddy well-being fluxes through me—the high that disciplined fasting supplies. How buoyant and pure I feel.

Sada's hands make shapes in the air—rock, paper, scissors, what?

"Are you talking with your hands?" I say.

Rock. Helicopter?

"I don't get it. Sorry. Does something hurt?"

"Puh—"

"Don't talk. You could choke."

Her chin juts. "Kuh—"

"Nurse VanTurk?" I call. "Can you help?"

"Buh—" Sada rubs her fist against her heart.

Abel carries in a spoon and a bowl of milky pap.

"Is that sign language?" I ask.

Abel hands me the bowl, rests the spoon inside it, and drapes a towel bib across Sada's neck and chest. "That's right. She told me her late son had hearing loss."

"Omigod! She's been trying to tell me stuff for weeks. I couldn't read the signs."

"I'd like to drop by here again," he says, taking the bowl from me. "On my own time, if you don't mind."

Sada's fingers gesture.

"What she's saying?" I ask.

"She's sorry."

"Why?"

Sada signs more, looking at me.

"Sorry she is hurt. No—she's a pain . . . in the ass?"

Sada nods. VanTurk smiles.

I smack my forehead. "I'm the pain in the ass. Me. Was she worried where I was when I went out? I didn't go any place. I just sat. Tell her not to waste energy apologizing to me!"

"I don't need to. Nothing's wrong with her hearing."

HOW TO FEED A PATIENT IN THE ADVANCED STAGES OF PROGRESSIVE SYSTEMIC SCLEROSIS TO AVOID HER NEEDING A FEEDING TUBE

☐ Swag a towel under her chin to catch spillage and prevent dirtying her outfit.

☐ Serve liquidy vittles that go down easy.

☐ Spoon small amount into patient's mouth, press her lips together so food doesn't squirt out, lightly work her jaw in chewing motion, like Turk the Nurse demonstrated (swaying against me as he moved my hands to feel how to do it.) Stimulate the swallow reflex, he said. Help her throat move her food down.

☐ Don't panic and freak the patient out.

☐ Distract her from the feeding procedure. Recite favorite poem and once again wonder if it's about Emily Dickinson getting some beef in her taco.

☐ Repeat above steps, if possible.

Dear Boopy-Dupe

. . . says Bridgit's Oregon lumbermill postcard. My only non-junk mail in weeks. Written in purple ink.

No job or bandmates yet. I miss Calif. Is life treating you good?
My addy: Box 2991, Ashland 97520

xo, Bridgit

Hey B,

I'd reply if I had a postcard. Something with local color. Carol Doda's North Beach Strip Club, neon a-blazing. Or better, the Golden Gate Bridge—a beauty shot to inspire Bridgit to come home. On my flipside, I'd write—

Unlike your funemployment, I'm booking gigs for new clients,
(Instead of boring her with the truth.) And—
I'm dashing out to hike with Sada. Stay frosty.
Luv,
B.

Then I'd burn the pack-of-lies postcard in my ashtray.

Things Sada's Ceiling Cracks Look Like
at the Witching Hour

Zipper

Paramecium

U.S. West coast

Flex-straw

Bowie knife

'Less than or equal to' symbol

Frown

French fry

Sex Addict Fantasy Interruptus

I skip knocking and let myself into the shop office. Spaceman Steve is out cold on the red floormat, a sleeping bag pulled over him as if he's at a Boy Scout campout.

I fall to my knees beside his bivouac. The room smells like the cage of the hamster Ma bought to teach me responsibility when I was ten. The lesson didn't go as planned. I never remembered to clean the cage, and my hammie got infected and unceremoniously kicked the bucket. Bob shoved the carcass down the kitchen drain to Insinkerate. But a shredder tooth on the grinder broke. The disposal stopped running, leaving half-pulverized animal ick at the bottom. Bob got even madder. He'd "belt me but good," he yelled, if I didn't clean all that fur and guts out of the drain. There were no rubber gloves or paper towels or sponges in the house. I had to use my bare hands.

Happy to be grown up, with no ass-masters the boss of me, I slide the sleeping bag off Steve. He's lying on his side, like a nickel on edge, naked, silver. A boner twitches against his thigh. If only I could get that wet dream machine inside me without a hassle. And push rotting rodent from my thoughts.

"It's Boop," I whisper, wondering how my friend, Emmie, wakes her hubby when she's hot for him. Steve's eyelids tweak. For someone who claims he's not pharming anymore, he's hella faded. It'd be easier to kill than screw him when he's this un-rousable.

Though murder is the last thing on my mind. Steve's always been decent and friendly—even flirty—with me.

I'm wearing tight brown slacks that haven't fit this good in years and pretty gloss from Emmie on my lips. From my pants pocket, I pull a Three Musketeers impulsively purchased at One-Stop Liquors. I tear the wrapper off. The bar is pliant from my body heat. I squeeze it in one hand, cracking the glossy coating and kneading the chunks 'til they break down into a palmful of candy lotion. What better way to break a therapeutic, three-day fast than tongueing emulsified Three Musketeers off Steve's hardy!

But before tongueing it *off* can start, there's getting it *on* him to accomplish.

I sing the hit tune hook, *"I smell sex and candy,"* while I deposit a dab of chocolate silt on the bone in question. I hold my breath, trying to think of my favorite poem about doing the nasty, penned by none other than America's notorious spinster writer. But instead I sing more Marcy Playground—*"Mama, this surely is a dream . . . ."*

Emmie would have taken her clothes off first, I realize, not jumped the gun with the candy and the penis. But a better-planned redo's not gonna be possible, 'cause, getting my wake-up call, Steve rolls over and—

In the Mythic Land of Boop...

. . . amusing daydreams aren't interrupted by hacks, hiccups, and respiratory blockage caused by fluid in the lining of Sada's lungs. Pleural effusion, VanTurk, the nurse, called it, which makes me picture a tropical waterfall.

If I ruled the universe, pleural effusion would mean that.

Not this.

Hello, Goodbye, Sex
and Love Addicts Anonymous

"Hi, I'm Boop. Tequila binger, junk food abuser, rageaholic. And sex maniac, obviousmently. Addictions aplenty, all overlapping, much to cop to. Wow. I'm not sure where to start."

"This is fine. Which step are you working?" Jonathan helpfully asks from his center chair in the semi-circle.

"Let's say Admitting My Wrong. There's a pile of shit with my name on it that I'd better take credit for. Or should I say blame?"

All nine people at the meeting stare expectantly. It makes me clam up.

"Taking blame or taking responsibility how?" Jonathan says.

"By going public! Or is that not enough for you people? You want a shining example of recovery success? Well, I do have a little headway to report. It's about that tricky switch inside me that used to make me wanna you know what all the time. You know what I'm talking about. But now the switch is toggled off, keeping me out of fucking trouble. Ach! Sorry. I've got a dirty mouth. When I'm nervous, I can't fucking control it. Whoops!"

"Just keep going," Jonathan says.

I look at the ceiling instead of the audience. Two crudely-sawn beams span the room like railroad ties. Between them, a long gray shadow masquerades as infinity.

"This part's important," I say, feeling high as a kite from my no-food fast, almost too exposed alone up here. "I'm talking about just me now, not anyone else. The rest of you do what you gotta do, but for me, there's gotta be more than *just say no*. Just 'cause no one's ever loved me so far doesn't mean I don't deserve it. I do. And I want it. I wanna say yes. To all of it. Sex. Love. A relationship."

"Amen," one person mutters.

Does anyone realize what I've said? Out loud? I deserve love. *I DESERVE LOVE.* My eyes scan the group. "You're probably all, 'You haven't even been good for very long, so shut up! You don't deserve it.' Yah, I'm still trying to figure out how to not be a love junkie, but—" This should have been better rehearsed. What made me think I could pull this off or make it count? "Fuck it. I thought I could do this, but, frankly, I don't know if come-clean talk is even a good idea."

One thing I do know—not looking at Fred will make it easier to continue whatever this spiel is. That Viking's sitting far to my left and, in my opinion, he doesn't belong here. I won't look his way. I focus hard on Jonathan, who nods.

"No one thought I'd ever volunteer, right? Cha," I say. "Shows how little you know about me. Another thing you don't know? Any time I come to this meeting, my neighbor has to fend for herself. She's sick. Her esophagus got infiltrated, and there's extra-cellular deposits growing all over her. A load of badness waiting to turn to worseness. My friend in this group knows about this. You know, Emmie. The hot—"

I cover my mouth with my hand. Trying to be cute, I almost said 'Hottie bombalottie.' That would be objectifying Emmie as a sex object—not what a true friend does.

"I mean, my friend who didn't mention that she'd be some place else this morning," I say, experiencing twinges of guilt and hurt. "I was planning to give her a shout-out for helping me through some hairy stuff. If she wasn't my friend, I would've quit 12 Step by now."

Stop glancing to your right, I tell myself. *She's not here.*

"I haven't acted out once since joining. Way to go me, huh? Though, admittedly, my spotless record got helped along by bad luck."

Don't. Look. At Fred. Either.

I stare into space and think I hear a pen or pencil tap against the frame of a chair. "But smarter decisions are part of my 12 Step success, too," I say. "A nurse I met says to give myself more credit."

"Amen," the same mutterer repeats a little louder this time. The postal worker, probably.

"I wish my friend was here, 'cause it's just hitting me now that maybe I've wronged her and need to make amends." My hands rise like stop signs, flat and full. "By 'wrong her,' I mean in my mind, that's all, but a violation even so. Like when I wonder what it would be like to be her. Pretty hard *not* to think of you know what when a large part of doing steps is hashing over all the hanky panky from the past." I cross my arms over my chest. "Me and my friend are like sponsors for each other. She's told me her secrets, and, I'm not proud of this, but they've triggered some thoughts about sex. My brain keeps hankering for what my body's not getting anymore—fantasy being my last hold out in this anti-nympho transformation I'm attempting." I glance at the door. "Know what? I'm glad my friend's not here. I wouldn't know what to say to her."

Jonathan says, "Everything you've said so far is good." He looks down at his digital watch.

"Our other friend didn't show up, either," I say. "It's like they're in cahoots on a don't-show-up-and-don't-tell-Boop evasion scheme. They're friends. I'm not." I gulp back the bitter taste of betrayal. "Boy, are they making a mistake, though. They're treating sexahol-ism like sexahol-WASM. Like they're over it." I plant my hands on my hips, trying to deflect my disappointment. "Who cares what they think? It's just pitiful that of the two friends I've got right now, the one who's not dying is deserting me . . . ."

I unthinkingly glance at Fred. He flashes me a poison smirk and leans forward in a threatening, ready-to-pounce pose that turns my self-pity into anger. My head whips toward Jonathan, who opens his mouth to speak, but I yell right over him. "I already know, Jonathan! 'Time's up, thanks for sharing.' You say the same ridiculous thing every single time, like you barely even mean it! Like it's all just motions here, no connection that lasts. Well, don't worry, I'm done volunteering—as a matter of fact, I'm done with the group. Enough. Whether or not the meeting's over, I'm out of here." I stride toward the door. "I belong at home with my neighbor. Gotta be fucking more to life than 12 Step."

Cable Movie of My Life

Act 5. Scene to End All Scenes?

EXT. MECHANIC SHOP – DAY

Boop, in the same clothes she wore at the 12 Step meeting, knocks on the building's regular-sized door. She shakes with urgency.

>   BOOP
>   Be home, Stevie-Cakes.

She tries the handle. The door unlatches, just like in her fantasy. This moment, however, is real.

INT. SPACEMAN STEVE'S SQUAT

Steve's bedding is flung apart on the floor, unoccupied. The bell tower at the University of California TOLLS: DLONG-DLONG-DLONG.

Boop kneels and talks to the sleeping bag.

>   BOOP
>   Out dumping and hauling, old friend?

She drapes Steve's sleeping bag over her shoulders like a cape, twirls to billow it, and gazes at a figment of her imagination in the room.

>   BOOP
>   (sultry voice)
>   Hello, Steve. I'm Emmie, Boop's friend.
>   Remember how you came to my rescue at
>   Mariner Hall? How do you like me now?

Boop lowers the sleeping bag and speaks somberly to it.

                         BOOP
         I gave Boop a poetry book as a goodbye gift.

                    MALE VOICE O.S., MUFFLED
         Who's that?

Startled, Boop pivots around, sees no one.

                         BOOP
            Steve?

                       KITTEN O.S.
            Meow.

On the bottom of the metal staircase stands a scrawny calico kitten.
It turns a pink nose up to Boop as she cautiously stalks it.

                         BOOP
            Hello, fluff-bun.

She nuzzles the animal, engrossing herself in innocent fur.

                    MALE VOICE O.S., ABOVE
         Bring that stray upstairs.

                         BOOP
            Steve?

                    MALE VOICE O.S., ABOVE
         Watch the toolbox on your way up.

Boop peers up the shadowy spiral of steps.

                         BOOP
            Who's up there?

                    MALE VOICE O.S., ABOVE
         Friend of Steve's.

DESCENDING FOOT CLOPS. STEVE'S FRIEND—20s, shirtless, dark-nippled, with bruised-looking tats on both shoulders—appears on a stair above Boop, smoking.

> STEVE'S FRIEND
> (points cigarette up the stairs, laughs)
> I'm subletting the penthouse. What are you—
> another stray?

> BOOP
> Where's Steve at?

> STEVE'S FRIEND
> Dunno. He was out all night. Knocking boots
> with some babe or other.

> BOOP
> Tell him Boop wanted to see him.

She holds the kitten out, but the man doesn't take it. The moment she sets it down, it streaks up the stairs. Steve's friend turns and follows it up.

> STEVE'S FRIEND
> Grab that thing, would you? It's hungry. I'll
> open its food.

THE "PENTHOUSE" LOFT

A mattress on the floor is spread with a plaid blanket. A rattan table is heaped with sundries and trash. The kitten crouches next to an open suitcase. Boop scoops the animal up.

> BOOP
> I'm hungry, too, little baby.

Steve's friend drops his smoke in a beer bottle and ring-tabs a Feline Feast can open.

The kitten squirms with anticipation in Boop's hands.

                    STEVE'S FRIEND
          Sit on the bed and hold her.

Boop avoids the bed and lowers herself across the stairs' top riser,
her legs stretched in front of her. She restrains the kitten in her lap.

Steve's friend sits on the floor above her. His pinky pries out a morsel
of molded brown cat food that he lets the kitten lick off.

                         BOOP
          I like her geigercounter purr.

                    STEVE'S FRIEND
          I like your eyes. How 'bout we go get a couple
          of beers?

                         BOOP
          I don't drink. Move that can, would you? It
          stinks and is making my stomach feel sick.

                    STEVE'S FRIEND
          Stinks? This stuff is premium. Fit for human
          consumption!

As if to prove the point, he digs up another gob of the food and hooks
it into his mouth, to Boop's disgust.

He grabs her wrist and pulls her toward him.

                    STEVE'S FRIEND
          Give me a kiss, so you can taste it.

                         BOOP
                (trying to pull her arm free)
          You're crazy! No.

                    STEVE'S FRIEND
        (swallowing, grinning, grasping her tighter)
        You said you're hungry. I'll feed you.

She shakes her head as he removes another clump of Feline Feast
from the can and lifts it to her mouth. He releases her arm and
softly, tenderly strokes it as he smiles and cajoles her.

                    STEVE'S FRIEND
        You're a good pussy. Show me your rough
        little tongue, and I'll give you a treat. Come
        on, open up. That's a girl.

She sighs and opens her mouth. He pushes the cat food to the back
of her tongue, laughing, entertained by his success. Boop gags, rears
her head back, and spits the food into Steve's friend's face.

He BRAYS, swats his eyes, reflexively thrusts his leg hard,
unintentionally kicking Boop in the chest.

The kitten jumps free as Boop flails, loses her balance, and tumbles
backward down the steep stairs. She thumps end over end, with
nothing to catch hold of.

Two-thirds of the way down, she lands hard on a metal toolbox . . .

                        BOOP
        Unh!

. . . and bounces farther down to

BLACK OUT.

1, 2, 3 VOICES

A voice fades in and out like whale calls penetrating a deep ocean. I want to swim to the cadences. I want to rise to the surface, to light. But I'm cloaked in darkness. I can't move. The frequencies' sharps and flats coalesce with splashes of words.

"Anonymous drop-off . . . ER . . . dangerously low blood pressure . . . abdomen distended . . . surgery . . . bleeding . . . four pair of shoes ruined when they cut her open . . . ."

There's contact against my hand, a warm brush of skin. The vanilla scent of graham crackers evokes memories—first grade, familiar perfume, Emmie.

"Ruptured sheath . . . spleen . . . post-op fatigue . . . full recovery . . . ."

Other smells announce themselves as Emmie speaks. Latex tubing. Starched laundry. Antibacterial soap. Rubber wheels.

"How does a spleen rupture?" a second, less tender, voice asks.

"The nurse said common causes are virus, cough, blunt force . . . ."

"Blunt force? Did she get beat up? You know she gets a charge out of being antagonistic. Remember when she threw a brownie at me?"

Roxanne's here, too. The third mouseketeer from 12 Step, once again giving me no benefit of the doubt. She doesn't know about Steve's weird friend at the squat, about the cat food. If not for that kitten, I'd have gotten my ass out of there. I wasn't beat up. I wasn't acting out. Please, Emmie, don't believe Roxanne.

"None of the medical personnel mentioned evidence of a physical assault," Emmie says.

The clack of a monitor keeps physiological time. This is a hospital. Another sweep of flesh feels warm on my hand. Emmie says, "I think the antagonism comes from her defensiveness. And frustration. She wanted to open up to you, to both of us that day in the bakery, but, you know how hard intimacy is. Especially for addicts."

"Sure," Roxanne says. "Though our girl here pushes defensiveness to a kind of aggressive brinksmanship."

Stale coffee smells. Air refrigerant. The smell of Roxanne's doubt. A weak glow penetrates the black against my eyelids. I lack the strength to open my eyes to meet it.

"You should see her tough little rooster of a stepfather," Emmie says. "This guy demeaned her all through childhood. That takes time to get over. You have to start from scratch to trust people."

Emmie understands me better than I understand myself. That's a friend.

"You met her family?" Roxanne sounds surprised.

"A couple of times. After my wedding, I stopped by their house to . . . ."

"Wedding?!" Roxanne blurts, surprised.

"Yes, I'm married!"

I'm happy for Emmie. In my mind, I'm levitating.

"We would have been in Fiji today," Emmie tells Roxanne, "but a business emergency postponed the honeymoon a few days. I called Boop to tell her, but her phone is disconnected. That worried me, so I went to her apartment. A nurse was looking in on the invalid that Boop takes care of. He was waiting for an ambulance."

I try to grab Emmie's hand, but I still can't move. Ambulance? Ambulance?

"Boop takes care of an invalid?" Roxanne says.

"The woman, Sada, was dehydrated and agitated," Emmie says. "She had no idea where Boop was. I promised I'd go check with Boop's parents. I drove out to their house, and the stepfather said his wife was asleep and whatever trouble Boop was in, she could get her own damn self out of."

"Nice guy." Roxanne, sarcastic! About Bob!

Emmie grunts. "This morning, still no sign of her. So I filed a missing persons report. The police cross-referenced a hospitalized Jane Doe matching her description, which led me here."

"What an effort on your part. And still such a mystery."

"She's getting off the Critical Care wing today. It's just a matter of time before she can explain what happened."

"Maybe I haven't given her a fair enough chance."

"If you'd look past the brashness . . . ."

"When she gets back on her feet, I'm willing to try another breakfast."

Emmie yips a little cheer. "Right after my honeymoon, okay?"

I want to congratulate my friend, but my lips don't work. How messed up am I? Do I have a face anymore? My foolish, heart-shaped face.

"Knock, knock," a man's voice says. "How's your friend?"

"This is the nurse from Boop's apartment," Emmie tells Roxanne.

"Abel Van Turk," Abel Van Turk says.

"She's taking her time waking up," Emmie says. "How's her neighbor? Have you seen her?"

Thank you, thank you, Emmie, for asking the thing I want to know.

"Yes," Abel says. "They have her resting comfortably one floor up. Ms. Pollard developed aspiration pneumonia and had to be intubated. Her condition is deteriorating. I've asked an orderly to move Boop into her room."

My eyes scream open. The room is dim, green, cold, sterile, one floor down from Sada. Emmie and Roxanne sit in chairs, nodding somberly at Abel. His hair is in a ponytail, and he's wearing a red turtleneck and looking me straight in the face.

"Miss Park? You're awake! How wonderful you look. Why don't your friends go get you some ice chips while you and I talk?"

Dear Bridgit,

[goes the note I actually send]

Guess what? I busted my spleen. Got a massive blood transfusion and emergency surgery. All from a stupid accident. Roxanne from 12 Step discharged me from the hospital and is helping me deal while our friend is on her honeymoon. Don't worry—I'm recovering.

Hope life up north is better. If you feel like it, write again.

Love,
Boop

PS—I inherited my neighbor's car and some funds left in her estate. The plan is to try college again, like Sada would want. She died a week ago. Sorry to be the bearer of bad news. I needed to tell someone.

THIS FORK OF MINE AND THAT SPOON OF HIS

"Rady, nooo!" a fisherman hollers as I try to shove a factory-fresh wheelchair between two massive wooden posts at the end of the Berkeley municipal pier. Bay combers furl and smack the wharf pilings, flinging cold spray to the concrete platform. The Chinese meddler has torn across the walkway to foil my mission.

Yesterday, California Wheelchair finally delivered the "high performance" manual Excel—too late to carry Sada one final time to the shorebirds she loved so much. Knowing I would full-rip hate having to see the hack standing empty and useless in my apartment, I got the deliveryman to leave it in the Nissan trunk.

Today, a man in the marina parking lot unloaded it for me, and it's been easy enough to push. But the frame won't fold compactly enough to clear the opening at the end of the pier. The push handles catch on the thick posts. What the hell kind of performance do they call this? The best place for this lousy piece of "personal transportation" is the aqua-brown depths of San Francisco bay, sunk from sight. Grabbing a handrim and crossbar, I lift the bulky rig to knee height.

"Why you do clazy thing?" the elderly fisherman screams.

"Worthless piece of shit." I heft the monstrosity to waist level. A just-discharged spleenectomy survivor has no business tangling with anything this cumbrous, but prudence isn't about to stop me.

"It wolth a lot fol someone. No thlow it off!"

My arms vibrate as I jack the chair chest-high. Two small brown Asian hands reach out, entreating me to stop, but agitated as the buttinski is, he doesn't dare touch me. Above us, seagulls beat their wings against the squall and cry as if demanding help.

In the hospital, they kept me sedated while my surgical site healed. Every now and then, I came to for a spell. One time, I saw Sada lying in a bed beside mine. Wizened, gray, she slept strapped to a ventilator mask, but was choking on the flow of oxygen. I slid off my bed to adjust her pillow and reposition the mask.

A black-haired kid approaches us, the fisherman's grandson from the looks of him, his flat face indifferent. My weak arms still support thirty-three pounds of metal, latex, and disappointment, like a giant squid I've hooked and don't want to keep.

"Rady!" the old man cries as he tugs my sleeve.

I scream a racial slur at the kid. "Get your chinky-dinky grandpop off me!"

The kid stares back inexpressively, a bamboo fishing rod in each hand.

When I stepped to the hospital linoleum, pain floored me. I collapsed between our two beds, my IV plug dislodging from the tape over my forearm skin and clattering away. I lay listening to the ventilator sputter and opened my mouth to tell Sada that she saved my soul, that I owed her everything and never had the chance to prove it. But all I could vocalize was a moan.

An echo of that moan fills my head as my arms collapse and the Excel thumps to the promenade, partially unfolding as it crashes down. The fisherman grabs the armrests and hunches his upper body over the seat, staking a claim on my brand new discard. But here comes another trotting man, making this a fisherman convention.

"What's crackin?" this African American man says, eying the Excel like it's the convention floor prize. He sports a Raider Nation cap and snazzy fishing tackle.

Mustering strength I didn't have, I rose to my bare feet and planted a knee on Sada's mattress. I goosed myself up. Right away, my incision ripped apart, the staples popping free. Under my gown, warm blood coursed out of me in buckets.

These two fishermen came to the bay to catch some mercury-tainted bay fish for supper but instead are facing each other down to catch a never-used wheelchair.

"I stop rady push it ovel," the Asian informs the black guy, not letting go of the armrests, improbably asking for a dustup with this much bigger and younger brohanski.

I back away—spent, cold, broken-hearted—leaving the pair of sheisters to whatever squabble they're about to have.

"Don't mean t'get up in your kool-aid," the black guy calls to me, "but whose wheely is that?"

"No one's."

"Me and my whodie don't mine takin' that chair off yo hands," he informs the Asian fisherman with fake friendliness that veils a threat. He points a little ways up the pier to a concrete platform with spouts and drains where his refrigerator-sized buddy performs a fisherman's chore.

Sada's hand found my leg and tried to sign a message on my bloody skin. The flat-line tone filled the air. ICU staff came running, barking instructions, tending to Sada as I silently bled. I don't know for sure what she was trying to communicate as her life ended, but I will always believe it was the word "love."

The air stinks of shredded seaweed and flinty shore pollution. I walk away. As I trudge past the "whodie," he's wielding a vicious hunting knife on a small silver fish. "Have a nice day, Ma'am," he says in a godlike baritone. Though I feel as gutted as his splayed, filleted catch, I nod.

Shore birds zip and bank and cackle with a brio Sada surely would have appreciated, if I'd been able to render the small service of getting her out here. I reach the asphalt parking pad, gaze back at the angrily flashing bay, and before unlocking the Nissan, deeply inhale as Sada's proxy. She's gone. The chair is gone. I'm still here. The car is here. And my fury? Good riddance to that, too.

***

Uptempo music wheezes through the hall, originating from Sada's unit, of all places. I pound on her door.

Nurse VanTurk opens up, an accordion around his neck.

"You?" I say. "And what in tarnation's all this noise?"

"Zydeco." He grins and pushes back his hair. "Good to see you. I tapped on your door a week ago, but your friend said you were sleeping."

It's been almost two weeks since my release from Alta Bates Hospital, six days since the steri-strips fell from my wound, sixteen since Sada breathed her last. With no surviving Pollard family members, no funeral was held. Even if one had taken place, I was too incapacitated to attend. A few days ago, Emmie returned from Fiji, tan and glowing. She packed Sada's belongings into plastic sacks. The building supe delivered her clothes and goods to the Salvation Army. The bed and dresser were left for the "next tenant."

"You're the new tenant?" I say.

Abel gestures me into the apartment, where his possessions are stacked all around. "You don't mind?"

My jaw goes woppy. Leaning against a wall is a giant wooden spoon. Not the exact vintage as my fork—the spoon is stained a lighter variant of teak and appears shorter in length—but still. "What a beaut." I trip toward it.

"Just out of storage."

"Where's your fork?"

"Ah, termites nibbled my fork to tinders." He plays a sad, buzzy riff on the accordion, a melody I almost recognize. "Insects lunched on my Jensen, too." He points out a George Jetson-ish, Scandinavian-sleek desk in the middle of the floor. "See the indentations along here? They reduced this beautiful desk's value by half."

I lean down to see tiny pits in the wood.

Abel sighs and pats his accordion. "My only collectible still in pristine condition."

"The spoon looks good."

"Fairly good, but even if I had the mate, its main value would be sentimental."

I wave my arm, inviting him to the door. "Come with me. Want to show you something."

Nurse VanTurk unstraps his pearly white squeezebox and follows me home.

Grinning sideburn to sideburn, VanTurk props my giant fork on end. "Hello, next-door, mid-century vintage!"

"Found it junked on the street. Pretty great, huh? Though the bottom got scraped."

"These things happen. My spoon suffered a nick while stashed away the past few years."

"You ought to sue that storage company for damages."

"There was no company. Just my ex-wife's attic. I can't sue her."

"You were married? To a woman?"

He chuckles and sets the fork gently back down on my wood floor. "'Til I screwed up, and she walked out on me. I'm holding out hope for a second chance with someone else."

The crooked smile he offers gives me the impression Abel's thinking the same thing I am—that sooner or later, despite their low market value and rough patches, this fork of mine and that spoon of his will unite as a slightly mismatched set in one or the other of our apartments.

In case there's cried-out eyeliner smudged on my face, I use my thumb tips to scrub under my eyes.

Abel holds his hands in front of his stomach, as if he's playing an invisible accordion.

"I used to be a fan of Those Darn Accordions," I say. "You know that band?"

"I played with them. Back in '92."

"You're shitting me!" We gaze at each other. It's as if Sada predicted this. As if she's watching over us. "Why don't we celebrate you moving in with a beverage? Roxanne brought fresh-squeezed juice."

In the kitchenette, natural as can be, VanTurk starts washing the dirty cups in the sink. How comfortable my neighbor looks, depositing each clean glass on paper toweling while asking if my post-op wound is healing, if I've heard from the probate lawyer, what I plan to study in college, and if I've considered the field of nursing.

I snatch my dish towel off a cabinet pull and dry one of the steaming-wet glasses, convinced Sada somehow arranged for this apparently heterosexual ex-Darn Accordion to move into her apartment, hit it off with me, and help plan my future.

"You have a talent for taking care of people," he says.

How could VanTurk's former wife leave someone who's this supportive?

"Plus, the pay is good," he says.

"If nursing's such gainful employment, why'd you move into this crumbling old building?"

"For the architecture. And the neighbors."

"I hope you like cockroaches."

He laughs. "Low rent's just what I need 'til I clear debt from a gambling problem I used to have."

Aha. I set the dry cup on the counter. "Which is why your wife gave you the heave-ho?"

He sighs. "By the time I gambled away all of our savings and security, she'd had enough." He hands me the next washed cup. "I'm in GA now, in case you're wondering. Gamblers Anonymous."

"You go to meetings?"

"Every week. And you?"

"Sada told you about SLAA?"

"You mentioned meetings when we first met. Don't you remember? Takes an addict to know one." He blows a soap bubble at me. "And to like one."

"But I went through 12 Step for all the wrong reasons! Sada promised me her car if I went." I cover my face with the towel. "She didn't deserve me faking recovery."

He tugs the towel away from my face and uses it to blot away a teardrop on my cheek. "Over time did it get less fake?"

I go to the 'fridge, thinking about the past few months. Cold air bathes my burning face as I reach for the juice container and stare at the light bulb in the 'fridge. "Yah, eventually, I took it serious and let it work, in the end. What still hurts so bad is that I'm not sure Sada ever knew that."

Abel closes the 'fridge door behind me. "I think she hung on 'til she felt assured about you. That was her closure." He gently unscrews the plastic jug in my hands. "Even without a spleen, mark my words, you're going to be fine, neighbor."

He picks up two clean cups that I pour into. The cold juice exudes a palmy citrus odor as it hits the warm glass. This must be how optimism smells. Abel hands me a filled glass and clinks his to mine.

"To Sada," I say.

"To life," he toasts, clinking my glass again, producing a merry chime.

"To love?" I say, surprising myself with a comeback that feels so right.

"I'll drink to that," he says and does.

And so do I.

THANK YOU TO

My agent, Don Fehr, for his tenacity and loyalty

Sarah Vollmer, for championing this book and giving tidbits of great advice

My writers group, especially Myra Sherman and Seth Fleisher, for their editorial astuteness and gracious encouragement through several versions

Mitchell Zimmerman, for generously providing legal expertise

Carl Peel, for sharing useful music biz info

Tim O'Brien and Michael Cunningham, for helping me trust my writing instincts

Vidya Tolani and Tim Crandle, for technical support

Rod Moore, Bonnee Elterman and Ellen Douglas, for reading a much longer early draft and still cheering me and the novel on.

My family–three wildly impressive men who make me laugh and for whom my affection is limitless

About the Author

Photographer: George Draper

Born in Manhattan and raised in Los Angeles, Mindela Ruby has worked as a motel maid, market researcher, SAT tutor and radio DJ. Having completed a Ph.D. at University of California, she currently teaches college and moonlights as a writing coach and editor.

Her short fiction and nonfiction have appeared in print, online and mp3 journals. *Mosh It Up* is her first novel.